Philip Dundas

An Exhampton Press Book
First published 2021

Book design: The Scrutineer, Rachael Adams
Illustration: Robert Littleford
Printed and bound by IngramSpark, United Kingdom
ISBN: 978-1-5272-8493-7

Bobby Grierson 1955-2020

Daniel, at sea

Daniel, at sea

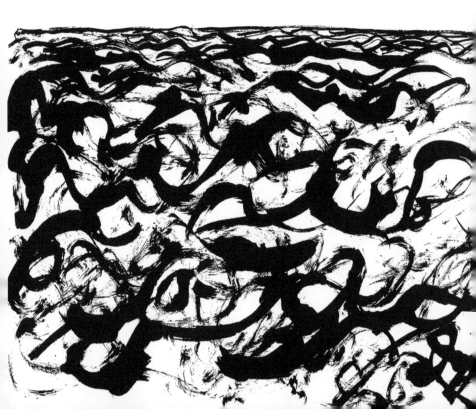

There is no Silence in the Earth — so silent
As that endured
Which uttered, would discourage Nature
And haunt the World.

Emily Dickinson

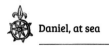

Daniel, at sea

Chapter One

Daniel Sale sat in a chair on the broken porch, staring into the garden beyond, missing the reassurance of his wife. Time stretched out, like those vacant boyhood hours spent gazing into the constellations of the night sky. The feeling hardly lasted a few minutes, but in those moments he felt himself disintegrating from the world around him. When he was young, the weathered teak table at which he sat was a vantage point, the crow's nest of his imagination where, cross-legged, he plotted his course over a thousand maps. Then it was aloneness that stirred his imagination into distant dreams. Now, after more than 70 years, the unbearable loss of his wife had shaken his grasp on life.

Lydia had died two years before. The night Hurricane Sandy smashed the Eastern seaboard, surging along the coastline, ripping everything in its wake like a vengeful god. Long Island Sound whipped into a foment, sending water high into the town through the waterways and lakes. Even houses on the hill, away from danger, were damaged and here at Gideon's Farm, the far end of the porch gable still bore splintered timbers like the yawning hull of a shipwreck.

That night Daniel sat it out while the old part of the house strained and groaned around them. He kept his vigil in candlelight, holding her hand in the storm, half-perceiving the gentle heave of her dying lungs. As the storm lashed out, in a low voice, he recounted shared pleasures aloud, not knowing if she could hear but knowing that any moment her life would slip away completely.

The decline had been mercifully short. In fact, the time she had left to her after the diagnosis had been so short, such an excruciatingly brief moment for them both, that he hardly had time to understand what was going on before she was gone. Two years later the wound in the gable of the house was still unrepaired and he was not used to her absence. The deaths he had known before, his mother and even before that, had left him with a sense of failure, that somehow, he had betrayed their trust and that they had died too soon. He felt that his life had been a gathering up around him of the tail end of things, the accretions of lost time, his failure to be himself, the disappointment of his mother and most of all the love lost deep within him that summer, half a century before.

But now, at last, that fall he was rallying again, possessed by a need to take action, to shake off the fatigue of loneliness. He was tired of seeing the clear plastic tarpaulin covering the gashed end of the building. After months of sun and rain it had become opaque and brittle like parchment and its incessant flapping in the slightest wind annoyed him. Progress on the reconstruction of the house had been delayed all this time by the insurance companies. And though he might easily have afforded to proceed without them, it lifted his mood to wage war against their relentless corporate ignorance. As it was, the local builders were hard to pin down. They had been the first victims of the cancelled construction projects of the recession. But with two hurricanes in successive years they were suddenly having an equally unexpected upturn in business. On this morning, he had been assured, the project would resume.

In truth, the damage around Greenwich from Sandy had not been so bad as the previous year and neither of these storms wreaked such remembered disaster as in the 1930s, when terrific havoc swept in from the ocean. This storm, known as the Long Island Express, was still part of local folklore. Every family had a story of heroism, disaster and survival. Daniel's mother was proud of her daring efforts to rescue her neighbors from the flooding and mayhem. Gideon's Farm was not exposed to water and sat on a spur at the edge of four acres of woodland, behind a wall of copper beeches and balsam poplars, halfway up Round Hill. So, she hauled a 200-year-old ceremonial Pequot canoe from the wall of the study and dragged it into the pick-up used by the gardener, then drove down to Cos Cob where the river waters were washing high into the houses of her friends. In this barely floating coracle, she ferried children and grandparents to safe ground, while she waded alongside in her trademark jodhpurs, sleeves rolled up. Until the National Guard appeared, she had supervised the local operation with imperious enthusiasm; a quality with which she approached every eventuality of her life.

Daniel still felt her presence around the house. After 40 years in the grave, time had not rubbed the patina of her from their home and the land on which it was built. Gideon's Farm was a living character in his life, it was where he formed his being, the outlook, temperament, demeanor, the inner and outer detail of how he grew into and became part of the world around him. The habit of its geography and architecture were etched into his life and anchored him. The endless details of its structure and shape, the thrum of his hands across its countless surfaces, the daily revelations of windows and doors, the unspoiled surprise of corners and stairs, the musk and odor of its rooms, gave him certainty and reassurance. After a lifetime spent in this place, it had never betrayed him, always giving up its care to him. And now more than ever.

Gideon's Farm bordered Gardiner Court estate, the huge mansion which Daniel's mother, Mary "Mae" Farwell had sold after her husband's death, leaving her a considerable settlement in addition to the Sale trust and a large share portfolio. She had renovated the original farm buildings with an authentic mid-century revival but added a bold modernist addition at the back; vast glass and stone angles stretching out onto a wild garden beyond. She relished the outrage caused by what many of her neighbors saw as an architectural travesty. They could not foresee that one day her project would be copied from Pasadena to Provincetown.

Mae Farwell had never truly been part of the Fairfield society in which her husband was so prominent a figure; so much younger than him when he died, she was glad to be freed from those allegiances. But not before he had given her a son. She was left a rich widow, free to pursue her ardent interests, which included men, jazz, art, sailing and Daniel. In no particular order.

A truck rumbled into the white-graveled drive. Ade Milič was originally from Croatia but in barely a few years, since Daniel had first met him, had become almost entirely American: his clothes, his booming voice, the earnest way he looked directly into Daniel's eyes while speaking, pushing his face forward insistently like a suburban pastor, as if somehow it demonstrated his loyalty and trustworthiness close up. The young in their ascendance, often forget, he thought, that old people prefer restraint over enforced intimacy. However, Daniel enjoyed this confidence with the younger man and having been alone here since his wife's death, he was pleased that finally there would be some activity around the place again. They agreed that the external restoration would be completed before Christmas.

As he wandered off, Daniel could still smell the tobacco from Ade's breath. He appreciated a hard-worker, someone who used expert hands to secure a livelihood. He held his own hands out. He could see every year of his life in the deep furrows, the worn skin, the contours of the veins, the swarthy roll of fingers and nails clipped low. More than any other part of his body, these bore the record of his lifetime. They had been willing assistants navigating unknown territories, hopeful allies grasping his purpose and

once, many years before, they had been the soft hands of a lover, gently moulding another's body into his.

Inside the house, a telephone rang. Daniel ignored it and walked down the drive, to the mailbox.

It was a surprise to him just how lonely the funeral had been. Death left him stranded, impossible to reach. And though it struck him as rather obvious, no matter how much people tried to genuinely and politely console him, he felt further away. Like a boat that's lost its mooring, floating out into the beyond.

He noticed that among his few acquaintances, it was only the bereaved who didn't try to offer any words of condolence. They caught his eye across the room, from the middle of the lake, offering a salutary half-smile. Not knowing or comforting, just acknowledging him silently from afar.

He hadn't wept. It had been a heartbreakingly short illness, working its way suddenly into their lives, separating them from what they had before. Like awaking to an unwanted stranger living among them, brooding, silent and malign. They had, of course, their moments alone, when the stranger seemed to have departed. But he soon returned bearing the ominous inevitability of a losing battle.

For these two gentle souls, this was a cruel parting. Particularly terrifying, as they knew few people well. Those who knew their habits and saw the grace of them together, respected that. The neighborhood acquaintances who seemed always to acknowledge their need for self-sufficiency without ever making them feel odd. And, of course, her colleagues in the faculty, with whom she enjoyed collegiate geniality. Indeed, her greatest loves, above even Daniel, were the writers to whom she had dedicated her life. And they had all departed long before.

The disease had come, like a rival, to steal away everything he had ever known of contentment. Now there were no gestures or familiar tones to remind him. Her death just ended in his aloneness. Something that comes, not from the ensuing silence of a life passed away but from a mute wall of separation from the lives of others.

Daniel was a pragmatist and always did precisely what was necessary to ensure that his patient was comfortable and peaceful; which despite the disease that tore them both apart inside, wasn't hard because they were a peaceful couple. She had once said to him across the sitting room, looking up from a book: Our life is perfect equilibrium. And without a sound carried on with whatever she was doing.

Looking back, he remembered how indignant she was at the invasion of alien objects into their home; the impermeable polymers of home hospitalization, the smells of chemicals competing with uncalled human effluent. The sanitary props which have the effect of colonizing their environment like the bacteria they seek to keep at bay. The house filled up with pharma packaging and crude plastic totems of human degeneration. Gideon's Farm, a house that had always given solace – that was built for the very purpose – like its inhabitants, was rendered helpless under this regime of sterility. The occupying nurses were too large for their uniforms and bustled with the static rustle of sheer nylon as they went from one task to another. They took on death with bossy efficiency and insistent good humor, poised to mop up the untidiness of mortality at a moment's notice.

It had been a shock for Daniel to see his diligent wife blown so completely off course without warning. As the end rapidly lurched towards them, they could bear it no longer and ordered out the enforcers except for a careful young male nurse, who was sensitive to their last days. He managed them quietly and respectfully and was liked by their regular help.

Daniel required more attention than Lydia; reminded to rest, encouraged to eat, to take a bath. All his instincts seem to have deserted him. There was nothing he could find to mend this life of hers. It could not be restored. His hands, used to conserving things, were helpless in this. Now, outstretched on the bedclothes in front of him, closed over hers, they were finally only useful for the prayer to wish away her pain.

Although they hadn't been church-going, he wanted to bury the body in the family plot next to his mother and father. He wasn't ready for her to be reduced to ashes in the wind. But almost as soon as the casket was lowered into the ground to the lilt of unfamiliar liturgy, he regretted his decision and couldn't bring himself to look into the void of earth.

Now he wanted to free himself from the whole event. He nodded bitter approvals at his comforters and left the graveyard seeing only the vast emptiness that lay ahead of him. This was familiar territory, there had been other deaths to set him adrift; this was not new to him. But she had been the one to save him from them and he felt old and alone now, convinced his memory was gradually failing. She had been that balance for him. Sharing their lives, never questioning or making demands, it was true, they had an equilibrium. A kind of singular focus that a person can only ever give once in a lifetime. Their love had grown from familiarity, from common

experience, from sadness. And now, after everything, all the years of simply caring for one other, he had always hoped they would die together. Not like this. So that having given all that to each other, having reached out, neither would have to be alone.

Chapter Two

Almost exactly a year after Daniel was born, Thomas Blackett Sale died, aged 44. The engine of his plane caught fire and exploded as he landed on the runway of the local airstrip and he was killed immediately. All that was left of the aircraft was the aluminum propeller which was found buried in the grass 300 feet off. It was given to Daniel's mother by the members of the flying club with a silver panel riveted to the shaft. On it they had engraved the words "For God, For Country and For Mae". She hung the propeller from the ceiling in the Cabin.

Daniel had always sought out something of his father, a private memento of an existence he knew nothing about. Some way of attaching himself to a past beyond this room and his mother's smothering occupation of his life. There was only a shadow of him here, only an imprint, nothing physical of him that Daniel might cling on to. He couldn't think of himself as having had a father at all. The little his mother had to say about him, was without any feeling of belonging, just a sort of wistful affection, like the sadness of describing the misfortunes of a complete stranger or a long since faded matinee idol, not her dead husband, his father.

After her death, Daniel found a dress box full of photographs and clippings. Scraps and shards, the broken mirror of their lives; school portraits, vacations spent skiing and sailing, family parties on the lawns of Gardiner Court, everyone dressed in white. Until then Daniel only knew two images of his father sitting in silver frames next to the liquor tray. One of a handsome young man in a flying suit and open-necked shirt, the other of a glamorous couple sitting in the back of a car with the sea behind them, his parents on honeymoon. Sometimes, in her later years, Daniel would find his mother mixing her second lunchtime cocktail, talking to the photograph of her dead husband.

She had built this home, so that she and Daniel were not lodged in a place of mourning. It was not that Mae had deliberately wanted to excise her husband from their lives but as the daughter of a widower, her mother's absence had been constant companion to her youth, and she had not wanted that for Daniel.

Her early marriage to a man 20 years her senior, although short, gave her all the implicit experience of the duality of womanhood. She had decided that she could give no more as either wife or mother and having the opportunity, she chose also to remove death from her household. And as she had not been raised with any instinct for the protocols or niceties of traditional grieving, the conditions of widowhood did not occur to her. After Thomas' death she simply moved on as quickly as possible. The best she could do was to create a home for her fatherless son. Now her life was her own and Gideon's Farm became their haven, a point of departure into a new existence.

So, Gardiner Court, rebuilt in the mid-1920s on the original plot bought by Thomas Henry Sale more than two centuries before, was sold. The family had been in Connecticut since the Dutch withdrawal and there were those in Fairfield County who believed this departure from tradition was a betrayal of an unbroken covenant. But Mae Farwell had no time for such pretensions, preferring to concentrate on building an architectural gem in the woods further down Round Hill. The Sale mansion was bought by a wealthy family from Hartford who had lived in the area for less than a century and believed themselves worthy of better things.

She never had time for the petty snobbishness of local hierarchy and knew her husband had little respect for a meaningless honor placed upon him by birth. In only a few years of marriage, encouraged by him, her fearsome independence of spirit had flourished among these people. The men were fascinated by her ability to challenge them in conversation and while very beautiful, she exuded an almost manly sexual vigor. Most of the wives, pretending bemusement, were envious. And though she had withdrawn from the county's social scene following Thomas' accident, they continued to see Mae and her son Daniel as one of their own. 70 years on, their children and grandchildren were still sending invitations to Gideon's Farm for their vulgar weddings and brash parties. Daniel Sale was a part of the heritage of the old ways, like a shaman in the woods, to be revered.

As a girl, having cared for her brother and father, Mae began her adult life with an intolerance for the dependency of men. And though her father became a relatively successful automobile trader, her intuition told her that if she didn't strike out on her own, his intention for her life would be suffocating. So, she moved from New Jersey and after secretarial college found a post at Buller Sale Engineering, near enough to visit, far enough to leave when she wanted. Here she quickly put everything she had learned into practice, making herself invaluable and attracting the attention of the people who could promote her.

Mae Farwell had a protean talent for being able to judge the balance between having things exactly as she designed while appearing to give others just what they wanted. Being good-natured, efficient and willing to help meant that others were always pleased to help her because she made them feel good. People liked to see something of themselves mirrored in her optimism. What she hid, was her determination to succeed.

Her elongated limbs were like a dress designer's sketch and she knew how to stand out while appearing modest; the simplest clothes looked chic on her graceful figure. One morning a few months after she was hired, Thomas Blackett Sale walked into the administration office of his company to find a tall gamine, who wouldn't be out of place on a Paris sidewalk, running the show.

They were unembarrassed at the speed of their romance. Thomas was long, broad and dark-eyed, the perfect match for Mae. The fact that he had remained a bachelor for so long, made him even more desirable to her than a younger man. She had every intention of marrying him from the start and in her he had finally found his soulmate; someone he could talk to as an equal. Her penchant for acquiring knowledge of new subjects and willingness to take on the new customs of his life was accompanied by a fast humor. Often, she'd study a subject sufficiently to surpass his superficial knowledge but never let on. Then she'd ask for his advice and this flattered him because he believed himself a teacher. She had enough experience of men, to know that to be content they needed to feel useful, comfortable and unchallenged.

Socially she was masterful, initially allowing his friends to patronize her, gaining their trust and eventually their admiration. When she'd transgressed some established etiquette, she'd make a joke at her own expense, which made her hosts like her even more. What an extraordinary woman, they were soon saying, what an ideal of what it means to be young and American. They were pleased that she should be the one to make Thomas Blackett Sale happy, where they had failed. Soon they welcomed her into their homes and more importantly, their confidence.

Once married, Mae never worked again, pleased to have a life of her own. She wasn't lazy but her life became a campaign of active self-indulgence. Their marriage proceeded elegantly with no fuss and a honeymoon in Europe. Mae remembered being happy every moment of that time, hungrily devouring the riches of the galleries and studios they visited, learning greedily about modern painting and sculpture. Thomas attended her with effortless ease, though he considered these arts a distraction from real life. He came alive in the evenings when they attended theater, ballet, opera and recitals. Introductions through the embassies and friends from university, opened many doors and they were eventually exhausted, pleased to be in the south of France, where they spent a month in a rented villa. Here the beau monde bustled and gossiped about Germany, the Nazis and the possibilities of another war. When Mae and Thomas were invited to dinner at the home of a famous writer, she stayed up all night reading his books.

Mae relished her partnership with Thomas; his decency and the unspoken understanding between them. He made no demands of her and she revered him. Whatever the uncertainty that might have hung over his personal life before they married, they were very much in love. Mae had always understood that Thomas also had interests elsewhere, but her concerns were dispelled once the two of them settled into a life of comfort at Gardiner Court. And she ensured that she was carrying his child soon after their return.

She did not see his other interests as a challenge to her position. She'd been used to men's need for physical attention. It was a sign of her prowess that she could share him without jealousy. As the men in question were young, charming and adored her, their dinner parties were immeasurably more entertaining than the dreary conventionality of Greenwich society. These young cards always deferred to her position and she knew how to play the game.

As an expert flyer, 20 years earlier, Thomas had been one of the first flying aces when America joined the war. They were a group of wealthy young daredevils, who had the money, the energy and the bare-faced courage to go into battle in the air. Many were killed in combat, but he survived and continued flying with reckless energy, taking part in races and competitions as well as developing designs for new aircraft.

Raymond Buller was Thomas' business partner and oldest friend. They had played together as their sons did later. But unlike those boys they were exactly the same age and temperament. Raymond was shot down into friendly territory as the Americans attempted to march on Metz but escaped without injury and returned to Connecticut to marry a society debutante and have several children. The two men went on to found

Buller Sale Engineering and with Thomas' genius for aeronautical design and Raymond's aptitude for business, they became powerful players in the development of new aircraft.

The day of their engagement, Thomas flew Mae along the coast of Long Island as far as Newport. She loved being airborne for the first time, free of the earth which had always seemed to resist her. After his accident, she took to the sea, where she felt more capable with the depths beneath her.

At the memorial service, Raymond unnerved the assembled Fairfield worthies eulogizing that their friendship had been such that part of him had also died on the airstrip that day. Mae wanted Thomas to have a simple headstone at the family plot in Sound Beach cemetery. Raymond wanted a more demonstrative memorial but respected her right. He visited or sent flowers to that plot every week until his death some years later and it was true that he walked with a little less endeavor after Thomas had gone. Later he became prone to melancholy, distracted by adultery and alcohol. But he supported Mae through the move from Gardiner Court which he sanctioned despite the disapproval of his wife and their friends. His judicious handling of the company financial affairs gave Daniel and his mother a legacy that would outlast both of their lifetimes.

Chapter Three

He walked slowly back up the driveway; by now the grass was growing up around the fallen beech. It had symbolic proportions, like a shattered thunderbolt. He always saw symbols in things; it was his life's work, piecing together marks and inscriptions, the significance of which was often lost, worn down through history and time, leaving only imagination to interpret their meaning.

As he entered through the kitchen door, his hand reached for the reassuring coldness of the marble on the huge kitchen dresser. He set the letters down, unopened. The dresser ran along the whole of one wall, its shelf as thick as a man's fist. Of all the furniture in Gideon's Farm, this had been the measure of his life boy and man, a point of departure and arrival, a place to leave keys and notes, something to hang from as an infant and now to support him as an old man; a staging post for every important domestic event. It was reputed to have been hewn from a single tree and brought to America by a French sea captain. His mother had it extracted from the kitchens of Gardiner Court when they moved here.

Along its upper shelves were meat salvers and rows of dusty china, none of which had been used for years. Daniel and Lydia hardly entertained, so there had been little need for it since his mother died. But the dresser still played a part in their daily routine; new mail would be laid down and seldom move, so the lower shelves were like a library catalog system stuffed with postcards and letters, some dating back many years. This often led to confusion when at the last minute before departing, one of them rushed back into the house to confirm the details for some event or other, only to find that the retirement party or wedding anniversary had passed them by on a different day or at another time.

He walked across the room to the range, lifted the cast-iron kettle onto the hot plate, took three pinches of tea leaves from a battered caddy, placed them into the open palm of his other hand, then threw them into a small pitcher and waited for the water to boil. He was never very far away from tea; his elixir, Lydia had called it. Apart from a brief period in his youth living in another country, he drank very little alcohol. His mother had done so with the particular energy of her generation. Before being taken out by one of the countless suitors she kept at arm's length, she'd come to say goodnight to him, as beautiful as a goddess, reeking of tobacco mixed with the scent of lily of the valley, always drink in hand. Until her last day, she had at least one martini at lunchtime, often more. He was never really certain what had happened on the *Dabbing Duck* the afternoon she drowned.

It was certainly these part-memories that put Daniel off drinking to the point where he felt intoxicated, though occasionally a glass of whiskey was able to send him to sleep, without resorting to pills. Tea, however, filled him with warmth and certainty. Rich broken leaf Assam in the morning and light fermented black Keemun in the afternoon; strong coffee, usually at an espresso bar. He poured the water and while waiting for the brew, wandered over to relieve the answering machine of its insistent red flash. Daniel, it's Nate. You had better believe that I have something in my possession that is going to get you excited. When are you coming into the city? We should have lunch. I want you to meet someone. Let's eat at Cafe China on 36th. Their pork buns are wonderful. You can have a turn around the Morgan beforehand. How about Tuesday? Call me.

Daniel sat down at the scrubbed table. He was always pleased by Nate's energy. They were almost the same age but Nate had a tireless enthusiasm for new things. They had been friends since the 1950s when they were both studying at Exhampton and though Nathaniel Defarge had far more native scholarship than Daniel, he had too much intelligence to be harnessed by an academic life. Daniel had always preferred the pace at Gideon's Farm and though for many years he had kept a small apartment midtown, unlike Nate he was never quite at home in the city. He felt it had the power to overwhelm him. Meanwhile his friend, who thrived on exactly that sensation of vertigo, had become a much sought-after dealer of rare paintings. Now retired like Daniel, he was busier than ever.

He stared at the six large white oblongs of his open diary. Five for the weekdays and one left over for the weekend. It had always puzzled him that the two days most likely to be filled with events, were reduced to a weekly footnote. But these days his schedule seldom had much to report.

Suddenly the room seemed to zoom out of focus and he slumped back into a chair. There was the ringing in his ears again, the sensation of being drawn into a blankness. He could almost see outside of himself, staring at the white paper, tightness in his chest, his breath growing short and fast, his gaze narrowing, until there was only a sense of being trapped in light and stillness, like a single sunbeam cast through a curtained window. A high-pitched sound seemed to surround him and continued for a few minutes until it was the sensation of his thumb intensely rubbing on the pencil in his hand that returned him with a bump to reality.

He knew this feeling from previous episodes and had no idea how long he remained in that small shaft of light.

Then there was a feeling of utter gloom that always followed these moments. It was more or less the same thing: a physical lightness, like gravity lifting, the sound of numbness ringing in his ears, then a blank inertia of forgetfulness, before something triggers him back to himself and the present slowly re-forms around him.

Compressing his face, squeezing his fists and stretching open his eyes and mouth, he returned to himself. Like the circulation returning to a limp arm. Is this the deterioration of my mind or just the life of an old man rushing in? Then pressing hard on the pencil, he wrote in the block Tuesday, September 14, 2014. *Lunch. Nate. City.*

Daniel did not go to the Morgan that morning as Nate had suggested. He hated the way the insufferable Rudy Brubaker lorded it over him when he visited. In the old days, all the curators were professional colleagues and the Director had been an old friend from university days, but they were gone and now this infuriatingly pompous boy, whose doctorate he'd supervised, was running the show. If he just wandered in, Brubaker, now Head of Collections, seemed to find out and would emerge from behind the scenes, taking Daniel by the arm in a gesture of affected warmth, steering him around the building and crowing about some new acquisition. Everything about him was fake, from the polished buckle of his loafers, to the pocket watch chain tucked into his ridiculous silk brocade vest and his round gold-rimmed glasses. Even his pretentiously long swept-back hair seemed to conspire in a coiffure of well-groomed irony. It was a strange paradox, Daniel thought, for a place celebrating authenticity and uniqueness that it should be presided over by such a buffoon. Even while researching his doctorate, Brubaker was aspiring far more to what he thought the behaviors of a curator should be than to serious scholarship. Museums were full of his kind, with their elongated vowels, eager wives and season tickets to the Met, fluttering around their wealthy benefactors like butterflies. Of course, Daniel understood how essential these people were to the business of great collections, he just wished Brubaker's ambition didn't make him feel so queasy.

Instead he ordered espresso in the cool marble of Graybar Passage, took the escalator and turned left out of Grand Central on to Lexington. He walked the few blocks to a dealer at 39th and there he passed the best part of the morning admiring a number of rare books, including a handsome early edition of *Moll Flanders* in two volumes still in its original calf binding. It was the sort of thing he would have bought for Lydia's birthday and she would have been happy, poring over it for hours before her conscience got the better of her, then she would chastise him for buying a book that ought to be in a collection. All of her own books were scrawled-on cheap editions, spines broken and dog-eared. He laughed because he loved to see her pleasure in their history. Defoe was one of Lydia's literary heroes; she had argued in her own work that he was a proto-feminist in his portrayal of women in crime. He'd remind her that they planned to leave their books to the library anyway, so that made these indulgences worthwhile.

Nathaniel Defarge was the son of a disgraced Louisiana congressman. When his older brother was killed in the war, Nate's Creole mother found a new husband and his father slowly drank himself to death. But not before his younger son had secured himself a scholarship at Exhampton in Art History. After their first semester, Nate had exhausted his early hopes of love with Daniel and committed to a friendship which survived their whole lives. They had learned to depend on each other from the outset.

He was a frequent visitor at Gideon's Farm and knew how to make Mae Farwell laugh. Her disregard for anything approaching the conventional strained Daniel. Nonetheless, after a lifetime of cohabitation, Daniel needed Nate to hold him together when she died. He was Daniel's only intimate connection with life and though they were close, his friend understood completely the boundaries of that relationship. Then when he announced he was getting married, though it puzzled Nate, who suspected more than Daniel had ever explained, he respected his good friend's silence and remained loyal and strong for him.

Something had happened during that time in Spain, something that changed Daniel. His friend had never told him what it was and he never insisted on knowing the details. But he knew that he had suffered something deeply wounding and that to bring it again to the surface of his life might destroy him completely. Their friendship was such that neither could imagine their lives without the anchor of the other. Nate would do nothing to risk that. For Daniel, the secret that lay hidden deep in his inner being, that love lost half a century before, had never been exposed to the light of day. And though some part of him, long lost, may have lain inconsolable at the foot of its petrified remains, it was deeply buried and could never be allowed to come to the surface. Nate knew from Sonny's stories of his mother's slavery, just how deeply pain could root itself in a life.

At midday Daniel walked the two blocks over to Madison, where Nate lived. He had moved into this apartment in the late 1980s with his partner. Sonny was probably the first black American to apply and certainly the first to be accepted by the building's board. The fact they were gay was overlooked on the basis that many of the residents were regular customers at the Defarge Gallery and they were by no means the only male couple in the building. Their neighbors rather congratulated themselves on the reputation they gained on the social scene for being liberal, though then in his 60s, Sonny hardly represented a threat to propriety.

Sonny was a well-known session saxophonist. He and Nate met one night at the Five Spot. Daniel had been there with his mother when she was chasing round after some abstract painter from the Cedar Tavern set. Mae didn't think it was a bad thing for her teenage son to experience the Harlem or East Village jazz clubs and so she left the car outside and he sat at the back by the door while she flirted wildly, commanding the eyes of the whole establishment, like a wartime entertainer at a forces show-night.

Five years later, Nate and Daniel, who had come to love jazz, were squeezed onto a table back in the Five Spot, smoking and drinking glasses of beer, trying not to look intimidated when a tall and very handsome man came down from the stage, sat down and started talking to them. He was a little older and after a drink or two he leaned over and whispered to Nate laughing in his honeyed baritone; are you two wet-behind-the-ears college boys fucking each other, or just come here to tempt me?

Sonny J. Franklin and Nate Defarge made an unusual couple. For 30 years they happily shared a tiny midtown apartment and though Daniel and Nate saw each other regularly, he hardly ever met Sonny. We come together at home but at the sidewalk we depart into different lives and it's the way we like it, Nate used to say. Early on, Sonny had avoided the drug-induced angst of his peers and after some wise investments set up a record label and launched the careers of some notable jazz talent. By the time they moved into the Merrill Building on Madison, Sonny was white-haired, well-off and the world had changed. He died of pancreatic cancer 12 years later. That summer they played a memorial set for him at the Newport Jazz

Festival.

As he got in the lift a tiny, ancient looking couple followed him in. He stood in the low light and looked down on their heads, noticing beneath the man's fragile strands of hair, the paper thin skin of his head. She had a silk scarf over suspiciously voluminous auburn hair and was wearing huge wraparound sunglasses, like a welder's mask. When they arrived at the twenty-second floor, they got out before Daniel and walked past Nate's open door, where he greeted them as they passed. He met Daniel's quizzical look with raised eyebrows and closed the door. Van Deusen is a tupperware billionaire, Nate said. And she has the best collection of Meissen in the city.

Daniel followed the parquet corridor into the huge living room that Nate used as his gallery. He didn't cook, so the kitchen had become a drinks dispensary from which bottles of Saint Veran issued with alarming repetition. Every inch of the walls was occupied with paintings, mostly early 20th-century American impressionists. At the end of the room framed against the light of the window, Daniel made out the figure of a younger man, admiring a picture resting on an easel. Come and see my new acquisition, he said, deliberately vague. When Nate had acquired a new work or on the rare occasion a new person, he was giddy, wanting everyone to share in his pleasure.

Since they had known each other, Nate had bought and sold many paintings for Daniel. In fact, his journey into the gallery world began at Gideon's Farm when Mae had asked him to catalog what remained from the Sale collection. She had little interest in the old masters and family heirlooms assembled by generations of her husband's family and threw herself into supporting new artists. She wanted to make room and liked to sell before she bought, a habit that Daniel inherited. Nate had recognized the importance of keeping what they owned together, but learned his business by extracting certain works without disturbing the whole collection. In later years, Nate had also gotten along well with Lydia and they would often have expeditions to salerooms up and down the coast.

Over lunch at Cafe China, Nate's high spirits over his new purchase were infectious, but he explained that he wanted to discuss something more serious than the double-cooked pork buns. The younger man was introduced as Chester Bowery, a lawyer with expertise in antiques, who had some experience in helping clients with arranging their estates for bequest. Nate was considering what to do with his paintings, those – rather too many in Daniel's view – he had never wanted to part with. He also wanted to sell Sonny's collection of vernacular photographs and had asked Chester to help him organize an appropriate tax valuation process. Wouldn't Daniel also benefit from similar advice on the Sale collection?

Daniel was usually shy with strangers, but found Chester delightful company at lunch and at Nate's behest over jasmine tea, he invited him over to Greenwich. Truthfully, it was pleasing to find someone interested in his research. By the time the three men parted ways, plans had been hatched. Daniel returned home on the 5.45 New Haven line clutching a small parcel containing *Moll Flanders* and, perhaps more remarkably, for the first time he could remember, experiencing a rare sensation. For some reason, he felt hopeful.

Chapter Four

The summer he graduated from Exhampton, Mae Farwell decided that it would be good for Daniel to travel to Europe. By now, she'd resigned herself to the unexciting truth of his considerable intellect and she'd arranged for the faculty to offer him a fellowship to research his doctorate once he passed his examinations. Though, more than anything, she'd liked for him to have been a painter or musician, someone for whom she could become a muse, there was nothing for it but to reorder her expectations around his becoming an eminent scholar; yet with uncompromising determination she wanted to ensure that Daniel had experienced a broader landscape than New England, so she insisted he did not begin his first postgraduate semester until the following year.

One evening, drink in hand she sat down with some maps on her studio table and once again plotted a course for Daniel.

Following up on some Sale family connections, Mae discovered that a second cousin, one of the Denton Sales, was an attaché in the recently reopened consulate in Barcelona. She had loved Paris but had been irritated by the self-regard of the French and, as a maverick gal from New Jersey, considered it an irony that a nation of revolutionaries could have so perfected the art of being superior.

To her Spain seemed to offer more opportunity for vicarious swashbuckling and Franco had recently signed an agreement with the Americans, so she made contact with cousin Robert to ask what opportunities might be open for Daniel. He replied that his interest in academic research might be valuable to the Association of Collections and Museums Council, newly reformed after many years of closure since the Civil War. The US government was in the process of establishing a new cultural exchange program and Daniel might be an early beneficiary. A second letter clarified that the local government had released a large number of private collections of books and manuscripts which needed cataloguing, and might this not suit Daniel well, while giving him time to explore. He could easily ensure that Daniel was granted a visa for a year as an invitee of the Consulate, which would doubtless add to his academic prospects, as this kind of experience was unlikely to come the way of most young men.

Mae ignored the slightly pompous insinuation of family favor implied in his letter. The Sales, she thought, had always considered themselves highly in the world and never more so now their light was waning. Once one of Connecticut's brightest stars, since her husband's death and the sale of Gardiner Court, outside Greenwich society they really had no bearing on events at all. Nonetheless she was torn between her contempt for their old-fashioned fustiness and assuring Daniel his rightful place in the family hierarchy. Resisting the temptation of a withering parry she responded in good humor, cheerfully accepting the offer with gratitude for his efforts.

Mae's aversion to flying was matched by her enthusiasm for the sea. And she adored the idea of ocean-going liners. She wanted Daniel to join a cruise from New York which would allow him a tour of the Mediterranean before arriving in Barcelona. Though the prospect of six weeks on board ship depressed him, he was equally keen at 22 to escape the thrall of his mother. He was curious about Spain anyway, which he knew little about so continued to accommodate her intrusion into his career, knowing that once back at Exhampton, he would be relatively safe from her clutches. What harm could there be in exploring out there in the world? He was excited at the prospect of venturing out on his own.

Mae had cleared the table and they opened the maps showing the route across the Atlantic past the Azores and Madeira and then past Gibraltar into a familiar world for Daniel from the early *mappa mundi* and portolan charts he had known so intimately. First along the coast of Africa stopping at Algiers, across to Odessa, back to Istanbul, down to Alexandria and Haifa, then Greece, Italy, France and finally creeping round to Spain. They marked the course like admirals planning for battle, reading the descriptions of each port of call in the brochure. Mae looked with glee at Daniel, while he summoned the necessary level of fervor to please his mother. Duly a ticket for a single standard cabin was booked to leave in mid-September arriving around the beginning of November in Barcelona.

During the summer, Daniel helped Nate to move into his first solo apartment in the city. Making house filled him with warmth, a feeling of domesticity mostly denied him at Gideon's Farm. When he was alone he loved to escape into the warmth of Marta's kitchen, the only place where nothing was on show and everything was on the move. He helped her to scrub the table and organize the kitchen implements in their correct cupboards, drawers and hooks; she would reward him with some delicacy freshly warm from the stove, and tea, iced or hot and sweet depending on the season. Settling in with Nate came naturally to him. Together they arranged flowers in a carnival vase they bought from the flea market and fussed over which way the bed should face, finally congratulating themselves with beer from cracked mugs and Thelonious Monk on the tiny record player balanced on a stool in the corner. Days passed and they explored collections and galleries, read *The Great Gatsby* and Henry Miller, ate in their favorite diner and talked about the cities Daniel would visit. Sometimes he slept on the floor, relishing the discomfort, the freedom of city life.

By now Nate had started an affair but decided not to tell his friend. There was still too much unspoken between them on that subject. He had secured a junior position with one of the auction houses and every morning, dapper in his pinstripe suit, a line of white handkerchief peeping from his top pocket, he was embarking on his own voyage. He'd never been certain if Daniel had felt slighted or betrayed by his lack of candor regarding Sonny. Though it was never said and their friendship always remained untroubled, Nate wondered if Daniel might have revealed more of his innermost feelings later on, had he entrusted his own to him, at those early exciting stages of love.

The evening before the ship sailed they went to see Ethel Merman in *Gypsy* and after dinner they drank mint juleps. They were all in high spirits; Mae was seeing her most successful project entering new horizons. Nate was thriving and Daniel full of nervous energy was casting off into a new life. They agreed that in the morning they'd see Daniel to the quayside and leave him to embark, without long farewells. So the next day they drove down to the pier in a gentler mood than the previous evening; Daniel shook Nate's hand, then dutifully kissed his mother before turning round and disappearing into the crowd.

For Daniel the prospect of six weeks alone at sea had been made more acute in the knowledge that he would be surrounded by strangers. That in itself he didn't mind, but what concerned him was being singled out as a lone traveler, prey to the attentions of inquisitive fellow passengers. He set about keeping a journal in a small leather-bound notebook, which he took with him everywhere so as to look occupied at the imminent advance of any unwanted approaches. He spent long hours reading in the recently refurbished and luxurious library that became his regular haunt.

One afternoon walking on the deck he fell into conversation with a young woman, also in her early 20s he assumed, whom several times he had spotted reading or walking alone. He'd noticed her too in the dining room sitting with an older couple. It turned out they were her aunt and uncle, whom she had been staying with in Philadelphia. They had decided to take the return journey to England with her and were doing so in a great deal of luxury.

He liked Lucinda Draycott because she seemed sensible and had none of the irritating and predatory flirtatiousness he saw in the daughters of the rich thronging the ship. She was bookish like him and to pass the time, they started to follow each other's reading, meeting after meals to discuss their thoughts on the novels and the writers that interested them. As well as the classics, the library had been stocked modishly with modern authors from the best publishing houses who came under their eagle-eyed scrutiny. They revelled in a slightly competitive but light-hearted literary pedantry, hardly noticing each other as two more romantically inclined young people might have done.

Two particular books had a noticeable effect on Daniel, or at least their protagonists. The solitary esoteric Prince Fabrizio in *The Leopard* chimed with his yearning for knowledge and peace amid the maelstrom of family politics. He could feel the sweltering heat of Sicily in the long descriptive passages and felt his struggle between escape and duty. Later he suggested that they should read *The Bell*, but having done so he felt it would be awkward discussing it with Lucinda. He had enjoyed the frisson of chaotic unorthodox relationships in other books, but he noticed his jaw tightening up at the sexual indiscretions of Murdoch's characters. In fact, Daniel was both attracted and discomfited by the rather tragic histories of these people, who despite their innate Englishness, he half-recognized as characters from home and even among his fellow passengers. Daniel was well aware of the competing sexual dramas of adult life but so far he was unprepared to face them, even if in the abstract, and certainly had no plans to act upon them.

At some point Lucinda asked Daniel to dine with her aunt and uncle. He understood, she hoped that this would simply be a gesture of kindness on his part to ease an otherwise tedious routine on hers. He agreed and spent a painless evening at their table discussing some of the timeless archeological treasures they looked forward to seeing over the coming weeks. The aunt was bursting with pride that, as she saw it, her rather dull unattractive niece could snare a handsome young man like Daniel. But she had little interest in the historical significance of the ancient artefacts and landmarks of civilization they might glimpse on the trip. Apart from my husband, she laughed raucously, I have no interest in old things.

So, the time passed amicably as they made their way across the Atlantic. Daniel loved standing in the early morning light, gazing into the churning waters left in the wake of the ship. He'd read accounts of sailors in tropical seas experiencing a delirium called calenture. Suffering from fever in the heat, men would be inexorably drawn to what they perceived as the cooling comfort of the soft waves beneath, sometimes throwing themselves headlong from their ships into the water. One morning, he came on deck at dawn to find a handsome man standing in his evening clothes, smoking a cigar. He looked like a film star with slick black hair. Moments later a woman with a fur stole around her shoulders came up to join him. It was as if they were making a movie, right here on board ship. They turned and walked along the deck towards him, the man looked at Daniel as they passed, his mouth twisted slightly in a cruel smile. Daniel blushed and looked away, as he always did when anyone gave him more than a passing glance.

They swept into the Mediterranean and began the coasting of North Africa, the Middle East and Turkey. For the first time in his life Daniel experienced a real sensation of history, that this was a geography he had studied in detail on his maps. He was constantly surprised just how accurate the ancient mapmakers were, how they learned to represent this on their maps and how successfully man had become a seafaring creature with his combination of unending curiosity for detail and desire to discover uncharted seas. At every point he'd come across an obstacle he couldn't fathom, he had deployed his skills to devise ways of being better at survival. From the beginning of time, existence had always depended so much on exploration and the further he strayed from the safety of his known world the more he had to learn to depend on something far more powerful than the evidence before him. Discovery, Daniel thought, was what this journey meant for him and he enjoyed the experience, the physical realization of places long in his mind's eye as much as their heritage.

At Piraeus, Lucinda and Daniel disembarked together, making their own way into the city to explore the Acropolis, while her relatives joined a bigger guided group. As soon as they set foot on land as they had in several ports before this, they both gave eye-rolling sighs of conspiratorial relief and fled unnoticed so as not to be associated with their fellow passengers, the loud Americans gathering on the quayside. They had both been anticipating Athens with more excitement than any previous stop but as they meandered

up the pine-clad slopes below the Parthenon it dismayed Daniel how much of this seat of civilization was crumbled on the ground, reduced to dust beneath their feet. Still the very scale of what remained, these vestiges of ancient Greek greatness and power captivated them as they walked silently, open-mouthed, gazing at the terror and beauty of the pagan images, graven now before their eyes; images he had only previously seen in print.

After they had lunch together, on their way back to the ship Lucinda asked Daniel if he would write to her about his experiences in Barcelona. He knew quite well, even as he promised to do so, that he had no such intention. This trip was to be his own adventure. He'd enjoyed talking to her and sharing their interest in books, but he wanted the time ahead to be something completely new for himself, free from the obligation that dogged him under the reign of his mother, a sense of duty that had worn him down forever. One thing he was sure of, after the years of being her vassal, now was his time to be completely himself, unfettered by Mae.

Chapter Five

For 30 years, Daniel was professor of maritime history, more correctly of early maritime cartography, the study of old sea maps. His specific interest was in a form of early hand-made chart, called a portolan. These ingenious ciphers of sea travel were used by mariners navigating their loaded ships from port to Mediterranean port as early as the 12th century. And this art of mapmaking, the specific details of its practitioners and their schools, was a dimension in which Daniel could lose himself.

Nautical travel in the Mediterranean, mostly involved keeping the shore in sight during daylight hours and anchoring fast by night. Only the boldest sea captains would risk their cargoes, sails and oarsmen to make a straight run across an unknown sea with only the Pole Star to guide them. From Libya to Constantinople and Genoa to Malaga, sailing was an endeavor fraught with dangers, not the least of which, even if you survived hostile harbors and catastrophic storms, was the unknowable precariousness of uncharted waters. The portolan as a powerful tool of sea travel was, in Professor Sale's view, the single most important key to the growth of trade and colonization across the globe.

Over a career spanning five decades, he focused on his subject so completely that he was able to entirely absent himself from the business of life, the society of other people. The secrets he guarded from his youth, when he had travelled abroad, were now embedded, far from daylight or scrutiny. For Daniel, an unexpected brush of intimacy could cause him such a jolt of pain that it was safer to pose as a man of few words who preferred to be alone. A life of research, teaching and the pursuit of his few interests was the perfect cover. In fact, he had always loved conversation and company but by now, only with those who appreciated the boundaries with which he kept people at bay. He mapped the contours of his own emotional landscape quite secretly, so much so that those unexpected moments when he laughed brought a wave of relief to anyone around him. And for those who knew him well, his limpid eyes were an open book of his mood and purpose. At the end of a lecture or when a conversation was complete for him, he would gently close them in a gesture of humility and clasp his hands as if in supplication. The meeting was done, he had said all that was to be said on the matter at hand, and now he would retire to his

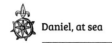

place of inner safety.

Portolan maps were carefully inked onto vellum, a form of parchment made from animal skins. Thus their shape when they were rolled out, starting at the neck, had the appearance of a wide bottle. Until the 15th century the chart makers concentrated on the Mediterranean, but later the maps followed the progress of sea explorers on their routes to the Indies, round the horn and cape of Africa into the Indian Ocean. Then slowly but surely, the trade winds chased these ships from Gibraltar across the Atlantic to discover South America and the West Indies, whence the currents pushed them further north, blowing in the arrivals and hindering the departures from the new colonies of America.

Daniel's interest in these strange ciphers of seafaring started with a portolan made in the 17th century, which had been passed down through the Sale family since the time of Thomas Henry Sale. It was said to have been found by Daniel's father, wedged into the lid of a family strongbox. The chart was ascribed to a mapmaker in London. It was not vellum but made from heavy linen-rag paper mounted on hinged wooden boards. The Sale Portolan was a particularly fine example. Apart from the deterioration of the hinges and some cockling to the edges of the paper, the map and pigments were still in fine condition. When Mae Farwell Sale presented it to the Exhampton library collection upon the acceptance of her son to study there, she ensured that it was given a prominent position among the dreary collection of New England manuscript artefacts, town charters and land treaty deeds. It was also an act of patrician generosity with which Mae hoped to establish Daniel, who given his disappointingly lack of creative or sporting talent, might make a respectable name in the field of cartography.

At the time, he was mortified at the unwanted celebrity it drew to him. But quietly he enjoyed the status amongst his peers within the history faculty. And there had been some private arrangement with his mother who felt he should have the opportunity to research the portolan as part of his dissertation, despite there being no-one able to supervise his research. In effect, she had now planted Daniel safely in a field of study in which she could approve. What she didn't know then was that it was at the Exhampton Rare Manuscript and Book Library, later named after their family, that he was to stay, apart from a short interlude, for the rest of his working life and where he would build one of the greatest collections of antique cartography in North America.

As a boy, one of Daniel's favorite books was *Robinson Crusoe*. He re-read it many times. Lydia was something of a Defoe fanatic and later, when they were married, she often called herself his woman Friday. Being alone on a wooden boat in the searing heat of the sun on a calm, flat sea was a recurring dream throughout his childhood. Though Mae loved going out on Long Island Sound on her little yacht, he could never share her pleasure. She would throw it around the waves, catching a current or a breeze, while he sat at the edge of the boat, looking at the sea with rising vertigo, fearing that any moment they would sail to the edge of a vast watery precipice. He was not frightened of the sea, never felt seasick and loved swimming, but he found sailing with his mother too unpredictable and couldn't wait to jump off and lash the painter to the little jetty by their Long Island beach house at the end of the afternoon, feeling his bare feet on the warm planks.

One summer, she lost the control line on the mast boom and it swung round catching Daniel's head before he could duck out of the way. He was knocked clean cold and the doctors told Mae he was lucky to escape with a temple wound, concussion and a burst eardrum. Those were the end of his sea-faring days. Privately relieved no longer to be the audience for his mother's hobby, he sported his bandage with pride and his childish play turned landward, building an elaborate stockade in the woods behind Gideon's Farm, knowing that like Crusoe he wouldn't try to leave the island until he was sure of safe passage.

The liner had been held back in France because of stormy weather, not docking in Barcelona until the early evening. There was a slight chill in the fall air, the dim lights from Montjuic peered from the hillside like curious eyes waking to a new presence among them. Daniel was alert to his surroundings but any hope of arriving incognito and merging into the new city was spoiled by the obvious figure of his cousin standing on the quayside. They had met only once before at a family gathering in New York, but he hadn't changed.

Daniel derived comfort from anonymity, he had a skill of disappearing into the crowd. And although he was not a particularly anxious person, he did not relish unsolicited social interaction, worried about looking unfamiliar and hated standing out. It had something to do with the exotic dominance of his mother, always being made to feel he was an object of attention because of her. Mae had seen a vibrant city life as an essential element of her son's upbringing. She hated the idea of him becoming one of those county-stuck Sales who barely knew the streets of Manhattan except for Wall Street and their Fifth Avenue clubs. So, she had forced Daniel out onto the sidewalk and together they explored the bohemian and risky quarters of the city; sometimes they walked and sometimes she made Daniel drive, even before he had a license. She had a keen eye for dress sense and made sure her son had something approaching the urbane about him; though Daniel preferred his threadbare tweed sports jacket with the leather patches, she would encourage him to offset this with modish pants or shoes. By the time he was 20 he had adopted a cheerfully dowdy but studied elegance which he liked because it set him apart from the conventional without making him seem outlandish.

On board the ship he'd felt safe, mundane even, among the other passengers. But here in this new city, where he was to live, from the moment his feet touched the ground, he couldn't escape the feeling of being continually observed. And with the imposing corpulence of the crassly American, cigar-smoking Robert Denton Sale standing beside his car on the quayside in short-sleeved shirt and fedora, there was little chance of being anonymous as he disembarked.

While they moored and the gangway was lowered, Daniel noticed the industry of the barrel-chested natives hauling cargoes onto waiting trucks. The flat evening light created a somber atmosphere and behind in the distance was a sea of gray created by the huge warships moored cheek by jowl on the other side of the old port. He'd read that Barcelona had become a base for the US Navy's Sixth Fleet and though technically peacetime, the presence of the ships and the large observation towers, which once housed cable cars, looming over the harbor like giants astride the port, gave the sense of a city under siege.

Daniel made his last journey down the gangway of the cruise liner and the two men greeted each other cordially, rigid arms fully outstretched, hands grasped in a gesture of distant suspicion but with just the appropriate appearance of warmth so as not to appear complete strangers. This choreographed Anglo-Saxon form of familiarization already seemed out of place here. After exchanging pleasantries on various aspects of family life in Connecticut and Daniel's small case had been placed in the car, Robert drove him into the city to his apartment near the top of the Passeig de Gràcia.

It was an apartment 'interior', which had seen better days. Rather gloomy, they were designed to keep out the Spanish sunlight but also failed to warm up during the nights of the colder months. Arranged over the second floor of the building, accessed from the hall by a separate staircase, the principal apartment was wrapped around the interior patio in the middle of the building. Despite the rooms being large and retaining most of their ornate 19th-century decor, Daniel had been allotted a tiny room to sleep in with an internal window, next to a basic washroom. Given the rooms that could have been put at his disposal, he quickly interpreted this as a sign from his cousin that he shouldn't get too comfortable. He wondered too if it was a gesture of contempt from a part of the Sale family which had long considered itself hard done by in some historic dispute. Mae had always repeated what Thomas told her, that the distant branches of the family had failed to distinguish themselves in business or in the service of the nation and begrudged the enduring survival of the Blackett Sales in Fairfield County.

Robert extended the dismissive attitude of a colonial conqueror to local domestic customs. The people here had dinner unusually late and rising early, broke the activity of the day with an extended lunch. He compromised by eating around 8 in the evening, allowing Senora Merce, his housekeeper to finish for the day and return to feed her own family at night. Once Daniel had unpacked, a meal of bread with a stew of peas and pork was served at the dining table in the large room at the back of the house. The floors were ornately tiled, and coals smoldered in a grand fireplace with a carved wooden surround. Large doors opened into a covered glass gallery at the back of the building. Apart from two sofas and the long dining table and chairs where they sat, the room had no other furniture. The two men sat at one end of the table and drank red wine while Robert explained that the whole building once had a single owner, who owned a textile factory at the bottom of the building and others in the north. But the family had been exiled after the Civil War and never returned. He was renting it through a contact who was involved in the project to reunite the private collections held by the city, with their original owners. This was the project which Daniel was to work on, and he should have no doubt of the efforts by which his cousin had secured such a wonderful opportunity for a young researcher.

Robert hadn't demonstrated any specific ability at Annapolis, physical or intellectual. He was lacking talent of body and mind but was in possession of an arrogant entitlement which never gave way to self-awareness. His naval training, left him without either leadership skills or an aptitude for

seamanship and his diffidence for learning anything made him hard to place. After an undistinguished desk posting at fleet headquarters, came the offer of attaché at the newly reopened consulate in Barcelona, an undefined position which he could make his own. Most of his days were filled with organizing itineraries for visiting US dignitaries and resolving minor municipal arguments between the navy and the Guardia Urbana. More recently he found a way to extract himself from these acts of counsel to dally with a new cultural exchange program being established between the two countries.

After supper, when Robert went to his room, Daniel took to the streets. The salty thinness of the air reminded him of Long Island. It was colder outside than he expected as he wandered down the wide paths of the street towards the main city square, Plaça Catalunya. The streets were lined with plane trees; finally, he thought, a foreign land beneath his feet. It struck him how out of place he felt. In a Harlem jazz club like the Five Note, he stood out as a white boy which was an obvious and allowable invasion for an enthusiast. But here, as soon as he found himself among people in the square, he stood head and shoulders above everyone around him. He had to have another way to fit in, so he hid his guidebook in his pocket, adopted a purposefulness in his walk and tried to look as if he knew where he was.

Chapter Six

Daniel took his tea into what Mae had called 'The Cabin' at the back of the house; a long open space with glass from floor to ceiling either side, supported by brick columns and long wooden beams above. The room, with the facing end wall lined by huge oiled teak bookcases, was designed to surprise. Sometimes at night when he was a little boy, the branches of the trees outside leaning into the glass, came alive with faces, like illustrations in his story books.

Along the length of the windows ran low ebony box shelves, inlaid with chrome around their outer edges on which sat the ceramics and small sculptures he and his mother had collected on countless gallery visits. It was a passion they had shared, acquiring objects like totems, objects that signified happiness in his childhood. And under the shelves were still the magazines, art books and photography catalogs he scoured, lying on the vast alpaca rug, chin in his hands, losing himself in the tinted images of people whose lives he imagined, souvenirs of somewhere else.

Low sofas sat back to back down half of the room, opening out into a square around a long, wide glass coffee table. Two glasses and an unfinished bottle stood on the table, where Daniel sat down.

The most surprising thing about the previous day was how much he had enjoyed having a visitor in his home. Probably the first person since Lydia died and certainly the first friend. Thinking of Chester Bowery as a friend, so soon, seemed somehow immodest. But something particular and intimate had quickly grown between them that day.

In the days and weeks since they met at Nate's apartment, Daniel had been looking forward to meeting the younger man again. He thought about his demeanor during lunch, the constant smile, looking as if he was preparing to say something funny. It reminded him of someone he had known years before. Above all, he was interested without being inquisitive and could hold a conversation without talking about himself, unlike Nate who was sparkling company and whom he loved dearly but who was exhausting and self-centered.

Chester arrived at Gideon's Farm one Saturday, driving a restored classic Rambler station wagon and wearing a blue wool suit with suspenders and an open-necked blue checked shirt. Daniel noticed the details of people.

When interviewing staff or students at the university, he could judge someone within moments of their entering the room. Apart from anything else, he believed that for a library of precious manuscripts and maps to be conserved, its guardians must themselves be immaculately presented and at least appealing, if not secretly attractive, company.

He thought how stylish Chester looked, with his clipped beard, swept back hair and broad shoulders. He'd brought red lilies, their blooms just open, which Daniel thrust into a glass vase on the table in the hall. There had been no small talk and they immediately struck up a rapport. After exploring the house from end to end, they sat on the porch eating the lunch of soft rolls and chowder Daniel had prepared. He'd been to the fish market early in the morning to buy the crab. Though he wasn't an ambitious cook he found preparing the simple dishes he loved a kind of creative act. He hadn't had anyone cook for him since Marta retired.

Chester had an infectious enthusiasm for everything Daniel showed him and fell in love with the house, wanting to know every detail of its history and restoration. At some point Daniel had retrieved the architect's plans for this most daring of his mother's projects, leaning on the kitchen table, with their knees on the chairs, poring over the details of the alterations and the original drawings for the bold triumph of glass and steel box she had added to the back of an early settler farmhouse. There was also a folder of cuttings from newspapers and magazines going back to the late 1930s. They laughed at some of the articles, local papers criticizing the despoiling of the Connecticut vernacular of Gideon's Farm or the great design and style magazines of the day celebrating a home that was now considered to be a unique fusion of architectural modernism and settler style. When Daniel imitated Mae dismissing her neighbors as 'aaaawfully feeble-minded and uuuuun-interesting', it made Chester giggle.

Friendship had never been a state of being that Daniel either courted or encouraged. Apart from a very few people in Greenwich, this rule was certainly enforced among his neighbors. He'd inherited from his mother a dislike of community camaraderie, the assumption of friendship that comes from mere acquaintance and proximity. He was coolly equivocal at the attempts of his neighbors to collate a specific picture of his life. Do you have a timeline on the repair work on your porch, it must be quite extensive? Your wife's illness was mercifully short. How are you coping? Is retirement suiting you, you must come to our local history lectures? We noticed a nice article in *New England Living*, what a beautiful collection you have. It's wonderful how you manage without a full-time housekeeper.

Daniel did not want these people to know how much money he spent, how he felt after losing Lydia, what he did with his time, who cleaned his house or where his collection would end up. He was happy to maintain the mildly militant career of isolation upon which his mother had embarked. After becoming a widow, she would follow her life entirely as she wanted without the approval of Fairfield society; her affairs were not to be exposed to the unsolicited scrutiny of bored county housewives and then discussed at the country club or with their bored husbands over dinner. Daniel was pleased to have inherited some of her maverick status. The Sales in Greenwich stretched back to the 17th century. They would end with him, the only son of the last marriage to produce a child. About that Daniel had no qualms.

He trusted Chester straight off. A conspiratorial warmth had grown between them from the moment they met. Towards the end of the afternoon they had looked at all of the furniture and paintings and Daniel was pulling out the folio drawers set into the bottom of the bookcases, to show Chester some family documents. He noticed his breathing beside him, strong and calm. Though not as tall as Daniel, he was solid and broad. He had the healthy smell of cut hay, old leather and cologne. Being next to him, gave Daniel a familiar feeling of safety, dredging a sensation from his memory, something happy and boyish. It had been a long time since he'd experienced that.

At the end of Chester's visit, Daniel suggested they go to the cellar underneath this part of the house. It was a rare excursion and he knew very little about wine, in which he had no interest. Thankfully Chester knew something and they pulled out a bottle of 1954 Pauillac, took it upstairs to the sofa and opened it. The wine was slightly brown and had a rich sherry taste, not unpleasant. Daniel was amused when Chester told him before he left, that he was anxious about letting him open this bottle, it might have been worth thousands of dollars.

Chester was fascinated by the family strongbox, in which Daniel's father was said to have found the portolan. He wondered if Daniel would mind if he took it away with him? A conservation studio he worked with had developed a new process using forensic infrared processing which might show up something interesting. The strongbox had always sat in Mae's

studio, which later became Lydia's office and Daniel had never really paid it any attention but he was happy to find a reason for Chester to return to come back, so they wrapped it carefully in a blanket smelling of mothballs.

They stood on the porch for a moment in the last of the evening light, before walking over the lawn where the station wagon was parked under the poplars and as Daniel held his hand out to say goodbye, Chester grasped him with both arms and hugged him with a smile through his beard and got into his car. Thank you for a wonderful day, he said rolling down the window. No, thank you.

When he'd had the Rambler restored, Chester decided to have the best in-car sound system he could afford. As he drew out of the drive down Round Hill, the broad smile still on his face, he flicked his phone to his favourite Country diva and reflected about this amazing day at Gideon's Farm. As *Walkin' After Midnight* blared out of the speakers, there was a thrill in his heartbeat.

He'd been fascinated by Daniel when they first met in Nate Defarge's apartment and later over lunch they'd laughed together at just the right moments. Chester noticed how intently the older man listened when he was speaking, taking in every word. He had a knack of pitching exactly the right question in response, purposefully designed to elicit the most knowledgeable answer. This skill had partly come from Daniel's years of teaching and a desire for his students to perform at their best. But it had also become an effective means of preventing too many unwelcome questions. Chester quickly sensed the slight distance Daniel created around him. It wasn't cold in any way, just a no-man's land, a safe separateness which seemed to make it easier for him to interact. Unusually, Nate hardly got a word in edgeways as the other two talked that afternoon. But something in his demeanor, a slight smile at the edge of his mouth, betrayed that this might just have been his intention.

This easy rapport continued during the visit to Gideon's Farm. He came away feeling that he hadn't really had a conversation with anyone so completely before. He was fascinated by the details of the property as Daniel showed him round every inch of the place explaining how his mother had restored the original 18th-century farmhouse, brilliantly merging the new construction into the sloping bank below it, working with the New York landscape architects West & Horowitz, lions of their day. A bronze sculpture dominated the lawn at the front of the house, and she had later commissioned works from some of the best artists of the day including a vast abstract canvas from Philip Guston which hung beside the staircase, on the facing wall of the hall, marking the transition between old and new. The objects and furniture in the bedrooms upstairs and around the original part of the house were all elegantly proportioned colonial pieces taken from the mansion. But nothing was fussy or overbearing and even 70 years later, Chester wondered at how perfectly modern and stylish it all seemed. Daniel explained that his mother had always had the touch, as with her own appearance, to bring out a minimal but essential beauty in things. But in the modernist extension Cabin there was far more misrule in the way she had chosen the pieces to keep after her husband's death. She'd wanted to preserve things that would give Daniel some sense of his family's part in the history of Greenwich but also to make his young intellect alert to the craft in art, the esthetics of design, ceramics, photography, and sculpture.

The Cabin was set on two floors, the long library sitting room upstairs and the rooms below, accessed by a polished iroko and stainless-steel spiral staircase. On the way down, Daniel pointed out the furrow worn down into the soft curve of the wood by his thumb from boy to man. The cellars of the farmhouse had been preserved when the foundations were exposed and a low wall of matching stone ran from the original building. Glass doors opening straight onto a terrace overlooking the wild meadow garden, ran along the full length of this lower floor. The windows looked out across the end of the terrace to show how Gideon's Farm was perched on the apex of Round Hill with a long view over the canopy of trees to the sea in the far distance.

When Lydia and Daniel married, she fell in love with the study at the front with its precipitous view and spent her life in this look-out immured by her books, emerging only to eat, to sleep and to make conversation with her beloved companion. After retiring, Daniel created a conservation studio behind.

Chester had noticed the sadness about Daniel too. How quickly he shied away from any discussion of his wife, pointing with a wistful glance to her bedroom on the tour of the house. What would it be like to be suddenly alone after a lifetime of companionship, he thought? Chester missed having someone around after his divorce but at 43 he still had the youthful optimism that a good relationship was only a reach away.

In the kitchen, Daniel had explained that as a boy, this was the only room

where he was safe from his mother. She was perfectly capable of cooking, having done so as a girl for her bereaved family. But as soon as she had cast off her girlhood responsibilities, she assumed a state of domestic liberation and never cooked again. When they moved to Gideon's Farm, Daniel had been looked after by a nanny, a small, ruthlessly efficient English spinster who had come with them from Gardiner Court but who was a cut above cooking and by the time he was seven, had returned to Dorset.

Cooks and housekeepers came and went, either terrified of Mae or unsuccessfully attempting to confront her dominance. She would tolerate neither. Then, just as Daniel was off to boarding school, she found Marta, a 19-year-old girl with a head full of good sense before her time. She brought an important balance to Mae's life with an uncanny ability to understand where her employer needed her most at any given moment and became her most trusted ally. But when Marta disappeared into her kitchen, Mae would not follow.

Daniel immediately fell in love with Marta. For a little boy used to his own company and constantly in the shadow of his mother, she provided refuge from Mae's wanton energies. Mae gave no quarter, even to Daniel. If you can't keep up, step back, she'd say. She loved her son with a fierce energy, as an ancient goddess might rule her mortal subjects. There was little in the way of tenderness or untrammelled affection. So he in turn both feared and adored her. But never sought protection or comfort from her. Marta was a gentle antidote to that and her influence on the home was like her food, necessary nourishment.

Chester couldn't help noticing the confidence with which Daniel maneuvered his tall, lean frame around the kitchen, reaching across the shelves above the range, ducking into a cabinet below for a tureen for their chowder which had been simmering on a low heat when he arrived. A batch of freshly baked rolls were plucked from the oven, their soft, yeasty fragrance filling the room, like a censer's incense. When it was all assembled on a large wooden tray, with a bowl of salad and a pitcher of lemonade, Daniel washed and dried his hands, ran his hands through his silver white hair, untied his apron and smiled. The look of a boy still in his eyes, Chester thought.

Most of the afternoon, they sat together at the large table on the porch in the fall warmth, looking through the existing inventory of the contents of the house. And when the light began to fade, they moved to the Cabin and sat on the terrace. On their way back upstairs Daniel took Chester into the cellar and suggested he choose a bottle of wine from the piles of half-open wooden crates and racks of dusty, mildewed bottles. He knew very little about wine, but he wanted him to have something as a thank-you for coming out here. Chester was politely embarrassed but Daniel insisted and so he in turn agreed only if they could open it together. So, they drank a glass of what was probably an extremely rare claret while sitting on one of the sofas in the Cabin, looking over the wild garden, listening to *Diz and Getz* on the record player. They laughed and decided that the wine tasted of dust and old suitcase.

Chapter Seven

It transpired on the day after his arrival in Barcelona, that the professor whom Daniel would be assisting had been called away to Madrid and the young man would have some free time before starting work. Daniel set about exploring the city, following the lines of the tram routes, walking through the grand streets to Sants next to the Plaça Espanya with its vast bullring, round the gardens of the Ciutadella park, down to Barceloneta where the factories and shanty towns stretched into the distant wasteland beyond the beach.

He found parts of the city rather menacing but immediately fell in love with the district of Gràcia below the Parc Güell where the houses were squeezed together along narrow streets, opening out into the squares where people gathered and where strangers to the city were seldom seen. His reasonable grasp of Spanish, learned mostly in the kitchen of Gideon's Farm from Marta, meant he was able to ask his way and eat. But his conspicuous presence was noted and at supper one night, he was surprised at his cousin's warning to be careful of his safety around the city when he was alone and to stick to the areas more familiar to foreigners. Senora Merce had seen him dozing on a bench in Plaça del Diamant. Of course, Daniel, though he was not courageous, was quietly incensed at being told what to do and with the adamantly independent spirit inherited from his mother, nothing would stop him from exploring. He started to look more boldly at passers-by.

Out of the center, away from the sullen-eyed office workers, in the local barrios he noticed the occasional nod and approving smile. He strained to understand the cadences of words he didn't know, strange to his ears in the insistent conversations at the café tables of these hidden places and in a few words passed between passengers on the top of the double-decker buses that took him around the city. One afternoon walking back from lunch, waiting for the policeman in his white helmet, tunic and gloves to give the signal that he could dash across the street through the chaos of buses, trucks and cars, he heard a voice behind him speaking clearly in a language he hadn't heard. Looking behind him he saw a fair-haired newspaper seller standing outside the offices of the *Vanguardia*, holding out a magazine smiling. How are you my friend? As he was taking change from his pocket, a fat man in a suit and a panama hat cut in, looking contemptuously at Daniel and demanded a newspaper. Daniel lost his nerve and walked on but the image of the boy stayed with him all day.

A few days into the following week Daniel was instructed to visit the office of Professor Josep Patxot i Manent, a small, gray-haired, slightly anxious man in his 60s, who reminded him of newspaper photographs of some dissident academic. Patxot inhabited a building on the corner of a wide street in the Eixample, which had originally been built as the College of Architects. Each floor had offices behind the imposing doors of what had once been lecture halls and meeting rooms. Stern looking women in austere black outfits carrying boxes of papers moved silently along the corridors. Everybody spoke in hushed tones, though not to Daniel, who was ignored with haughty suspicion when he arrived.

Through some doors beyond Patxot's office was a set of airy rooms, all lined with bookshelves stuffed and overflowing with boxes, folios and books, cascading down onto the long reading tables. This had once been a library paid for in the 19th century by an eminent industrialist but now it housed the confiscated or unclaimed collections of books, manuscripts and maps belonging to exiled and murdered Catalans which Daniel was to catalog. They hoped he might find and rescue anything rare. The exercise was partly the result of a program of restoration atrociously managed by Patxot's predecessor, who had ended up out of favor with the local powers and was removed under some suspicion, without ever reuniting a single item with its original owners. Because of this a committee of museum curators, local worthies and conservators with the support of a little American cultural research funding, was attempting to find the right homes for these artefacts.

Despite the chaos of historical documents that lay strewn around the room, Daniel was undaunted by the task on which he was to be employed, enjoying the idea of being responsible for wrestling the untamable stacks of paper into order. Mostly what he loved was opening books, sheaves of manuscripts and unrolling maps tied with string or sealed by an archivist decades earlier and seeing their inner secrets come to life. He could never know what he might expect to uncover in this trove, amid clouds of dust and the smell of dried parchment. It was a pleasure he had enjoyed in the rare books and manuscript library at Exhampton but there the undergraduates were always observed under the hawk-eyed disapproval of the librarians who believed that no student, or professor for that matter, should be allowed to violate the sacrosanctity of their precious charges by actually touching them. But here there were no white gloves or book rests,

Daniel just took care of the treasures the best he could.

The professor occupied his office in the room next to him with a feverish energy as if in the constant expectation of invasion. He'd spend his days on the telephone talking so fast, Daniel could never tell what he was discussing. He would pace up and down the tiled floors furiously smoking his pipe and dictating letters to his secretary who sat bolt upright like a crow on a fence, clattering out letters on her ancient typewriter. Although at first she looked on Daniel with pitying disdain, he soon discovered her weakness for chestnut *torrons*, and would offer her an occasional square of the chocolate, which all her sternness could not prevent her from accepting. Eventually she learned a soft spot for the boy and brought him coffee from the stove pot downstairs where the secretaries gathered to smoke and discuss the varying hierarchies of importance among their bosses. It was never expected that Daniel could complete the Sisyphean task he'd been given but that hardly bothered him, and he approached each day with a cheerful purposefulness that everyone admired. None among them could understand why this intelligent American was squandering his youth in a moldering library. Wasn't America the land of the free? Shouldn't he be traveling and seeing places in the world more suitable to a young man? Though it might seem odd to anyone else that Daniel had just swapped one library for another, he found the world in all its variety and adventure in that room and started to love the life he was quickly adapting to in the city.

Around two in the afternoon the whole building would fall silent as its occupants emerged from their work into the streets to find lunch, or walk to a café with their sweetheart. Every day it was the same ritual and it might be two hours or more before people began to return to work. Daniel followed suit and soon found a restaurant that he liked down some steps, next to the flower market. There was sawdust on the floor, which hung from the drooling muzzle of a huge dog that lay unmoving between the kitchen and the bar. It was run by a couple, he at the bar smoking constantly, cutting sweaty slivers of ham, pulling beers and dangerously balancing drinks on his tray while he served the tables and took orders. She came out of the kitchen only to bring food to the tables, plates of greasy, cheap home-cooked local dishes. This was all a revelation to Daniel, for whom the wife developed an affection, bringing him extra plates, indistinct bowls of gray broth with mushrooms or fatty meats, lathered in gelatinous gravy, patting him on the shoulder and showing her incomplete gums as

she smiled, as if she was feeding her own son.

One afternoon when Daniel returned to work, there was a group of men talking excitedly in the professor's office. As he entered and walked past them, they looked at him benignly while continuing their unbroken chatter. Eventually Patxot came into the library with a couple of men and introduced him to an Italian, apparently a well-known art conservation expert, and the other a well-dressed handsome man in his early fifties who looked out of place among the ancient museum curators, with a name he couldn't remember. He explained in perfect English to Daniel that a building in the old part of the city, which they were restoring to house an important modern collection of paintings, had revealed what they believed to be medieval frescoes under the plasterwork. They now had to embark on the painstaking process of uncovering and removing them. The problem they were discussing with such concerned animation was that the restored palace was to house the works of a hugely important but controversial artist, and the government in Madrid were edgy. If they lost too much time, someone might veto the project. The Italian had arrived from Siena the previous day to assess the discovery. He would need a team of people to help and it might be that Daniel will be asked to help, if he would be willing. Until they knew more it would be sensible to say nothing, particularly to the Consulate. Would Daniel accompany Professor Patxot and the rest of the group to the site of the palace on Calle Montcada, the following afternoon?

Daniel hardly noticed his first few weeks in Spain. So much was different and small things needed getting used to; the currency of daily habits. Not least that for the first time in his life, he was able to loosen his tie and feel no obligation to his mother. Theirs had become a symbiotic relationship where he provided the necessary structural foundations for her life, which though she lived it with wilful energy was entirely occupied by schemes to avoid the encroaching boredom she found with men and society generally. Though Mae didn't need his company all of the time or even at all now that he was an adult who had inherited a good deal of her obstinacy, his gentle nature was a rudder for her periodic waywardness and harum-scarum enterprises. Though he lived independently, in a kind of reversal of maternal obligation, she had taught him to always need to know where she was. In later years, after her accident, he blamed himself for letting up that guard.

But now he was far from everything he knew and taking pleasure in a perceptible change he felt happening to his nature. As if by opening the top buttons of his shirt to the warmth of the city, he was coming alive and tiny atoms of curiosity and optimism were coming to life in his blood. Barcelona was an alluring city of contrast, with its unexpected solemnity. The other ports he had visited during the cruise were teeming with color and activity, they seemed exotic in comparison, just like the historic records of voyages and trading expeditions he had read. But here, perched by the sea, the city was like an unwanted cousin of the Mediterranean and resisted the easy familiarity of Athens or Naples. Barcelona was retiring, haughty even. He felt at ease with that.

The weather during the day was still warm but when the sun was low the streets were in shadow and the rooms which most of the year had their balcony doors thrown open, were cold with their tiled floors. Here no-one seemed to spend any time at home and from mid-afternoon, around six, the cafés and bars filled up; people spilled out of their offices and workplaces, occupying the avenues and boulevards with noisy chatter. Daniel found himself becoming more open and cheerful. He even occasionally sought the company of Robert, who had ascertained that his younger cousin had no intention of overstaying his welcome and so responded by suggesting that they walk around the city to look round some of the barrios where he might like to live. They even went out of town in his car to a nearby village where they had lunch and strolled by the sea. But they were both private men, with a preordained rivalry between them, which could never be breached. Despite the superficial pleasantries they tolerated each other's company with mutual respect, but no more than that.

One of their walks took them past Plaça Catalunya, down the Ramblas veering left to the Cathedral and beyond into the winding streets through the Gothic quarter, where Daniel felt excited, even a little alarmed as they rounded the shadowy cul-de-sacs full of dampness and the odours of buildings sunk into the ground centuries before. He was all too familiar with the ordered urban vision of the 19th-century New York industrial magnates with their grand open boulevards and imposing facades. But in these narrow alleyways, history – old history – stretched from far beneath the ground upwards, sometimes eight or ten floors, teetering towards the gap of blue sky wedged between roofs above.

That history, those ancient struggles, intermingled with the ravages of the recent past and a sense of unease with the present, was engraved on the faces of the people who lived here. All their daily efforts, nightly squabbles and angry retorts, occasional neighborly kindnesses, shadowy love affairs and lurking secrets skulked under their caps and scarves as they made their way under arches, through doorways and up the many flights of stairs. He was fascinated by that feeling of precariousness, not dangerous exactly – he never felt he would be harmed here – but that his own self-preserving need for privacy could coexist quite simply here, without social formality and that by being among them, without actually watching each other he would be able to become part of the lives of others going about their daily business.

The room in which the frescoes had been discovered was a large vaulted chamber deep in the building which had been a palace for centuries, now rather unceremoniously known as Montcada, 15. It had passed between noble families since the city had been a great independent maritime and trading power, ruled by a monarchy of its own. Floodlights had been set up in the room, illuminating the mildewed walls where the paintings were still intact, covered in lime and plaster. There was a palpable sense of excitement in the room as the workmen busily placed duckboards on low trestles alongside them. The conservation team, four men and a young woman in white coats, huddled in a corner talking hurriedly, occasionally issuing a warning to the builders to take care. Professor Patxot explained that these could turn out to be the most important medieval frescoes discovered in the city and that their preservation and removal would take months. It had been decided to continue with the building renovations in the rest of the palace in order not to lose time, while this project was taking place. He had been in Madrid to ask for more money to pay for the work but none had been forthcoming, so the university and museums would pay though they were strapped for cash. He had been impressed by Daniel's work so far and hoped he might be willing to support the conservation team by cataloguing each stage of their work.

Daniel was thrilled to be asked and immediately agreed, his calm expression breaking into a broad smile, which reassured the professor who thought the young man was a little too placid. As Daniel walked through the building works and out onto the street, it was with a feeling of importance, that he knew this is what he longed for in a life of academic research. Precious objects, the silent witnesses of time past, needed to be cared for and he was being recognized as someone who might do this well.

He finally had status in the world, something of his own, with no bearing on his family or name. Meandering happily through a tapestry of streets, he came across a square with a tiny café and sat under an acacia tree to drink a beer. As he looked up through the branches, he saw a painted sign offering a room to rent on the balcony of the fourth floor.

So when Daniel returned that afternoon and insisted that he'd found decent lodgings in a room belonging to a reputable widow in La Ribera who owned a laundry behind the Santa Caterina market, Robert decided to silence his misgivings and immediately gave his approval, relieved that he too would soon have his life back to himself.

Chapter Eight

Daniel could hear the workmen setting in place the straight new lumber pillars. He went outside onto the porch where the smell of paint mingled with the sweet mulch of fall. The tiles on the sloping roof had been painstakingly replaced and the men had already started work on rebuilding the floor and the railing screens. He was pleased with the progress and was fond of the young builder who he believed was trustworthy and reliable. The only obvious giveaway that he wasn't an affluent native were his tar-stained teeth. But this is why I come to America, he'd laugh. He was completely open about the price of assimilation, happily telling Daniel in his careful accent, after the teeth I will get a really American wife and really beautiful children and to forget I ever came from Croatia. There was a great deal of specialist restoration to do on the Cabin, Daniel said, so if he wanted there would be plenty of work and that dream could be closer. Ade smiled broadly shaking Daniel's hand and revealing his wonky teeth to his employer's gaze with reckless humour.

After they'd passed time on the porch, Daniel took a wide basket down the side of the house through the wild garden, where helenium, goldenrod and hyssop were still blooming on the land that ran from the east over the spur down the hill towards the town. As the path cut through the tall meadow grasses into the dense forest between Gideon's Farm and the rest of the world, Daniel closed his eyes and drew in the smells he had known so well for a lifetime. Further through the oaks and down a small incline, the sun broke through into a small coppice of black walnut trees. Every fall around this time, he would make his way carefully down here to pick the fallen nuts. As a boy and then later with Lydia this harvest would be ready for Thanksgiving and Christmas and last year after her death he continued to do so because he needed to keep something of their routine together. And because he felt he'd lost so much here, it was important to connect with the land he lived on with all of its seasonal changes. This was an act of pagan duty. He knew that when he died, the plot would be sold to an investment banker who would tear up the garden to make a pool and tennis courts for his ill-mannered children and that the ritual of collecting these walnuts every year would be forgotten. But he was alive and intended to be so for some time to come, so the nutting would go on.

After collecting a basketful, Daniel sat down on a tree trunk, looking down the bluff into the undergrowth beyond. He lost focus on the shafts of sunlight catching the gleam of rose hips. Something was rising inside him. Indistinct emotions awash in memory quickened his heartbeat. He could hear the faint voices of children ringing in his years. His eyes filled with tears and for a few minutes he sat unmoving, gazing unknowingly through salty droplets, the past clawing its way up the hill before him.

He came back to reality with the usual quiet bump and sat breathless for a moment collecting himself. In his mind's eye he could see Sheldon here, all those years before. Sheldon was Raymond Buller's youngest son and had been Daniel's childhood friend. The Bullers lived in a large stone house on the other side of Round Hill, off Clapboard Ridge, called Mount Wales. During the school vacations, Sheldon would escape the tyranny of his older siblings and cycle through the lanes to Gideon's Farm where he and Daniel would pass hours playing in these woods. Daniel was tall and skinny, Sheldon was a year older, more solid, more daring and had to show off his bravado all the time. Even when he was little, this used to upset Daniel. Sheldon never let up his need to be top dog. But they came and went as boys do, acting out scenarios freshly sown in fertile minds with strong imaginations.

When he brought the nuts home, Daniel placed them in the flat stone trough at the back door of the kitchen and then smashed the skins away from the hulls with a large stone. This done, he took his haul downstairs to the studio where he laid the fleshy innards to cure on sheets of newspaper. It hadn't ended well with Sheldon. They were good friends, but the older boy loved to torment Daniel and was developing physically much faster. One hot afternoon, during one of their play battles, he pinned Daniel's arms to the ground with his knees and was pinching him mercilessly all over. Then he started slapping his hands covered in moss and mud on Daniel's face, under his shirt and then inside his pants. Feeling this unwanted intrusion, something savage welled up in Daniel. Squirming from underneath his captor, in one heft he wriggled free and swung a branch at him half-playfully. With no intent to actually harm his friend, the branch slipped from his hands and lurched into his chest, throwing him to the ground. He lay there winded, unable to speak. Daniel ran terrified to Marta who called a doctor. Sheldon had to be taken to hospital suffering from a collapsed lung. Though he went to see him in hospital and Sheldon did come over to visit when he was better, there was something awkward in their friendship now and it did not recover.

He sat in a wicker chair and looked out across the sea of reds and ochers in the lowering afternoon light. He was becoming anxious that these moments with the ringing in his ears, the blank forgetfulness were signs of the approach of something more serious than the confused reveries of an old man. As his mind returned to the sound of the wood thrush, it brought back the words of Thoreau:

Whenever a man hears it, he is young, and Nature is in her spring. Wherever he hears it, it is a new world and a free country, and the gates of heaven are not shut against him.

He enjoyed seeing the twilight here, the way the dying embers of light from the west reflected on the trees in front of him. Just as all his beginnings were on the porch, this side of the house was a place of contemplation and rest. The evening of his mother's drowning, he'd returned from the morgue after identifying her body and had come to sit here. The morning after Lydia died, he came down with his tea, desolate, alone again. He knew the pattern would never change. Going into the woods brought back the ending of things.

Though Daniel thrived in the relative solitude of Greenwich, he still loved going to the city. Once he'd sold the apartment, he stayed overnight in one of the cheap rooms at the Exhampton Club on Fifth Avenue, breakfasting early in the morning room before taking a walk in the park. Sometimes he'd go up to the Metropolitan where as a Friend and benefactor of the Thomas J. Watson Library he could take advantage of early access to the galleries. He increasingly found the monumental stagings of canonical work too much to take in on a walk through; now he was happier settling for one object at a time, seeking out a single act of genius to sit in front of and fully absorb.

At 77, the contrast between the urbane and the simplicity of his life in the country gave Daniel a kick. His youthful passion for jazz continued at home but he'd stopped buying new records or going to concerts back in the 1960s, when most of his heroes were dying off. The artists who were playing bebop these days were pastiches of what he'd been used to and his interest had waned with the arrival of modern fusion and abstract electro. At the same time Lydia, though she shared a generalised pleasure in the ruckus of jazz, had opened his ears to classical music. The supreme monoliths of the 19th century, she pronounced them: Schumann, Bruckner, Mahler and Sibelius. And then a special obsession with Schubert *Lieder*. Daniel

knew when she had finished working for the evening because he could hear those familiar melodramatic tones signaling that she was emerging from the chrysalis of her study. She said that Schubert interpreted poetry in ways she could never reach.

To mark her 60th birthday, Daniel made a generous endowment from the Sale Trust to the Brooklyn Concert Society in their fundraising program for a tailor-made concert hall in a refurbished cloth factory in Williamsburg. They wanted to name one of the large public spaces after her, but he knew she would want something more discreet. So, he decided on the Lydia Sale Studio, a rehearsal room where there would be masterclasses and small recitals. She was delighted when she arrived entirely unsuspecting, to the launch of construction for the Cloth Factory. She became deeply involved in supporting young musicians and singers, particularly from the poorest parts of the city, setting up bursaries to help them study and following their progress with genuine care and excitement. One of their beneficiaries was now a leading operatic tenor. Daniel was not ostentatious but privately thought this was the best thing he had ever done with his family's money and resolved to leave the society a legacy in his will. He still attended concerts regularly; a difficult reminder where he felt Lydia's absence keenly.

Late that October, a few weeks after Chester's visit, Daniel walked down the drive to collect the mail, frost crunching under his new boots. He wedged two letters and a package under his arm and marched back to the kitchen, hands deep in his lumberjack jerkin, feeling the crisp air catch his nose and ears. Sitting at the table with toast, a pot of Darjeeling tea, poached eggs and bacon, he opened the letters.

The first confirmed that his doctor had made an appointment with the consultant at the Exhampton New Haven Hospital Geriatric Unit, which though he knew he was healthy, irritated Daniel by association. He was anything but geriatric and had kept himself well-tuned, walking wherever he could, still hiking up into the Berkshire mountains every year and he swam regularly as clockwork in the local club. But Daniel had always faced difficulties head on. He knew it was important to have these tests, grateful on the one hand to move things on, but terrified of the unwelcome possibility of what he might have to face.

The second was a hand-written invitation from the Director of the Brooklyn Cloth Factory for the following Sunday to hear a recent graduate from the Juilliard rising talent program sing *Winterreise* in place of the string quartet who had been booked to play but who were stuck in Tel Aviv with no visas. Nate, who was his usual companion to concerts these days, was out of town, wintering in Palm Springs. He'd been going there since Sonny died. I have a whole other summer social life, darling. Meanwhile you are freezing your balls off with the rest of your Connecticut worthies. Daniel was not persuaded to visit, suspecting he wouldn't cope long with gossipy octogenarians, incessant cocktails and worst of all bridge, the prospect of which terrified him. As it was, he enjoyed the state of winter at Gideon's Farm. He made a note of the concert in his diary and resolved to invite Chester who he recalled lived in Brooklyn, around Williamsburg.

He turned the remaining package round and for a moment Daniel's heart stopped. He swallowed. It was postmarked from Spain. He slowly held it out in his hands to examine it, noticing his fingers were still chilled from the walk to the mailbox. A brown cardboard envelope sealed over with tape at the top. The sort of thing in which books arrived. The address was capitalized in a peculiar hand. He moved aside his breakfast things and cleaning the knife on his napkin, he carefully slipped it under the tape. As he opened the flap, a knot rose from the pit of his gut into his diaphragm.

What emerged, in one moment reversed everything that had happened in Daniel's life for the last half-century. Fifty years spilled out of that envelope, like an avalanche pouring unstoppable down a mountainside. As he allowed the contents to fall out on the table, he saw his own handwriting, words he had formed years ago, written in desperation, the blood and tears of shame, guilt and pain. He started to tap his foot on the floor to regulate the breath trying to burst from his heaving lungs. After a few moments, he turned over the thin sheaf of letters tied together with a ribbon, the faded blue ink on the envelopes quite faint but still legible: *J. Ferran, Carrer Pintor Fortuny, 14, Barcelona, Spain.*

A thick leather-bound notebook, with the initials embossed in faintly perceptible gold leaf. D. B. S. His initials. With cortisol pumping into his bloodstream, the shock had turned to fear, mixed with outrage, not just that but despair also. He started to convulse uncontrollably. Everything he had turned away from, all the years of pushing away the pain, burying it further into the depths of his subconscious, were thrown at him again in a few seconds. Bewildered, Daniel put his hands on his head, elbows raised and let out a cry. From that place, submerged under layers of time, rose a sound, so preternatural and anguished that it might have broken every heart for miles around.

Holding the notebook in his hand, Daniel pressed the frayed corner of the leather between his thumb and forefinger, then lifted it to his nose and inhaled deeply. There were vague notes of camphor and beeswax like a forgotten religious artefact. He is moving backwards, losing the present. Now there is a room, lightless but for a yellowish afternoon haze filtering through lace curtains. Everything here is heavy; the brackish air, the oversized furniture, the thrum of a bluebottle slowly circumnavigating the room. In a straight-backed chair a young woman, severe and cruel, sits with tears in her eyes. She looks up accusing and he turns away quickly not even able now to slow the heartbeats racing through him. He can't remember what he wants to say, his tongue is swollen in his mouth, stopping him from voicing a name that keeps repeating in his head but which he cannot speak. Inside, silently, he is screaming. Then the image begins to fade and a fast frame of time rushes round him, his consciousness returns, landing him alone in the present again, still unable, or unwilling to speak the name.

He came around face down on the table with his forehead resting on his arms, teardrops stained the shattered leather of the notebook. This feels like a death again, he thought. The alienating intensity of grief that renders you incapable of fully connecting with what is going on around you. Only a few minutes ago, he had been having breakfast and looked down at the half-eaten toast, a futile act of human endeavor. Every action, movement, intention and decision he'd made in his life had been, in some way, to guard against this moment or at least to anesthetize the fear of its occurring. He'd sought peace from the constant pain of knowing that the life he should have had was stolen from him, had been taken as quickly and unexpectedly as it came. The draught of hope which he had drunk so deeply all those years before, had become a venom for which he had spent his whole life looking for an antidote. But it turns out that trying to wash it away had been a useless effort, for here he was after all that, exactly where he had begun.

Chapter Nine

On the wall of Daniel's room on Plaça de Llana there was a plain crucifix above the bed, which he left there out of respect for his landlady. It had originally been the sitting room of the apartment at the front of the building but a sink had been installed and the pipes came through a large hole and exited through the floorboards. Newspapers, now old and yellow, had been stuffed in the gaps and above the sink was a mirror and a shelf with just enough room for a glass, his toothbrush and razor and miniature model of the Empire State Building, that Nate had given him the night before he set sail. To remind you of home. So you don't forget me. On the wall next to the window he pinned a poster from an antique market in Glòries where an old man in a beret sat smoking, surrounded by junk. The picture was a stylized utopian image of a javelin player, dressed in white and had been a poster for some international sporting games before the Civil War. On a marble-topped chest of drawers against the other wall, he kept the few books he had brought with him and there was a square table and chair in front of the balcony doors. From here he would dash off letters to Mae, full of general observations and news of his activities. Not so much information that she could imagine the worst nor too little that she'd be concerned. Thankfully, there was no telephone in the building which made him feel safe from her intrusion. Mae responded with occasional letters briefly expressing her pleasure at his success and recounting her activities and small domestic dramas.

Just outside his room, next to the door of the bathroom, was a recess with an electric ring on a cupboard where he could make coffee. In the mornings, he would run down to the bakery in the next street for bread or croissants which he'd eat while a shaft of morning sun between the roofs of the surrounding buildings, beat down on his legs stretched out into the balcony. Then he'd rally himself and head to work in the library or some mornings go straight to Montcada. His task was to photograph and catalog every detail of the painstaking conservation process when a new section of the frescoes was carefully transferred from the wall. This was done by covering the painted surface with a layer of cloth and a heavy glue made from animal bones, which absorbed the pigments and when it dried transferred the painting to the cloth. It was kept in one piece by removing it with a thin layer of plaster, a traditional technique still used by the Italian conservator. He bustled around the room importantly in a smock, followed by an assistant who, whatever direction the master looked, followed his gaze as he issued instructions, which Daniel then recorded as best he could. The busy scene had the effect of making him look like a renaissance painter working on a grand commission with his studio entourage in attendance.

Once the sections of painting were taken down, they were transported carefully in the back of a van on wooden boards to a room next to the professor's office where they were laid out on the floor and cleaned ready for conservation. Daniel became part of this team, wearing the same dusty overalls while he worked and sometimes joining them for lunch. The young woman among them was called Natalia. She spoke excellent English and they soon became friends, spending evenings together watching westerns at the Capitol cinema. Daniel had been on dates with girls before, when he was at Exhampton and sometimes in New York, but they usually got bored as he had little skill in small talk and certainly never made a move to kiss them. Natalia seemed to expect no more than good company from her handsome American friend, so he relaxed, joining her for walks around the city, sometimes exploring places she'd never been. Spending time with Daniel reminded her of her trips to study abroad and his conversation was a relief from the demands of her family.

That evening he wrote to Mae. *I walked from the Cathedral with Natalia whom I work with at the museum. She's rather jokey with me and says I take myself too seriously. She talks about her studies in London all the time. I tell her to go back there but she loves working with Pitrelli. I think she hopes he might offer her a post in Siena. Walking to Montjuic, we saw a whole village of shanty houses not far from the summit. Natalia says they are full of Andaluz Gypsies who sell magic charms and dance naked round their fires. Visited the Poble Espanyol, pavilions built for the 1929 International Exhibition here. Now it is only full of mangy cats and barefoot children begging for a few pesetas. After this we had lunch of meat and cuttlefish in Poble Sec, a nice area beneath Montjuic Hill. She has a cousin who sings in a choir. Says she'll invite me sometime to the Palau de Musica. I am going to buy a ticket to see some jazz next week.*

Daniel seldom went anywhere without a book and he was reading the newspaper in Spanish to help his conversation, though he understood little of the politics and noticed that generally people he met steered away from any discussions like that. He would sit in the café under his balcony with a glass of red wine, smoking cigarettes, with his leather journal as companion, contemplating the activities of his day. Though his task was to organize and catalog the family collections, it wasn't so simple and he would be easily drawn into the particulars of a book or manuscript which might distract him for hours. He sat in his shirtsleeves in this dusty empire of moths with some yellowing parchment on his knees, holding his breath as he turned the pages. Occasionally a note or a photograph would fall from the leaves, records of the loves and lives of the lost owners. Many of the artefacts were in Catalan and were of little significance except to an enthusiast for historical ephemera – family documents, contracts, letters of commission, treatises and architectural plans. He could make educated guesses about their exact contents because the language had romance tones of Latin and French which he knew well and as he was writing up the catalog in English for later translation, he often described them as much by their physical appearance.

He knew that his job was really to identify if these assiduous collections contained anything important or overlooked. He wasn't ever sure if they had been confiscated or rescued but he loved this intimacy with their provenance, bringing him closer to the origins of these orphaned treasures. Though ownership was never clear, and he wished he knew more of the families who had left these objects behind, his instinct told him that there was more at work than the restitution of lost property.

Dozing in bed the following Sunday, the bells of the great cathedral down by the sea resonated through the buildings and the alleyways of the barrio as he flitted in and out of sleep. Yawning loudly, Daniel stretched his legs out, arched his torso and ran his fingers through his hair. There was a rare and unconscious smile on his face as he relived the events of the night before in his mind.

It was midday but he'd hardly slept, not arriving home until the sun was already well up. Ever since he arrived, he'd planned to go to one of the jazz clubs in Escudellers. Music was something he missed from New York City, the pleasure of getting lost in the simple clarity, the abstract rhythms and virtuosity of jazz. And he loved that this music brought so many different types of people together, regardless of class or color; enthusiasts who could find esoteric ecstasy in the bar lines and others who just got drunk on the mayhem of it all. All energised by its drive. A great jazz number is like a kaleidoscope, it takes you somewhere, bowls you over, turns you upside down, wrings you out and puts you back head up and alert to everything

in a new way.

The day had been hot for December and in the morning he had decided to walk down to the beach, emerging from the damp reek of La Ribera, past the old port. Here the fishermen's wives sat mending nets with their sleeves rolled up, wearing black from headscarves to skirts, their calloused knees and bare legs as brown as the earth. Their men gathered on the boats, smoking and arguing about the week's catch, the latest fish-market prices or last night's football. He couldn't tell which. It was a city full of industry and noise, the struggle of its past mingling with modernity, the port with its vast warehouses backing onto the railroad sidings, the horns of trucks blowing and the whistle of trains shunting cargoes in and out of the yards. Here everyone came together; ship owners and peasants, suited brokers and dockers, gangs of American sailors and the dark-skinned girls who made eyes at them, sighing from a safe distance.

Past the *chiringuitos* ranked along the front, Daniel found a spot where he could sit and watch the people encamped on the beach in the thin early winter sunlight. It was teeming with young people his own age which made him acutely self-conscious. He was strong and slim and at the beach house on Long Island, he would be stripped to his trunks and soaking in the sun all day. In December, the weather was cool in Barcelona and the older people sat on their beach chairs in their overcoats but for him it was perfect weather and he envied the gang of boys sunning themselves in front of him. Part of him longed to be among them, to be talking and laughing with them. But it would have been out of place for him. He was an outsider and however much he wanted to be brought alive by sun and sea on his skin, he'd be too embarrassed. As was so often the case in his life, this blond, fair-skinned foreigner stood back and observed the life he could see others enjoying. He tried to read his book but there were too many distractions to keep his attention on it for long. At one point a ball skidded in the sand, sending a shower of sand over him. A tall guy who looked his own age but with strong sinewy limbs and wild dark hair ran over laughing while apologizing to him half in Spanish and then in English. He turned away to return the ball to the shouts of his friends before Daniel had a chance to respond.

In the seemingly untroubled lives of the locals, he saw a simplicity, an easy way with things that he just hadn't known. That was certainly true of their social habits, where nothing happened quickly. He'd never experienced such long days that often didn't end until the beginning of the next. Life here revolved around eating and drinking with friends and family but with little formality and meals could take place over many hours. Work here was hardly ever discussed, toil seemed to be considered a mere footnote to the rest of the day when the most important thing was the uncomplicated society of others. Alongside this languid attitude, Daniel noticed how much they despised deference and authority. Nobody liked to queue, you just had to find your moment to get yourself on a tram or space at the bar. During lunchtimes, which was the only time he was ever in a group, no-one waited for their turn to talk, conversation was freeform. But despite being difficult to follow, he soaked it all up.

In the late afternoon, he had fried green peppers and salt cod at one of the sea-front places, before heading home to sleep for a few hours. He decided to wear a dark blue shirt, cream pleated pants with his favorite deck shoes and a sweater against the cold. With his hair slicked back he looked like the photograph of his father in France. He arrived at the club early to make sure he got a good seat. It was already busy, mostly with other foreigners but he found a spot at the side in an alcove with a direct line over the stage and ordered whiskey. The combo was led by a young blind pianist recently returned from a successful tour of America. It was a style of post-bop, a little different to the straight bebop on which Daniel had been schooled, here the band would swing in and out of rhythms and tempo in looser form. He liked the way numbers shaped themselves around the musicians, one moment the drums would lead out the band, then piano would slide back in and drive it all onward before the trumpet or sax sailed in take it off in a new direction. The whole atmosphere of the noisy, smoke-filled underground den delighted Daniel and for the first time since leaving home almost three months before, he lost himself completely in the moment.

A few hours passed until in the early hours Daniel emerged bleary-eyed and warm from several whiskeys into the busy street. The sounds of the music still ringing in his ears, he wandered into the big square where the restaurants were closing up and crossed under the palm trees, stopping to light a cigarette at one of the madly ornate street lamps in the middle. As he was looking in his pocket for matches, a young woman appeared from nowhere in front of him. He could see her eyes glistening in the dark under her black hair, pinned up with metal combs. Hey sailor, can I have one smoke? He stammered in Spanish trying to explain that he wasn't a sailor before submissively handing her a cigarette. His fingers struggled to light a match and he immediately regretted he'd said anything, wishing she'd go away. Sensing his unease, she smiled. You Americano yes? Yes, yes I am. I'm a student. You like pretty girls? Oh yes, I mean no, I'm sorry I'm going home now, thank you. He blushed wondering why he wasn't just asking her to leave him alone. I can come too, she laughed, putting the still unlit cigarette into her hair. Just as she did so a young man, Daniel's age, unusually tall, with long dark hair swept back behind his ears called the girl from behind as he approached them. She turned around unperturbed and they exchanged the usual nonchalant kiss on each cheek. He turned to Daniel and laughed. Hey, you don't remember me? Daniel was surprised and started to back away, unsure if he was being set up. I'm sorry, no, I don't. On the beach this afternoon, my friends were playing football. It landed next to you? I guess you wouldn't recognize me, I looked a little different. Suddenly Daniel saw the guy smiling at him from earlier in the day. Don't worry Lili won't bother you anymore, he spoke some Spanish to the girl and she wandered off to the other side of the square. My name is Xavi, holding out his hand. Hello, said Daniel nonplussed, aware that circumstances had slipped out of his control. But with hardly time to make a mental note that three glasses of whiskey were too many, he realized he didn't feel at all threatened and held out his hand. I'm Daniel.

Chapter Ten

Daniel withdrew the single sheet of white paper remaining in the envelope. He read the typed text, grateful for the grasp of something of the present among these moth-eaten relics. At the top of the page, the name Rosa Lopez Mestre, an email address, the date and a telephone number.

Dear Professor Daniel Sale,

I wanted to contact you last year, following the death of my mother Elena Ferran Lopez. I could not find the right way to explain what I have to write to you and it has taken me this time to prepare for the journey I will now take with my husband to New York in December. We are bringing my daughter, who is looking at the opportunity to study at Columbia University. I will be able to meet you in person and to talk to you of the things I know. I hope this will be possible.

As you may not know, I must explain that my father was Don Gilberto Lopez of Buenos Aires and he married my mother in 1963. Two years later I was born. My mother lived a long life and died when she was 84 years old.

Before my mother died, she made a confession to me. What she told me was very shocking as I had not known of the history of my family during the Civil War or the time of Franco. But most of all she wanted forgiveness for an act of betrayal against you. And to my uncle Xavier who you knew at the time. She told me you had all been friends and that she had not been kind to either of you. She had never spoken of these matters before and soon she was too sick to tell me anymore. I am sad to say that my mother died an unhappy woman, regretting things in her past.

She asked me to promise to return to you these letters and notebook. There are other matters regarding this history of my family but I do not wish to say more in this letter. I decided to send it first as I do not know you or what your life is. But I found that you were still living at the home of your family from some articles on the internet. I am sorry if this is a shocking letter for you to receive.

We will be arriving in New York on December 17 and visit for five days. If you will give me your contact details by email, I will call you when we arrive at our hotel.

The letter was signed by hand. Daniel's heart was still racing but he'd begun to feel calmer. Reading the names of these two people with whom his fate had once been so entwined brought a profound sadness and relief, as if he'd never wanted that story to end. For a while he cried the inconsolable tears of a child and when he was done, he stood up shakily, cleared the table, placing his breakfast things carefully in the sink and took these tatters of his past into the Cabin. The half-finished bottle still sat on the liquor tray, he was tempted to pour a glass, checking himself when he realized that despite reliving his whole life that morning, it was still only 11.30.

He sat down on the sofa and untied the fragile ribbon with which someone had so carefully tied up his letters, knowing that somewhere in Gideon's Farm there were more like these sent back to him years before. He had not shown them to Lydia, she only knew the scantest details of this episode of his youthful life. He did not wish to hide anything from her but to have acknowledged the detail would have exposed to the memory of what his life should have been and his responsibility for the death of someone he loved. It would have knocked him off-balance. The matters to which he had devoted his daily existence every day of the last 50 or more years: the maps, his work, first his mother, then Lydia. These things had saved him from this truth. What a time to come, he thought wryly, just as I am fearing the glue of my mind is weakening, this comes from out of nowhere. The final reckoning.

Over the coming hours, his youthful self, banished to a distant past, began to reform in his mind, like an alabaster statue slowly coming to life. Memories and scenes long consigned to his subconscious resurfaced. He had no idea what to do, nothing had prepared him for this. Everything he had done since returning home had been a superhuman attempt to suppress the truth of what had happened. He was weak and bewildered but at the same time, the light started to search inside him, like sunlight entering a long-forgotten corner of the forest, newly exposed by a fallen tree.

The next day Daniel woke late in the morning feeling knocked about inside. Having spent the intervening hours in a state of silent shock, he found the feeling returning to his nerve endings and realized it was time to reconnect himself. Exposed to the guilt and loss he had carried for so long, by now he didn't care if this knowledge could hurt him, it was too late to change anything and he was too old.

He resolved to attempt his normal routine, take a swim in the afternoon and call Chester about the concert. First, he made a pot of strong coffee, which he only drank at home on days when he thought courage would be required. He went down to his studio, where Mae had once painted rather badly and later developed the photographs for which she had more talent. Daniel in his turn had put it to more focused use as his map conservation studio. The room was on the lower level of the Cabin and had one wall of natural stone and the other of glass supported by two large steel riveted pillars. The glass was covered in a dark film to prevent the afternoon sunlight damaging the maps, so the light in the room came from square lumières on rails on the ceiling. The temperature in the studio was always cold, being carefully regulated by a humidifier, so he put on the vicuna sweater he left down here and a white apron. A large central wash table stood in the middle of the floor where his brittle orphans were bathed to bring them back to life and to enable the removal of centuries' old layers of dirt. This was surrounded by various trestle workstations, some on wheels. One housed a lightbox with a large sheet of toughened glass, another had a vacuum suction table for blotting stains from the fragile discolored paper and also a mounting frame for drying boards. Against the back wall were wooden folio rails with open shelves beneath, full of his prized maps and many of the photographs his mother had developed here.

Daniel was actually an historiographer but his years of working with conservators, starting half a century earlier in Barcelona, had given him a practical knowledge of preservation techniques and a fascination with restoring lost artefacts on paper. In retirement, he forged a reputation for reliable renovation. But despite being well able to afford them he wasn't vain enough to assume responsibility for really important sea charts, preferring the ones that appeared to be lost causes. He'd usually acquire destitute nautical charts through salerooms or dealers, carefully transporting these torn, mildewed and rotting objects to his studio; the place Lydia had called the Hospital for Broken Maps. Indeed, once he'd put on his white apron and sat down on the high stool at the workbench covered in the tools and paraphernalia of his trade and put on his magnifying visor, complete concentration in his eyes, he looked like a surgeon preparing for the most delicate of operations.

Over the years he'd patched up a good number, the best of which he'd given to permanent collections but most of the charts he catalogued and stored safely for his own interest. On the drying board was an 18th-century pilot's map of Narragansett Bay. It had been badly damaged with water staining to at least half of the map and the paper was frayed and torn with several pieces missing. The lengthy and careful conservation process starts by strengthening the front of the chart to prevent further deterioration, lining it with a delicate Japanese tissue paper. Then with perfect precision the map's original cloth backing is gently removed before immersing the paper in the shallow water bath, where the discoloration of all the years is painstakingly cleaned. The paper is then removed and before a new liner is added to the back, it is then laid on the suction table where remarkably the vacuum removes the worst of the stains onto blotting paper. The next stage is to reinstate the loose paper fragments to their exact positions, flatten the whole using glass weights and apply the new backing.

Although a professional conservator might take a couple of months to complete this complicated process, Daniel was happy to work on two or three charts in a year. And since Lydia's death, he had been disconsolate and easily distracted. He found it harder to be in the studio without the knowledge of her presence in the adjoining room. Both of them had always been occupied in the business of being busy, their minds too febrile to allow them to sink into any kind of torpor brought on by retirement. They allowed themselves very few vacations, the occasional conference visit and an annual trip to the Newport Jazz Festival. They both felt that life at home was as good as they might have it.

Daniel had not expected Lydia to die before him. It was a source of great dissatisfaction to him that in this aspect of his life he had also failed. But then he reminded himself that if he hadn't been around to see her through the last weeks, who would? And now this, he thought, as he lifted the mutilated chart and delicately placed it flat on the opal glass light-table, just as a surgeon might do with a new heart ready to transplant.

Later in the afternoon he drove the old pick-up to the swim club. He was greeted, as always, with jovial familiarity by the changing room attendant. Stan wasn't young but he had jug ears and a lanky boyish goofiness about him, which cheered Daniel up. He had clean towels next to Daniel's locker, as if he'd been expecting him. It's been over a week since I saw you, Professor, you're well I hope. We worry about you, you know, when you don't show up. Regular as clockwork I always say. I know you prefer to swim outdoors but hey, before you know it, just as you're getting used to being indoors again, spring will be right upon us and they'll have that pool open. We have Thanksgiving and the festivities to get through, I guess. Enjoy your swim, Professor. Daniel swam forty lengths freestyle in the same lane, breathing every five strokes, methodically pushing through the water, stopping a moment at every ten lengths for breath. Sometimes afterwards, if he had time before the local mothers brought their kids after school, he would take a Turkish steam, for which Stan provided separate towels and a pumice stone. As he left, without fail Daniel placed a neatly folded ten-dollar bill on the table where Stan sat. Goodbye, Stan, I'll see you later in the week, he said and smiled, wondering on what day of the week December 18th would fall.

In the parking lot as Daniel was about to open the door of the pick-up and climb in, he heard a voice, a child's voice, behind him. Grandpa, grandpa, why don't you look at me, grandpa? He turned and a little girl with pigtails, holding her swimsuit and a pink swim ring in the shape of a dinosaur was looking at him with inquisitive eyes, head cocked to one side. Before her mother could make it over to them, she looked at him again quizzically and started to cry. The woman apologized profusely as her daughter clung to her legs, explaining that her father had recently passed away and her daughter was taking it rather badly. Daniel smiled, leaned forwards and patted the little girl on the head. Afterwards he sat motionless in the truck thinking about the encounter and how his feelings as a boy had never been allowed to flow freely like that. Mae had occupied his childhood, it had been a campaign, one of the conquests of the men in her life. All his needy emotions were turned to stone by her Medusa touch. She impressed upon him that relying on love was impossible and would make him pointlessly vulnerable. Purposeful goals would make him happy and independent. Despite her, his instinctive emotions were often brought to life, but always briefly awoken by the sufferings of others, never his own sadness. Well apart from that one time in his life, which seemed to have come back to find him. Here he was, the ancient chimera of that young man long ago, free and happy. And he had no idea what to do.

Chapter Eleven

Early evening Chester was on his cell taking a client through the latest federal Estate Tax provisions for his classic automobile collection, when the landline rang. These days he hardly ever used it but was pleased to hear the voice on the line. Chester it's Daniel. How are you, Daniel? It's just great to hear from you, I was going to call you over the weekend. I think the lab might have come up with something on the strongbox. Chester I won't keep you but I wanted to ask, next weekend, Sunday, there is a concert in Brooklyn at midday I wondered if you'd like to come? Sunday, I have the girls over for the weekend Daniel, Christina, my ex-wife is away. We've planned to have Thanksgiving lunch then., Daniel and Christina, my ex-wife, is away so the girls are staying over with me for the weekend. Oh, please don't worry then, I just thought it would be good to see you. Let's find another time, why don't we talk next week? Well, I have an idea, Daniel. The girls are old enough to stay on their own and they love meeting new friends. Why don't we go to the concert, then afterwards we would love it if you can join us for our Thanksgiving lunch. Before Daniel had time to invent a reason why not, he found himself accepting. That's very kind of you, Chester; if you're sure I won't be imposing, I'd be delighted. Shall we meet at the Cloth Factory, I think it's quite close to you, say 11.30 on Sunday? Daniel, I can't wait. It's going to be great fun. The girls will love meeting you, thank you for saying yes.

His divorce had been relatively painless. He and Christina had married in their late 20s, swept along on the intoxication of middle-class convention and she'd power-birthed the girls in quick succession once she'd fully qualified from business school. It soon became apparent that they had little in common. They just didn't have enough of the shared aspirations and values that become the cement of long and successful relationships. She'd moved from LA after college to work with a major investment fund and latched onto the brownstone Brooklyn fantasy. But she was a West Coast woman and despite the best education and fine-tuning, even she was embarrassed by the way her own brashness echoed around those closed New York circles. She had that single volume-setting voice with a slight whining pitch at the end of each sentence, which was cute when she was funny and they were in love. Chester pretended not to notice, though he

knew his friends mocked her cruelly behind her back.

It started to unravel. One day when they were fucking, he noticed that she wasn't looking at him, in fact her eyes were pressed shut, as if she was enduring the sex. Deep down, he knew there was something about this that was wrong for him. He needed to connect with something to be happy sexually. Sex was the great leveler, it strips you back to your naked selves, where you are viscerally receptive to one another. She used to like him to look in her eyes while she was giving him head. She said good sex gave more meaning to their relationship. But by now they had let those early feelings subside. That left them in a place where intellectually and emotionally he could not thrive because the physicality had partly informed who they were. When he found himself no longer wanting to come up behind her, lift her hair gently and kiss the back of her neck, it left him feeling not impotent but inept, awkward like a teenager. As she withdrew, so did he. For him that meant they were merely treading water and he worried about his life disappearing. He was adopted as a baby and felt that he didn't want to waste time with experiences or relationships that didn't mean anything. He wasn't driven by doubt which is why he didn't have the desire everyone else wanted for him, to seek out his past. As a younger man, he carved his groove happily enough without drama or consequence, focused on his career and the family he was creating around him. Now, long-submerged feelings started to trouble him.

He'd become an expert in inheritance with a major law firm and by his early 30s had worked on countless cases for families who half the time didn't even know what they owned. Gradually he lost interest in the clients, becoming increasingly fascinated by the actual objects they were fighting over or trying to settle their tax liabilities against. Aged 36, he enrolled on a Masters in American Fine Art & Furniture, weekday evenings at Cooper Hewitt. Between that and looking after the girls, he had no time for anything else. By this point, he and Christina both realized their hearts were no longer in the marriage. Just as it dawned on him that she wasn't settling for his low-fi ambition, he made things worse by deciding to leave the law firm and set up his own business. So eleven years into their marriage, when she returned from a conference and announced she'd been having an affair, it came as a relief.

Chester adored Tabitha and Chloe. They were literally the apples of his eyes and they had worked out a happy arrangement for visits. Christina had agreed it would be better for everyone if she stayed in New York for a few more years until the girls finished high school, so he was able to spend plenty of time with them. Particularly as she was now enjoying the kind of life to which she felt she'd been destined with her new partner Thyodr; skiing in Aspen, summer weekends at the Hamptons, shopping trips to Paris and London. Thyodr was an oil-rich Russian and spent hours at an expensive gym, training his pectoral muscles to prominence. Being alone more of the time had allowed Chester to develop his new clients carefully, offering a specific service around valuation and growing his buying and selling skills at the same time. Which is how he met Nate Defarge, who had the kind of expertise that made him one of New York City's leading dealers in American Impressionism.

They were immediately fast and uproarious friends. Nate, almost 80, was a bon viveur and loved anyone who would listen to his stories over fine food and wine. He could read talent in this strong, handsome, funny 40-something. So, he decided to take him under his wing. At his age, he valued reliability and trustworthiness in his associates. Here was someone who was willing to learn, to whom he could impart the knowledge and opportunity he was ready to pass on. The same as Mae Farwell had afforded him in the early 1960s by giving him the chance to work on the Sale family collection. This one, Nate thought, was made for the job and not just that but years of discreet observation in his rarefied world gave Nate a sixth sense about the younger man. The way he saw it, his wing was free and fully extended and he wanted Chester under it. And Chester, always with an eye to new opportunities, reckoned meeting Nate was going to be a life-changing project.

Nate had been asked to arrange the private sale of a large collection of valuable 19th-century paintings by the wife of a rodeo-riding Texan oil baron now reduced to living through tubes in a wheelchair. She was an ex-model and cheerleader, and he'd been a hell-raiser. Concerned by the way the disposal of the estate was being handled, Nate spoke to one of the auctioneers who immediately recommended Chester Bowery, a smart young lawyer who had impeccable knowledge in his field and could advise on the intricacies of power of attorney and settlement conditions. Nate invited him over to the Merrill for coffee one morning the following week. Chester arrived punctually, dressed in one of his trademark vintage suits, hair swept back, beard neatly trimmed and tiny beads of sweat at his temples. Nate, who was no pushover but entirely trusted his own judgment

and usually went on first appearances, decided that he liked him.

The younger man was able to offer him just the clear advice he wanted to give the would-be widow. Unfortunately, he wouldn't be able to arrange the private disposal of such an important collection of American paintings. However, it would be a very successful sale with one of the big auction houses or a gallery bequest could easily be set against taxes and he knew a lawyer who could help her with that. He never heard from the buxom brunette again, although it came to Nate's attention a few months later, that a significant lot of mid-century work had been sold to China through an unknown auction house in Austin.

Nate consulted Chester on two more deals, cutting him a generous percentage of his sales. They developed a mentoring dialogue and often talked on the telephone late in the evening. The older man made Chester laugh with his manner which was both tacitly camp and ironically stuffy at the same time, calling him my dear boy with the emphasis on the long-drawn-out Louisiana vowels and then giggling irreverently at his own acerbic comments regarding clients, neighbors and almost anyone he chose to be the target of his knowing and piquant wit. The older man usually always had an ulterior motive where people were concerned; not in any sort of malevolent way, but his aim was always for the very best interests of those he loved and this was no exception.

After Mae Farwell Sale's tragic yachting accident, his friend had become increasingly insular. Though they still spent time together, Nate knew that something of Daniel wasn't ever completely present. Some fundamental part of his being to that point in his life, when most people are ready to launch into independent lives and careers, had been arrested in Daniel and had pressed him into the service of a past from which he couldn't escape. So Nate, despite his surprise some years later, and with considerable uncertainty about Daniel's real motives, had been entirely supportive of the marriage to Lydia and got along well with her. The two men continued their friendship as before, without too much connection with the other's domestic lives except when they all took the annual trip to Newport. Then Nate and Lydia created a spirit of camaraderie to distract Daniel, plotting everything weeks ahead. It was also the only time Sonny seemed to want to join them all. They would hang out backstage, enjoying the excitement of being among some of their favorite musicians. If they weren't actual jazz festival royalty, they were close enough. Elaine Lorillard had been a great friend of Daniel's mother and the Sale name still meant something, so they'd get invitations to Belcourt Castle for dinners and private sessions late in the evening, with some of the festival's special guests.

Other than that, life went on over the decades for the studious and private couple, so dedicated to their academic research. One event in his friendship with them had stuck with Nate and now he thought he'd found his opportunity to complete the circle. There was a small party at Gideon's Farm for Lydia and Daniel, to celebrate their silver wedding anniversary. They were the last people to bother with that kind of thing but somehow they felt prevailed upon by their friends and colleagues. So poor Marta went crazy when the catering company took over her kitchen forcing her to move the pancake batter and meatloaf for Sunday out of the fridge to make way for champagne. This resulted in Lydia having to form a truce and insisting that Marta was driven home, so she could dress beautifully as she was not working and would be a guest that evening. With much complaining and shaking of her head she agreed and the party came off splendidly. Halfway through the evening, Nate, on his best behavior, gave a charmingly pithy precis of the couple's life together to the small assembled company, commending their generosity and their support for colleagues and associates. His speech had just the right tone and was applauded energetically after they all made a toast to the couple's future happiness. It wouldn't cross Daniel's mind to ask anyone else but Nate to speak on his behalf, for though he could hide behind an academic paper or in his seminar room, addressing groups of people who knew him well at close-quarters made him anxious, as if he might betray something about himself. And naturally Nate was able to pitch it perfectly.

Lydia was a small, lively woman, with a dramatic silver bob and bright green darting eyes. She had an eccentric look, like a Bloomsbury throwback, on this occasion wearing a remarkable silk orange kaftan with a matching chiffon scarf tying her hair back. She glided over to thank Nate but before she could embrace him, he reached to the table behind him and presented her with a simple black leather box. This is for you, darling Lydia. A little something for being the savior of my dearest friend over this last quarter century. She opened it like an excited child, delighted to find a torsade choker made from woven strands of coral with gold and emeralds at the clasp. And you are wearing the perfect outfit to show it off, please, allow me. He picked up the delicate treasure, placing it round her neck from behind. As he did so, she placed her hand on his and without turning around, she spoke into the distance with such tenderness and wisdom.

We both know Nathaniel, that Dan is a wounded bird. Something has been taken away from him that we can never replace. But just as you've thanked me, dear friend, I also owe you so much for helping me to be his caretaker and companion all these years. You mean so much to him. She turned, took both his hands and looked gently at Nate, her soft wrinkled eyes shadowed in cornflower blue and sparkling with tears. If I should go first, please make sure he has someone to care for him. I'm not sure he'll know how to manage alone, without us. She smiled admiring the necklace in the overmantle glass. This is the most beautiful object I have ever been given, I will treasure it, thank you. She raised on her tiptoes and kissed him on both cheeks before stalking off to speak to her other guests.

Since Lydia died, Nate knew that what she had said was true; Daniel had lost his main connection with the world. He had thought a great deal about how he could help his friend and until now that hadn't been clear. One night, he invited Chester to join him for dinner at his favorite restaurant, *Le Veau d'Or*. Unlike Daniel, Nate nearly always took cabs and that evening arrived at this unprepossessing facade squashed between a drug store and a sandwich place on 60th, with only a few steps in the rain to reach this little bit of faux Paris. The uncompromising owner Monsieur Robert had died a few years before but his menu and the Languedoc-Roussillon wines in his cellar remained steadfastly predictable. Nate was welcomed and ushered to his favorite table in the corner by the bar, where he sat comfortably under a street sign for the Boulevard Saint Germain.

Chester arrived a few minutes later, just in time for Nate to suggest they enjoyed a glass of chilled Chambery before they ordered dinner. If Chester would allow him, Nate might suggest some of the better dishes on the menu. They don't do everything fabulously, darling boy, except when I specify. The food is painfully old-fashioned but it never changes and life is so full of surprises, I'm always quite glad to be able to order a dish without fearing what will appear on the table. Nate liked the conviviality of dining more than the food and he chose the best wines to accompany a starter of artichokes vinaigrette, a middle course of sole, and roast rack of lamb with dauphinoise potatoes to follow.

Over the chocolate mousse, by now the two of them were in full flow and Nate realized that Chester was heading over the other side of decently inebriated, becoming maudlin on the subject of his failed marriage. Over cognac, a little glassy-eyed, he looked at his dining companion and said Nate there is something I need to tell you, something I haven't told anyone. Nate laughed, my dear boy I simply never take confession after two bottles of Cru Corbières Boutenac and a good dinner. It will have to wait. Have some more coffee. As it happens there is something I want to discuss with you, and the conversation came round to Daniel. I have a close friend I would like you to meet. He has one of the best small collections of Cos Cob paintings, a raft of early abstract collected by his mother in the '50s and '60s and some very fine settler pieces you should definitely see. He was a very eminent professor at Exhampton but retired I don't know, late '90s sometime, I guess. Professor Sale comes from a rich, old New England family but he leaves no heirs. Lately he's been attempting to catalog his collection, I think rather half-heartedly. And very sadly his wife died two years ago. He needs some help putting himself back together and his house in order. I think you two would get along. Would you come to the apartment on Tuesday and I'll introduce you? We can have lunch afterwards. I have a painting I'm pretty sure will grab his eye.

Chapter Twelve

Daniel noticed the silver St. Christopher hanging from the dimple beneath the boy's Adam's apple. He wasn't sure what to think. The last few hours and minutes had left him unprepared for a passing conversation and he kept looking at the ground at a loss for what to say. The young man seemed pleasant and relaxed and he couldn't sense anything dangerous, so he smoked his cigarette and when he looked up it was with the reluctant smile that he gave people when he didn't want them to think he was being rude. It wasn't exactly shyness, more social awkwardness, the inability to resuscitate a conversation if he didn't know what to say. Added to that the effect of the whiskey and the music was still making his head swim a little. Xavi chattered for a few minutes explaining that Lili was from one of the shanty villages and Daniel was able to say he'd passed one on Montjuic. We call them *barraques* and most of the people round here at night come from there. They know me because I teach some of the girls to speak English.

He asked Daniel which direction he was headed, at which he pointed shyly to the other corner of the square. Do you mind if I walk with you? As they left towards the street leading to the Gothic quarter the girls under the arches shouted goodnight to them. They call me *palillo* or *pal* in Spanish. It's because I'm tall and skinny and they think my sister should feed me more. I live with my sister, over on the other side of the Ramblas, past the market. Do you know the area?

Daniel began to ease a little into the situation and explained that he'd just been to see the jazz concert. Xavi had heard of the young pianist. He used to play in a bar when he was just a kid, he's not much older than me. Then he got discovered and now he's a big shot. Daniel was surprised at how American his new acquaintance sounded and asked him how he learned English. He explained that at 14 he'd met a US marine stationed in Barcelona, a quartermaster on an aircraft carrier, whom he'd help get to know the city and for whom he'd sold silk stockings and chocolate on the black market. As they walked along one of the quiet alleys in the dim light, Xavi slowed and turned to face Daniel, who noticed the way his oval brown eyes widened under the flashing neon signs. Would you like to drink something? I know a place nearby. Daniel liked this guy and they found the bar, where they talked and drank coffee under the naked bulb, sharing

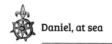

small facts about each other, nothing in particular but those indistinct elements of a person that quickly build a picture between you both, which then allows trust to germinate.

They continued talking until almost six and then walked to the square where Daniel lived. In the early dawn, Xavi held out his hand. Maybe I can come by and find you sometime. I would like to introduce you to my city, I know some places we can show you. I'd like that, replied Daniel unreservedly, not holding back his smile. Goodnight Xavi, I've enjoyed meeting you and climbed the stairs to his room, took off his clothes and fell into bed. He didn't know it then but his heart was opening to an unfamiliar sensation. The permanent knot of tension in his gut was starting to unravel and for the first time his whole body was experiencing something new, a feeling of safety. He felt warm and alive as he fell asleep in the waking noises of the street below. Somewhere, in the near distance, perhaps beneath his balcony, he could hear a kind and gentle laugh that he recognized.

Xavi's sister, Elena, owned a store selling fruit and vegetables on a street called Pintor Fortuny. You don't pronounce the *y*, he told him sitting in the Café Sicoris one evening later that week. Daniel had arrived home from work to find a note waiting for him, asking him to meet Xavi the following afternoon. He waited outside the university library while the students milled in and out through the vast wooden doors. He felt a tap on his shoulder and there was his new friend, in an American leather jacket, his hair falling in unruly curls around his broad open smile, books under his arm. It was almost Christmas now and it was raining heavily, so they set off at a run across the Plaça Universitat and down the Ramblas. Once they shook away the rain laughing, and settled into a table at the back of the café, without any awkwardness the conversation continued immediately from their first encounter. Xavi and Elena lived above at the back of the store, a building he called a locale and the rest of the building was owned by Don Gilberto Lopez, an Argentinian businessman who fancied his chances with his sister. But he hasn't got a hope. Elena is only 32 but she lives like a saint. She keeps a constant eye on her two workers from the parlor behind the store – immigrants from the south, who live in Hospitalet a little south of the city. Sometimes I help in the mornings when they arrive from the market. We have family too, up in a village in the north, they send us vegetables in a van sometimes. She never goes to the countryside but sometimes I visit them. The night at his small table, Daniel wrote in his journal. *Met Xavi again today. He writes his name Xavier, with an X it's Catalan which is not allowed on official documents, so it has to be Javier. Stood outside the university waiting for him. He majors in economics. Strange for me not to be studying but he said he'd show me the library sometime. Talked three hours in the Café Sicoris. There is a bad-tempered waiter there who smashes everything down on the table with a great clatter. X laughs at him which makes him even angrier. We ate tortilla and a tin of clams and drank beer. He's half French, his mother is from Roussillon and his father from a village in the Garrotxa, which is next to the Pyrenees. Both of his parents are dead. I think this gives us a connection. He hardly knew his father. So, he knew how to survive from a young age. I envy that independence and yet here I am thousands of miles from home, so I suppose I'm finding my own way to be free. It's been so wonderful to see him again. I feel with X that it's the chance to be a real friend.*

Sometimes Daniel would wait in the university gardens for Xavi to finish. Then they would sit under the trees exchanging their lives. One evening Xavi took Daniel to Vallvidrera, walking high into the woods below Tibidabo. They were meekly getting the measure of each other, Xavi gently trying to fathom the intense young American. They'd talked about the work Daniel was doing with the library. These families, he'd asked. What do you know of them? Very little, Daniel explained, sometimes nothing. Most of the collections were confiscated from the exiled families after the war. The lucky ones had time to put them in the trust of the Council of Museums. Daniel thought he noticed Xavi grow silent when they talked about this. He'd change the subject and start talking about something else. He often laughed about his sister Elena, the way she barked orders across the warehouse downstairs from his room as they cleared the stalls from the street. The way he described her contempt for men reminded Daniel of Mae. They compared the women supposed to be their guardians, who regarded their charges as part useless, endlessly in need of instruction and part obstacle to their true calling. For Elena, like Daniel's mother, that purpose in itself was indistinct. But she often berated her brother for his part in preventing her from taking blessed vows as a younger woman. Apparently he was very much his father's son and his spirit had never been crushed by his sister's emasculating tongue. Mostly he ridiculed her carping, reminding her that it was never too late to join the nuns and that at 23 he could manage well without her constant interference. Which in turn she dismissed insisting that he'd be helpless without her and that she had raised him and prevented his fall into delinquency. What's more, who would pay for your studies if I didn't labor all day in this store? Neither of which were based on anything but her fantasy. Xavi had a native intellect that allowed him to negotiate his young adult life with considerable success around the city and Elena spent most of the day in her darkened parlor at the back of the store, having little to do with any but her most valued customers.

Xavi and Elena had lost both of their parents in circumstances that would have been unusually tragic, were it not for the widespread and general tragedy of this nation during the years of their childhood. He hardly remembered his father Sergi who had inherited a thriving printer's business in Barcelona. Before the Civil War his father had supported the followers of Companys during the uprising and had even printed the briefly independent Catalan banknotes on his presses. After the Civil War the presses were destroyed and he was imprisoned in Manresa for two years, leaving his French wife Myrtille to bring up their young children and convert the printing workshop into a wholesale fruit and vegetable supplier. But as with so many fervent anti-fascists, being in prison only intensified their resistance to authority and on his release, he made contact with the maquis through his wife's family in France. The Ferran family had a farm in the north, close to the mountains, of which Sergi owned a share. They started to supply the store with produce and once, sometimes twice a week in summer, a truck would arrive in the city laden with artichokes, tomatoes, peppers, potatoes and great stacks of mustard greens or whatever else was in season and return that day with the empty sacks and boxes, often with a fugitive or wanted agitator hidden beneath them.

Sergi was increasingly absent from the family home, going off sometimes for weeks at a time before returning home and keeping a low profile behind the store. Myrtille Colombard's own family had been imprisoned in the Rivesaltes internment camp by the Nazi collaborators so she was quite happy to cast a blind eye on proceedings, focusing all her attentions on giving her children the best possible upbringing in the circumstances. She had trained to be a village schoolmistress before the war and with the undying fortitude of someone who has seen everything in their world reduced to rubble but with complete absence of any self-pity, she determined that her children would succeed where she had not been able to.

Until one day, Sergi Ferran didn't come home. He had disappeared, leaving his wife, three-year-old son and teenage daughter to fend for themselves without him. Despite many approaches to the authorities he was never found and it was not until a few years later that Myrtille had word. A package delivered by a distant cousin in which was a pocket book, hunting knife with his initials on the hilt and a wrist watch. An unmarked shallow grave had been found in the mountains near Figols, containing several bodies. It was believed that these were revenge murders against the maquis' bombing of an army convoy. His remains had been removed and buried discreetly in the cemetery at Sadernes where his family lived. She should be careful not to draw attention to this discovery.

The Ferrans who faced endless hardship had a tendency towards stoicism but the death of the distant hope that her husband was alive, killed Myrtille's stony resolve and a dismal cloud descended upon her life and that of her daughter. Xavi in contrast, resisted despondency, grew into his father's stature acquiring a possession of mind born from a careful measure of optimism and passion for justice. This was his means of survival, the antidote he needed to the shadowy solemnity that descended on their household. On the pretext of needing space to study, he was permitted to move to the old accounts office above the store. Elena meanwhile had retreated into sullen piety, leaning towards the trappings and rituals of the Church for comfort. Two years later, their mother had a heart attack, collapsing into a newly arrived delivery of calçots, and died a few days later.

Despite her insistence that she alone managed their financial well-being, in fact the Ferran children were not left without resources. Myrtille had some money from the sale of the Colombard estate in the Roussillon and after her husband's disappearance she ensured that the children would keep their stake in the family farm in Sadernes, cleverly offering the rest of the family a small share in the profits from the wholesale business to keep their loyalty. Their grandfather had bought the first floor of the building that housed the printing presses. This included the half-floor where Xavi lived, which he accessed up some stairs at the end of a narrow iron-gated alley at the side of the building and the first floor where Elena kept home. The remaining three floors of the building, accessed by the main door beside the store entrance, were owned by Don Gilberto who had come from Argentina to escape the financial crash and now imported Cuban cigars.

By this time Xavi was 14 and the US navy had just arrived in the port. He quickly saw an opportunity provided by the smartly pressed, handsome ratings looking for shore-leave diversions. He could speak English quite well and offered to teach it to some of the girls he saw loitering at Drassanes, on the edge of the *barrio chino* by the port. He could give them the basics of what they needed to ask their customers. He befriended a black marine called Bert for whom he sold chocolate, silk stockings and cigarettes in return for a cut. Bert would reappear with American magazines and newspapers for his young friend and Xavi became his official guide and companion. So by the time he was 17 he was a man of the world and had a good knowledge of the world outside his sister's bitter religiosity and Barcelona's depressing submission to an unwanted regime.

One of the promises that Elena had made her mother was that she would help Xavi in every way to study and become the man their father would have wanted. He was diligent at school and there was enough money to pay for him to attend classes at the university, where he showed sufficient promise in economics and languages to be given a modest scholarship. After four years he was continuing to postgraduate studies and had embarked on a newly established course in economics as well as Catalan studies program recently permitted by Madrid, albeit taught in Spanish.

Xavi joked that Don Gilberto's voice would often boom through the store enquiring if Elena would accompany him for a refreshment after closing time. He imitated her withering reply. Don Gilberto as the only person here doing any work, how would you expect me to contemplate social frivolities and the idle indulgences of others with nothing better to do than waste their waking hours on such things, when I have a business to run and accounts to keep? But perhaps you would like to call round in the morning and accompany me to mass?

Elena at 32 and without ever having been married or even in love, comported herself as a widow, though nothing she did would inspire gossip. Not a soul would have bothered to take notice of Don Gilberto escorting a spinster for a glass of tiger nut milk. Don Gilberto, in his turn, had given over much of his life to those pleasures which Elena claimed to despise and was indolent in his faith. But something about her insistence for his public companionship made him happy enough to oblige and allowed him the merest moments in her presence.

Daniel loved what he was learning about this new family, savoring each detail of his friend's description, laughing with an unguarded freedom he didn't recognize, like a jubilant bird first discovering the power of flight, bright and soaring. Here at last he was untroubled and could truly be himself.

Chapter Thirteen

Daniel's grandmother Meredith was in many ways a remarkable woman. Born into a straight-laced Vermont family, when she came to Greenwich as a young woman, she took private painting lessons from a well-known painter who had set up a studio in the area, with quite a following. In time, she became quite a collector and when the Greenwich Society of Artists held their first show, they invited her as a guest of honor.

She did her best to interest her son Thomas in art but with little success. Since he was able to read, his heart had been captured by the exploits of the early aviators. When she took him to France in 1909 aged twelve, after obediently trotting round the Louvre, he asked his mother if they could visit Le Mans where Wilbur Wright was demonstrating his new aircraft to the wealthy and powerful of Europe. She duly obliged, realising that her boy had the makings of pioneer, qualities no self-respecting Sale could ignore. Poor Meredith developed Alzheimer's long before she grew old and was lost to the world in her rooms at Gardiner's Court. She died soon after her son's wedding.

It was partly the affection in which she held her mother-in-law that persuaded Mae to bring the Cos Cob school paintings with her to Gideon's Farm. Though she wasn't particularly interested in landscapes or domestic scenes, she recognized their significance to the family collection and loved the painting of the boatyard where she enjoyed talking to the old boat-menders while they worked on the *Dabbing Duck*, an S-class yacht she had built from scratch. She was quite at home in the yard, just as she had been in her father's automobile repair shop as a girl. A place where she could curse as hard as the mechanics.

Daniel stood on the oak boards of the landing, in his bare feet looking over the banister to the room below, tea in hand. When she had remodeled this part of the house, Mae wanted to keep the architectural features but open up the space. She added a glass vestibule with French doors the full width of the house and took down the wall between the long sash windows where the front doors led to the porch. Four pillars supported the room where the wall had been and a long rosewood dining table, ten chairs on either side, stood on a rug thrown over the flagstones. On the other side where the room had originally divided, there was a fireplace with a gilded mirror above. There were various armchairs and occasional tables, giving the room an air of refined stateliness and it was full of oddities and trinkets the Sales had collected over three centuries, each one with its own story, washed up on this shore of time. Here, at night, when the room was bright with firelight and candles flickering against the glass and mirrors, music in the air, newcomers to Gideon's Farm could feel transported to a place beyond time, somewhere magical and other.

Mae would often have parties when Daniel was a boy. Despite her ambivalence for local society, she nurtured the Sale connection and enjoyed bringing her new city and old county worlds together. The driveway would fill up with cars and she'd greet her guests from the curve of the staircase leading from the upper floors, arms outstretched, while they marveled silently at her beauty. Everyone from the city sophisticates to the heirs of country estates wondered how she dared to be such an original human being. The house was always decorated with her favorite flowers, agapanthus, white dahlias and delphiniums and the dining table and sideboards were laden with food and drinks. She'd always book a jazz band to give the evening a kick-start.

But only the most favored of visitors were ever invited through the doors beyond this room, into the Cabin, which infuriated the curious denizens of Round Hill even more. They'd seen photographs in magazines, and in the summer parties, they'd looked up to the terrace from the gardens beneath. But they had never been invited into her inner sanctum. Behind their onyx beads, vapid smiles and crystal punch glasses, they gossiped about her, suggestively, which she liked. The next day, recounting the evening to Marta, she'd say, I'm the only person they know worth talking about. We have to leave some things to their limited imaginations after all!

Daniel felt the warm, uneven wood beneath his feet, a sensation he could remember since he was a boy, standing there in his pajamas. He watched these ladies come and go in their silks, jewels and furs, his mother floating supreme among them. After she died, he held the wake there but by that time she'd lost interest in the *beau monde* and had chased off the last of her most persistent admirers, so had few friends left; only the remnants of his father's generation. He stood in this same spot looking at the empty room below thinking that he wouldn't buy Nate's painting, there were already too many. He put off the landing lights and walking over to the low shelves outside his dressing room, he found his childhood copy of *The Adventures of Robinson Crusoe* with its shredded spine and loose pages and read late into the night.

The next morning, he woke with the lamp still burning by his bedside and the book on the bed next to him. He lay for a while listening to the birds outside, pondering the resilience castaways have to rely on for survival. As he showered and dressed he concluded that he could no longer separate himself from humanity; his unresolved past had returned, he couldn't escape that. The time had come to give himself a purpose, some kind of future. The guilt he'd been bearing on his shoulders, the feeling that he'd let them all down, Mae, Lydia, and before that. The belief that he'd deserved to be lonely, the fear of being discovered, forever clutching at his throat. He had to stop hiding now. He knew his wife would have been proud that he had come to this conclusion. That after all this, he had decided to live.

Crusoe, fearing danger had created a place of safety, deep in the island. Unknowingly, partly under the lifelong influence of his mother and partly from his own fear, he had retreated in the same way. Lydia had been dead two years and that had made it worse. They had both needed this companionship and he had not been ready to make it on his own. He became more bound to this place, unable to escape the accretion of objects and experiences. So many of those were not even his. He'd borne the weight of others, of people he didn't even know; the distant figures of his father and grandparents, the Sale ancestry to which he always felt impostor, swept along by his opportunistic mother, who had no regard whatsoever to the meekness of her wounded son or how he might reach towards a life where he might have flourished.

Now, quite imperceptibly, a part of him, another life, one entirely his own, a life which had been buried deep inside him and was long ago turned to stone, slowly breathed into life. Feelings smothered in childhood then briefly given a tragically short existence as a young man in Europe were now beginning to unfurl within him, like an ancient leviathan stirring after centuries of sleep. It was not a relaxing sensation. One moment his heart would start to race, riding on a wave of optimism telling him that everything could change. The next he would collide with an all too familiar despair. One he'd experienced for so long. A lump would rise in his chest, sending him back on that ebb tide of fear and guilt. A fear of the past, a fear of the scars cauterized under layers of time. The hours and days, months and years and decades all piled up upon each other. But this time was still not enough, it was clear, to bury the truth of his experience. He knew in his heart that despite all his strenuous efforts to lock away the memory of those few months, the only time he had known the exhilaration of true happiness, when he had truly lived if only for a moment, that the core of his being was now returning to the surface. He thought about Lydia and the tenderness with which she had been the caretaker of his lost self. He wondered what she would say to him now, how she would advise him.

At 9, he rang the hospital to ask for the earliest appointment. He had been referred by his doctor who was a golfing friend of the consultant. They could see him that afternoon due to a last-minute cancellation. All morning Daniel prepared his response, trying to calm himself with simple explanations of the sound in his head, the sense of disorientation, raised blood pressure and confused memory, determined to continue with a positive outlook, whatever the outcome. At 77 he'd had a good life, full of achievement. He had no plans to stop regardless of how hard it would be to accept whatever diagnosis was given. This was something that came to many people at his age and these days if you could catch it early, it was possible to continue to lead a normal life. For a time, at least.

But when his guard came down, the waking beast sent a wave of horror through him, bringing images from the past flooding into his mind. He felt adrift in the lake again, weighed down by a deep, empty longing, knowing that he could not turn back time. He would have done so many things differently. He wished he could have been a stronger man but there had been overpowering circumstances against which he was powerless to struggle. He should have been brave enough to give his own life for what he knew was right but then, at that time, it didn't occur to him. Instead he fled. He might too have been able to deflect the dominance of his mother but her love, twisted round him like a liana preventing his growth, was all he had. So, he'd remained drawn to safety and permitted her to take over his life to her own advantage and never a day went past when Mae Farwell Sale was not the center of attention. The emotional intensity of everything she had cast behind her, all the friends and lovers, were projected onto Daniel, who had no means to resist her. When she died, he was not bereft by her death, but by her absence and the relationship they might have had. And her legacy was to leave him with an indiscernible sense that somehow, ultimately, he had failed her.

He took a taxi to the hospital asking the driver to return in two hours, stopping for espresso on the first floor of the hospital. He took the elevator to the fourth floor where he was immediately conscious of walking past ancient people. People he hardly recognized as his contemporaries. From the corner of his eye, as he passed the care rooms, he caught sight of tubes emerging from behind gowns, saline drips on trolleys, scant white hairs barely covering liverish scalps; men and women navigating the precarious business of staying alive.

He was shown into the office of the consultant by his nurse where a pen-and-paper test was waiting for him. He would be along in around 20 minutes, take your time, no rush and just answer the questions however you best feel able. Daniel approached the test like a conservation project, assessing the whole before looking at the specific details and working out how long it would take to achieve each specific stage. He didn't think it was particularly challenging, but he was relieved when the nurse returned with water and put her hand on his shoulder before taking the test away. He could feel his heartbeat increasing and beads of sweat on his forehead. That all too familiar feeling where the room started to circle around him hazily. He drank some water and stood up, hands gripping the side of the table and stood looking out of the window at the gray November afternoon.

Soon the consultant came and they had an extensive conversation about Daniel's health, diet, fitness, exercise and so on. He ran a few tests putting slimy pads on his temples from which ran wires that fed into a monitor. He explained how the brain impulses worked and checked Daniel's blood pressure, while the nurse took some samples. When these were done, he interrogated him in detail about the episodes he was having and his particular concerns, continuously clicking his pen and scratching notes on his pad. Daniel hated being near doctors. He thought they had a particular way of disguising their specific indifference about symptoms with a look of serious and focused concern. The consultant furrowed his eyebrows when Daniel answered his questions to signify he was genuinely contemplating the issues they were discussing and not his golf match at the weekend or dinner with the nurse later. After around an hour, Daniel asked if there was anything immediately he should worry about, the consultant shrugged smiling, held out his hand and said he'd be back in touch in a few days, once they'd looked at the tests. On the way out, Daniel took the stairs.

Chapter Fourteen

His girls were Chester's chief joy. He could hardly believe that he'd been in anyway responsible for these beautiful human beings. Physically they had all the sporty, fine-framed litheness of Christina but his height and sparkling blue eyes. Everything about them belied children damaged by divorce. In fact, they seemed immediately liberated by the change in circumstances. A fresh dose of oxygen dispersed the tension that was allowed to hang in their home, suffocating both adults and children. They all found themselves better able to flourish and the girls acquired an assuredness enabling them to be the perfect arbiters between their parents.

During their weekends together he fell entirely into their plans. They worked him, seeing their Dad as a collaborator while at home they acquiesced dutifully to their mother's parental plan. They couldn't really even take him seriously whenever he wanted to have one of his talks with them. They'd sit on the floor next to each other, cross-legged and stare at him intently, nodding before collapsing in fits of giggles. This weekend he told them, we're having a visitor, a new friend called Daniel, Professor Sale, he's on his own and I thought it would be nice for him to join us for Thanksgiving. For some reason, they recognised the seriousness of what Chester was saying and nodded respectfully without laughing before returning to their extravagant decorations for the next day.

What they loved most of all about being in their father's apartment, was making a mess. He encouraged what their mother couldn't. She had them sewn to the hem in ballet, tennis and riding lessons, at which they excelled for her. But when they were with their father, they would be quite happy spending all weekend making crafts – painting models – anything involving glitter, glue, and scissors. Often Chester would be at a meeting, standing in a subway station or ordering a coffee when a tiny piece of glitter would fall from his wallet or a pocket, and he'd smile at the comfort of the presence of his girls. He encouraged the intuitive creativity he knew their mother couldn't; she was way too controlling to allow the girls to have unstructured time – achievement was everything to her.

Chester thought that Tabitha and Chloe managed the trade-off successfully, perhaps seeing the best of both worlds. Everything they did with Chester was calculated to be the opposite of their life with their

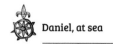

mother and Thyodr. But they never told tales about either parent to the other, only the scantest details would be revealed in this most careful of political negotiations. At 12 and 14 they recognized that this was both fair and advantageous.

Tabitha had come first but it was almost like they were twins because she just seemed to be waiting for Chloe to emerge before she really entered the race of life with any spirit. She'd spent most of the first 14 months of her life lying on her mother's belly, listening for signs of her sister's arrival. From the outset, they developed together. Tabitha brought Chloe along as quickly as she learned something, like nascent partners. Ladies and gentlemen, please welcome to the stage The Amazing Bowery Sisters Chester would shout when he woke in the morning; as signal for them to come rushing through to climb into bed with him and decide what excitement the day would bring. The sisters were exactly like an old vaudeville turn; everything they did was a perfectly choreographed success, as if they'd rehearsed it many times before. And it was all delivered with as much enthusiasm and love as they intuitively knew the adults around them needed to be happy.

When Chester had explained that he was going to be meeting Daniel on Sunday for a concert in the morning and that he'd invited him to join them for their afternoon feast, their eyes widened with anticipation at the prospect of a new adult friend upon whom they could work their vigorous charms. Their father asked them to go easy on Daniel, that he was older but that he was very kind and charming. They wanted to know everything about him and while Tabitha interrogated her father, Chloe put her arms round his neck and told him Daddy if Professor Daniel is a good friend of yours he must be very nice indeed and maybe we should make him a special pumpkin meringue pie.

They adored the boho chic of the street markets in Brooklyn and none more so than the Sunday farmers' market where they would shop for the amazing meals they had with their father. In New Jersey they lived on superfoods and pseudo grains, salad and juices because that pleased their mother. Even their baking was gluten-free. While with Chester they concocted meaty stews which they braised overnight in the warming drawer of his French range cooker, filling the apartment with fragrant aromas of the herbs, wine and spices with which they laced them. They fashioned pizzas with homemade dough and elaborate toppings, vats of rich tomato sauce for bowls of pasta and mountains of parmesan cheese, eaten on the floor leaning on their elbows or sunk into the huge sofa, shrieking with laughter in front of one of their father's favorite Laurel and Hardy movies. And best of all they plotted the creation of forbidden desserts which they would never ask from their mother..

There was an air of excitement that clear and sharp November Sunday morning. They woke early and stopped for breakfast and hot chocolate on the way to buy provisions for Thanksgiving lunch. Home they came laden with vegetables, fruit, bread and cheese. The girls started to prepare the lunch while Chester washed and got ready to meet Daniel. Together they covered the turkey with strips of pancetta; soused it with white wine and encrusted it with garlic and thyme, then he lifted it into the oven. At 11.15 Chester pulled on his blue cable knit sweater, a tweed cap and scarf, kissed the girls and on the way downstairs buzzed Rochelle his neighbor to ask her to pop up and check on them while he was out. He walked the quarter mile to the Cloth Factory, where Daniel was waiting.

The Lydia Sale Room had been a dyeing floor. Many of the features had been retained by the architects, preserved in the raw to maintain the ideals of labor and toil: the iron loading platform still jutted out of the white-washed brick walls and the old pulleys for hanging the cloth to dry still hung from the A-frame roof. At one end of the room there were floor-to-ceiling windows where a half-light came in from the yard at the back of the building. The highly varnished reclaimed wooden floor covering the large washpool set in the floors lent acoustic resonance to the warm voice of the young singer.

Lydia had been intimately involved in the renovation, poring over the architect's designs and more than once interfering in decisions being taken by the board. It was nothing to do with money but she figured that if her name was going to be associated with the room, she may as well get involved, determined to realize a neutral performance space where the history of the building might be celebrated without becoming a pastiche of its former life. She loved the thought of the women, barefoot, skirts tucked up, dyeing the great sheets of cotton cloth in the huge wash baths and passing them through vast steel rollers before hanging them to dry from pulleys. All that activity imprinted in the air of this room, now celebrating effort and determination of a different kind.

Daniel was captivated by the Norwegian baritone's muted tones exploring the wanderer's loss and disorientation in the freezing landscape of *Die Winterreise*. He preferred this to the virtuosity of the high tenor voice with its slightly strangulated edge of hysteria. In this performance Lydia would have loved the sonority from the tall, blond singer who interpreted the unending burden of loss faced by the mysterious lover wandering bereft in winter, as disappointment rather than grief. Who or what he searches for or what unease runs through his chilled veins in this desolate cycle of poems is never clear, but love and hope have deserted him and certainly in his late wife's view, nothing could compare to the poignancy of Schubert's telling of Muller's tale.

Chester hadn't expected two musicians to be able pull off something so dramatic, one moment peaceful and still like a Flemish old master, the next exposed and haunting like dry tundra. He did have a little experience of classical music as his mother had been a piano teacher. But for some strange reason, she had never encouraged him to learn. He assumed it was because she knew intuitively that he had no talent for it. In fact, she had felt slighted that he hadn't shown enough interest at an early age for her to want to encourage him. There had always been this undercurrent in their relationship, that he hadn't quite shown the necessary level of gratitude for the sacrifices she felt she had made to parent him. This resulted in an absence of openness, a failure of communication between them; just as she had no real instinct for parenting, he had none for music. But every night he would lie in bed, listening to her play on the upright in the dining room downstairs, wishing that he could find that harmony.

They were happy enough once he was grown up but after his father died a few years earlier, she found it harder to reach out to him. He remained everything she might expect from a dutiful son, enjoying his occasional visits but she hardly met her grandchildren, wistfully dismissing the fact to a neighbor, saying he'd moved on in life beyond what they'd had in common. Sitting there, he wondered if she'd be pleased that he was at a classical recital, something they could share, even now. The music here in the intimacy of the studio made the hairs on his neck tingle, with the performers so close and so expressive. He wanted to reach out and touch the sounds of the piano which were like porcelain in the air around him, accompanied by the manly baritone curving around and embracing them. Despite the melancholy of the music, sitting there Chester felt silently connected to his new friend, joined together in this shared experience.

Daniel who had a well-tuned ear for music was normally able to lose himself wholly. But he was nervous about the test results and he wasn't sure if his brief email agreeing to meet the Spanish girl had been curt. Images from the past kept crowding in on him as the music continued and he tried to focus on the lunch today, not wanting to seem like an anxious old man. As he surfaced back to his conscious presence in the hopelessness of the wanderer's lament, he felt the weight pushing into an empty space in his sternum. Here, in this room, so much of his life was being played out before him and the emergence of long-buried memories made him acutely sensitive even to the timbre of the air. He didn't turn for a moment after the applause but when he did, it was suddenly clear to Chester that more than this music or the significance of the room, deep down Daniel was bearing some profound sorrow. He was pleased he'd invited him home to Tabitha and Chloe, those two had an uncanny way of reading people and he was sure they'd do the same for Daniel. They'd unobtrusively scrutinize him calculating how to tend or entertain in just the right manner. But he had no need to worry for Daniel was also keen to impress them.

They beat a retreat through the fire exit to avoid small-talk with obsequious trustees who were always looking for more money and would want a photograph with Daniel for the newsletter. They discussed the recital as they walked through Cooper Park, stopping at a street stall to drink eggnog from polystyrene cups and then to buy a bottle of organic wine from the local vintners run by two women wearing vintage grocers' coats. During one of their phone calls, Chester had suggested that Daniel should sell his wine cellar at a collector's auction as most of it was valuable for its vintage and provenance rather than drinkability. While they were in the store, they struck up conversation and the girls were open-mouthed when Chester told them about the bottle of Pauillac he'd drunk on his first visit to Gideon's Farm.

Taking the elevator to the third floor, Tabitha and Chloe were waiting at the open door, perfectly buttoned and smiling, ready to greet their guest. The smell of food and glimmer of lights in the apartment against the gray skies through the windows gave an air of anticipated festivity. After they had all been introduced, Daniel fished out of his jacket pocket two rectangles of tissue with their names written on neat labels and handed them to the girls. This is a small token to thank you for inviting me to share your Thanksgiving lunch. Unwrapping them revealed in each package a delicately ornate jay feather braided on the quill with silver beading and colored threads. These were once part of the head-dress of the wife of Pequot chieftain, Daniel explained before the girls rushed off to look in their bedroom mirror, returning minutes later with their hair up and

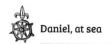

the feathers spiked through. Chester was stunned by Daniel's generosity, looking quizzically at his friend but the older man just shrugged and smiled.

Soon there was a buzz of activity in the large open-plan kitchen dining room. Chester at the stove and Daniel helping the girls to finish setting the table, while they chattered on, subtly interrogating him, which he rather enjoyed. He started to feel more youthful in this haven of chaotic domesticity and a few days later at home he reflected that what his mother had created was a prison, somewhere the world could not get in but it had also trapped him. And even when he returned, he once more became prisoner, a willing victim to its spell.

The four of them made for jolly company, the girls kept the conversation going, giggling and impersonating their school teachers. Daniel, spotting a 19th-century city plan of Brooklyn, talked about his maps. Chloe was fascinated, listening wide-eyed with her chin on her elbows to her new friend explain how the early sailors had only the sun and stars to guide them. Tabitha and Chester were putting the finishing touches to the lunch while they looked at images of medieval astrolabes on the iPad. This is the first Thanksgiving I have celebrated since before, well for a couple of years now. Daniel said raising a glass to toast his new friends, Lydia, my wife, she would very much have loved to be here and meet you all.

After the pumpkin pie, Daniel and Chester sat on the sofa drinking coffee. The girls were being collected by Christina on her way back from the airport so were gamboling around the house, throwing their things into bags. At the sound of the buzzer they ran to their father hugging and kissing him furiously. Daniel stood up, uncertain what to do. Without hesitating, they rushed to hug him too, grabbed their bags and fled through the front door into the elevator and down to the other part of their lives.

Chapter Fifteen

It had taken Daniel several days to pluck up the courage to respond to the letter from Rosa Lopez. He had thought about it constantly, carefully wording it in his mind, not wanting to reveal anything about his life and unwilling to commit to any specific explanation. His dreams were full of tumult and anger. One night he woke up, half-fallen out of the bed and tangled up in the sheets, convinced he could see a man, outline framed in the window, shining a flashlight into his eyes. He got up and sat rocking on the side of the bed his hands over his ears, specters of those long-forgotten times circling round him. Pulling on his thick pajamas, he went down to Lydia's study. Facing the bright glare of the screen in the dark, his heart racing, fingers trembling above the keys, he wrote a brief email confirming that the letters and notebook were his and inviting her to join him for lunch the day after her arrival. The sound of the email entering the web sent a tremor up his larynx and his jaw started chattering in the cold. He knew he was no longer able contain the inert emotion of the brutal wound he had sustained; for so long successfully boxed up, a tragedy forgotten and suppressed was about to take hold of his life again. As he wept, it wasn't clear to Daniel if this could be anything other than bad for him.

He returned to bed and passed off a few hours of fitful sleep, eventually woken by the telephone ringing. As he picked it up he glanced at the alarm clock seeing it was already 9.30 and he could hear Ade's men taking down the scaffolding at the last part of the porch roof beneath his window. It was the receptionist from his doctor's office. Professor Sale we have some of your results back and the doctor would like to see you at his office if possible rather than talk over the phone. He doesn't want you to be alarmed but there are one or two further tests which he'd like to discuss. They agreed a time for him to go in the following week.

Daniel made coffee for the carpenters and placed it with a tin of cookies on the table on the porch, the wood still rich in its winter coat of linseed oil. Here the men sat to smoke and tell dirty jokes in their own language, most of them it seemed were Ade's cousins or friends. But they were polite and gentle when Daniel was present, telling him about their wives and children in English. Today he wasn't able to tune into the chatter and went downstairs to start work on backing the map. But he could feel his blood

sugar was low and wasn't able to concentrate on this either, so took his coffee out to the terrace above and sat wrapped in a blanket gazing over the leafless branches of the trees. Then it dawned on him.

He went into the office and dialed Chester who was with a client. He'd return the call in a bit. While he waited reflecting on the conversation he was about to have, Daniel sat in Lydia's office. He hadn't changed anything, not entirely comfortable with trespassing in this room, merely layering over her things with his own. Papers and books littered the table overlooking the terrace. He'd spend hours reading fragments of research papers and longhand notes on texts she was editing. Just before the diagnosis, she was preparing an anthology of 18th century feminist discourses. When she knew she was going to die, she'd arranged to have her material passed to one of the faculty researchers at Exhampton but all the original handwritten papers were still here. The fallen leaves of insight she had so cherished.

Daniel answered the phone. He was determined to free himself from the vicious burden of guilt he had borne so long and so alone. He was about to do something he had never dared to do before. To ask for help. After thanking him for Thanksgiving dinner, in almost one breath he said Chester I have something very important to talk with you about. It has been preying on my mind for some time and I cannot go any longer without taking into you into my confidence. I know it is a lot to ask, you have been incredibly kind and thoughtful but there is something I need to discuss. I think that it will tear me up if I don't release it. Can I please ask you to come over here as soon as you can? If you would like to take the train and have dinner, I can cook. You'd be more than welcome to stay overnight. I'm sorry to ask this of you, but I have been shocked by some news I recently received. For the first time in many years, I feel helpless. I need a friend I can trust.

The whole day, Daniel was possessed with a nervous energy that didn't allow him to concentrate on anything much. In the late afternoon, he stood out on the porch in the dimming of the crisp December light, feeling the tip of his nose and lips numbing as he contemplated what lay ahead. The builders had gone, leaving the porch restored to its placid geometry. He admired their expertise in the restoration of its understated colonial flourishes, the imperceptible merging of new and old. Here, once again Daniel sat at the helm, alone, sailing into an expanse of undetermined waters. He was filled with both excitement and anxiety, unsure whether to be relieved or terrified that finally he was about to confess the past he had so carefully protected from scrutiny.

He was also surprised that it was to Chester, who he had only known for such a short time, to whom he was going to unburden himself. But Daniel had made few trusted friendships in his lifetime and though he had never contemplated doing so at this stage in his life, something remarkable had happened such that he was emboldened by their encounter. He might even go so far as to say, he had been made happier by it. It had been a very long time since he'd felt any new stir of connection like this. The last had been Lydia.

He could remember almost the same feelings the day she had first visited Gideon's Farm. Marta had come in early to prepare lunch for him to serve here on the porch and he had fluttered around the house trying to occupy himself, uncertain of how or where to be. When Lydia arrived almost without any noticeable shift of key, they were deep in conversation and laughter, the first he had ever truly experienced in this house. Oddly she seemed entirely at home here, when he'd always felt a stranger in his mother's home. Now it felt different, almost joyful and after only a few of these visits Daniel realized that his life could be transformed by Lydia's constant presence. She had a feel for this house, she intuitively moved about it with ease as if there were something she understood about the way it had been conceived.

They'd been introduced at the publication launch of a book Daniel edited. He normally made scant appearances at these events but over the last few years, since his mother's death, he tended to linger longer at the end of the day. To his surprise he found himself talking to someone he'd never met and they were almost the last remaining at the end of the reception. As he drove home he thought how much he'd enjoyed the conversation with the English professor and realized he'd forgotten to register her name. A few days later, the faculty assistant left a package on his desk containing a monograph on the work of Felicia Hemans with a note thanking Daniel for a delightful evening. The following week they had lunch on campus.

Though what followed was in no way a courtship, when they were together these two independent creatures loosened a little their prehensile grip on the serious business of their lives. They found that compassion and lightness grew between them and whatever had happened to make them previously dread the intimacy of random acquaintance, was diminished in the pleasure of two like minds welcoming each other to a place of safety.

It was not many months before Daniel had unearthed the courage to make a serious proposal to Lydia. She would understand, he knew, that he had never expected to have a companion and that he had only ever shared this house with his mother. Since her death, he'd found a routine that suited him but he thought that she was in a similar condition, so might they not create a home together from their lives. She laughed and said he made it sound as if they were mariners marooned on an island, an idea she liked. She kissed him on the forehead and held both his hands in hers. When she did this, the warmth from the stare of her bright green eyes comforted him. She could see that he fought back tears and was not sure if they were for the joy of knowing that he would not be alone in this place, or whether some hurt, much older and deeper wanted for air.

And now he was feeling all of this again. The reassurance that comes from not thinking of oneself as being entirely alone. He went inside and tried to distract himself with a book. He thought of swimming but couldn't imagine being able to coordinate the feeling of boyish urgency in his limbs. So he sat out the rest of the afternoon in front of the fire, listening to Miles Davis on the library sitting room record player and running over the story he was about to tell, surprised at how vividly the events of those days still appeared in his mind.

Daniel knew that Chester would be concerned at his sudden request and didn't want him to think of him as a frantic old man, so he resolved to manage the evening as if he were revealing something important to the future security of the estate. He'd state the facts of the story like the reading of a will, somber and exact, leaving nothing out. Chester could judge himself if Daniel was to blame. When Chester finally arrived. Daniel was completely at ease again. They ate on the sofa in front of the fire and when they had finished, Daniel made tea and placed the notebook and letters on the table in front of them.

Chester woke up on the long sofa with the smell of wood smoke in the air. He was wrapped under two heavy plaid wool blankets but the room was cold. Daniel had offered him a bed but he'd fallen asleep here in front of the fire, exhausted by the emotions he was feeling. From the sofa he could see the beech trees at the side of the house silhouetted against the dawn light as the events of the night before turned over and over in his head. Wrecking sounds from the depths of the house suggested an ancient heating system struggling into life. There was so much in the extraordinary story Daniel had recounted that he could barely piece it together. Except for one part, the most important part of the story, the thing he had least expected to hear from Daniel. He had always thought his friend was harboring something unrevealed so it hadn't exactly surprised him that there was an unknown secret. But his sober insistence that he was responsible for the death of someone else many years before had confused Chester. He still wasn't clear why Daniel was telling him, and it changed something between them the instant it was uttered. Daniel was shattered before eventually going to bed. Tears fell from his eyes as he quietly explained in detail to Chester what had happened in Barcelona that summer 50 years earlier. The tears seemed to emerge not from suffering but like spring water uncovered and opened to the air.

At four in the morning, finally Daniel handed Chester the leather notebook and two bundles of letters. He should read them for himself. From what they contained he would understand why he was forced to betray someone he loved. He could judge Daniel on that. Chester was also emotionally shattered by the revelations and as he lay there contemplating it all, Daniel came in with a mug of tea, steaming in the cold air. How are you? I didn't sleep but I do feel rested somehow. Thank for allowing me to share this with you. I hope that you won't judge me too harshly. I only acted as I thought right, as I was forced to do, at the time. I hope you will still be my friend. It has been a huge weight lifted from my shoulders. Having you here, being able to tell you. It didn't seem possible it could ever happen. But now I do feel differently, even if I am to blame. It seems like a vague shape of the future, is out there, coming into the light. Until now, until this morning, I was experiencing the opposite; my life was gradually disappearing in front of me, as if I was standing on a precipice in fog, my hands stretched out into the nothingness beyond.

Chester had to get back to the girls but promised to call Daniel the next day, reassuring him that nothing in his mind had changed. Though it had, dramatically. But it was not what the older man assumed. Even so, Chester couldn't express it. For him a surge of emotion with such force moved him further and stronger towards a precarious position in his own world. It seemed to be shifting around him, all the assumptions he had made about himself were now changing. Despite being the older man, Daniel now appeared to him so vulnerable and helpless and the whole of the evening he resisted the urge to comfort him. Something was forcing him to be

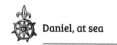

judicious. He knew Daniel needed him but wasn't at all sure quite how.

That would have to wait, first he must read what Daniel had given him, to judge for himself. He would need a peaceful space for that which wasn't possible with Tabitha and Chloe racing round the house. He waited until they were asleep late that night, took his cargo into the office, closed the door, placed them on the desk in front of him and began reading. First, he arranged the letters in front of him, around the notebook, all addressed to the same person. But he chose to start with the notebook because it felt less intrusive. Perhaps by becoming familiar with Daniel's narrative to himself, he might find the confidence to be party to the intimacy of the letters addressed to someone else.

The studied but emotionless observations on Daniel's entries in these first stages of his trip portrayed a priggish and buttoned-up young man, carefully detailing things around him with little sense of excitement or energy. The lists of books he read on board ship, the waspish commentary on his fellow passengers, his sneering at his cousin were all in a voice Chester didn't recognize. He guessed that Daniel was writing for his mother, still too young and too recently under her power to have formed a sense of worldliness not devised by her. Partly boredom from the first chapter of his adventure and partly too eager a desire to please her made the early diary entries seem studied, like letters. But as the days and weeks went on his style gradually changed, more observant of difference, less judgmental. Something of the Daniel he knew now was emerging. His observations were personal, full of feeling; He was starting to embrace what was happening around him; he seemed to be feeling life as he was experiencing it.

Chapter Sixteen

The friendship with Xavi rapidly took a hold of Daniel. He was not prepared emotionally or even practically. He had never really strayed beyond the confines of college fraternity loyalties. Daniel had seen these as merely association by proximity, just the sort of connections people from his background made. Connections made not through any bond of intimacy or genuine affection but for their usefulness in later life. Daniel's only friends had been local to Greenwich or study companions from his courses and seminars. From the age of 12 he had attended a private boarding school 30 miles away, where he had dutifully performed exactly what was expected of him and no more. He was neither bullied nor fêted by the other boys and had little of the natural competitive vigor that seemed to course through the veins of the elite. Quietly and assuredly he made his way through school, without ever attracting attention or forging strong bonds. It was Daniel's particular skills at not being noticed which gave his fellow pupils the impression that everyone else, except them, must be his closest friends. And so he easily maneuvered his way through the adolescent outrages and juvenile angst that most schoolboys suffer.

It wasn't at all that he didn't enjoy the company of his peers, just that Mae had taught him to be self-reliant, never to assume that because you were in the same class or even family, that those people would remain loyal or faithful to you. It was vital to seek out the people who would etch new meaning onto your life experience and thrust you forward into the world a better person. Better to do without people than have false friends. Learning this made Daniel more than just old beyond his years, which he was. It shaped him into someone who witnessed other's loves and friendships, but with few of his own.

So far, nothing had shifted the practical distance at which he kept other boys at arm's length since the incident with Sheldon Buller. Until at the age of 18, a freshman at Exhampton, he became the unlikely dorm mate of the ebullient and colorful Nathaniel Defarge, with whom surprisingly he immediately hit it off. Despite appearing slightly starched, Daniel was in no way prudish or ignorant on the subject of men's desires. His mother's social milieu was scattered with homosexuals and she herself was rumored to have had an affair with a cabaret singer. As a tall, lithe, blond boy with broad

shoulders and blue eyes he'd often had to tactfully repel the advances of some of her friends during parties at Gideon's Farm. Once in the vacation a writer lectured Daniel at lunch on the benefits of sexual adventuring with his schoolfellows, declaring that the next generation must rebel against the establishment through physical permissiveness.

Daniel was aware that the attraction for both him and Nate was more than friendship. But he was determined that by the time these college years were over he would be free from his mother and he knew that she would draw in anyone with whom he developed an attachment. Making her happy was its own imprisonment. With the cool rationalism she'd taught him to address all aspects of his life, he decided that romance would complicate that plan at the moment. And though the physical longings were sometimes demanding and he often contemplated revealing his feelings to his friend, at the point that might have happened, Nate was already enjoying his own freedom and passions on campus. So, their companionship never strayed beyond their many other shared pleasures. And throughout his life, though he never said so to Nate, nor indeed acknowledged the subject, Daniel was to be profoundly grateful that those strong foundations had never been physical. Years later, after graduating, it amused Daniel that he was aware of Nate's affair with Sonny J. Franklin long before his friend decided to tell him. But they were both cautious men in their separate ways and as someone who kept his own counsel, Daniel would never dream of questioning the decisions of the friend he most admired. Perhaps by then neither had wanted to change what it had become.

By contrast, Xavi's company grew on Daniel like a quick contagion. With him he had let his guard down and allowed the constant presence of his new friend to affect his equilibrium. Until now he had been a bystander. Feelings of affection he had intellectualized but never fully come to terms with, ambushed him overnight. For the first time, he was permitting fate to take its course with no thought for what might happen. He was at sea, where chaos and the unknown rule, with only the light of the stars to guide him. Happiness was entering his being in a wholly unexpected way, like a boy carved from marble given the breath of life.

But the self-possession in which Daniel had been trained over many years, did not completely desert him now. Despite the pleasure of this new friendship, he remained reserved as they got to know each other over those first days.

At the end of the week it was Christmas and Daniel had accepted an invitation from Robert to the coast, north of Barcelona to stay with the American Consul and his wife at a house belonging to some Catalan friends. Robert had arranged for them both to accept and Daniel weighed the outcome as being to his advantage. After spending the vacation together his cousin would be unlikely to disturb him again for some time.

Those three days were near purgatory for him sharing festive jollity with people he hardly knew, singing carols and wearing a paper crown. Still the wife was a good cook and he enjoyed her American dishes. She thrust a bag of leftovers into his hands as they left for Barcelona on the day after Christmas, declaring her concern for his welfare. Her husband hadn't shown the slightest interest in his work but they had talked about jazz, sharing a love of hard-bop and they found a copy of Cannonball Adderly's *Somethin' Else* with Davis guesting and Art Blakey on drums. He felt sorry for the wife, unable to speak the language, childless and with no real interest in anything but her husband's career. As they left, he offered to take her around the museum.

Daniel could barely contain himself as they arrived back in the city. Robert dropped him at Via Laeitana and he ran to Plaça de Llana, up the stairs, only stopping to give the food to his landlady. A note was waiting for him from Xavi, saying that he would come at the end of the day. Daniel asked his landlady to send up some hot coals in a *brasera* to warm the room up. It was a rather self-defeating exercise because it hardly threw out much heat and filled the room with fumes, which every so often had to be let out of the window.

Daniel missed listening to music when he arrived and though he seldom spent money on luxuries, when he moved in he had bought himself a record player from the local department store, carrying it to his room with the glory of a conqueror returned, his prize wrapped in brown paper and string. The next day he wrote to Nate asking him to send some of the latest favorites. Rollins, Davies and Coltrane arrived from New York a few weeks later and in the meantime he found a local record store in the city where he bought Charlie Mingus and Chick Corea, which he played over and over again.

Xavi wasn't schooled in jazz or really musical at all, so Daniel who was a patient and careful teacher, over the first days they spent time together introduced him to the key elements of the form, enthusing about the players and their sounds. Quickly his friend, who was an eager pupil, knew the right questions to ask that would make Daniel smile and fuel the brightness in his eyes.

He heard the familiar scatter of Xavi racing up the stairs, politely calling out to the Senora on the way past the second floor. He jumped to his feet and was there already to open the door. Unable to resist a natural inclination, without any hesitation or plan to do so, he leaned forward and kissed the man facing him fully on the lips. Xavi, as if this was the most normal reaction, put his arms around him and without taking his lips from Daniel's they moved as one into the jazz-filled room, kicking the door closed behind them. For minutes they stood, their faces touching gently, gradually encircling one another. Then Xavi stood back with a grin, holding Daniel's head in his hands, thumbs stroking his eyebrows, looking into his eyes and shaking his head. I felt it so strongly. But I couldn't hope. I didn't know. He kissed him again.

There was one chair, so they sat on the floor on a woolen rug Daniel had bought from the market. All night, they drank whiskey from a bottle and smoked, listening to the night outside, wrapped one to the other, kissing with the hunger of a love newly spoken. The smell and taste of body and sweat intermingling, the tender brush of skin under gentle hands, the holding of breath and surfacing for air, only to drown in each other once more. Later in the evening, they carried the narrow mattress to the floor and gave themselves, heart and soul, to each other. *He plies your mouth with his. Then, limbs entwined, your bodies unite. You push against each other, draw his body towards you, hungry for every piece of him, you exist for those moments. And in the morning, there lying on the bed is a knot of two lives suddenly entwined.*

Chapter Seventeen

The two young men sat at a table outside the Zurich with blankets around their knees and the sun shone over the top of the plane trees along the side of Plaça Catalunya. Its light hovered over a cloud of cigarette smoke and steam from their coffee and breath in the cold air, creating the effect of a halo over them. Bert, the tough black marine, had told Xavi that there was nothing unmanly about being with a man. You just have to decide how you want to move forward in the world. And though he had girlfriends, Xavi knew from a young age how he would do that. During those early years, he looked forward to the day when Bert reappeared, though now he was long gone, apart from a single postcard from Cincinnati. They used to take a room out of sight in a pension off the Diagonal, known to be safe for male lovers, though in this city you really never knew whom you could trust. Xavi kept a close eye on the man who owned the apartment, a widower who had been an anarchist before the war and seemed to have the right political views. His boyfriend worked here at the Zurich and it was possible to make arrangements using a special code, which sounded to everyone else like passing the time of day, while ordering your drinks.

Though on the surface Barcelona appeared open and relaxed, Franco's government reserved a special ruthlessness for the Catalans and under fascist repression, this kind of love had to be clandestine. Assignations were shadowy and fleeting and any overt displays were shunned. Xavi knew who the rent boys were, plying their trade in the Raval with visiting seamen and nervous travelers. They were friends of the girls in the *barraques* where he taught English. But he kept his distance.

There was cruising, out in the open a lingering nod or a hand raised to the ear could lead to sex. More immediate relief also played out in public lavatories, the back of cinemas, bus stations and parks, just as it did in cities everywhere. But here the risk of being apprehended was far more serious. Being caught could lead to a long prison sentence, if it even got as far as that, under the vicious justice doled out to gay men. The *Generalísimo* declares that if you are different, you are not just morally deviant, you are an enemy of the state. And Xavi knew of boys who had been raped in the basement of the police station on Via Laeitana, and several who had disappeared.

He was also familiar with another scene, where a more powerful and affluent group of men could afford to play out their social interactions but far more discreetly in the cultural gathering places where people were used to more open expression. He had been introduced to this highly secretive and sophisticated gay society at a party hosted by Sebastian Desvalls, an antiques dealer in his 60s from an old Catalan family, who had been sent to English boarding school and Oxford. The war left a certain class of men, people with social position who knew no sides and who carved success wherever they could while making everyone believe they were loyal. Due to one indiscretion or another, they were clearly unable to measure up to the strict moral codes of the new regime so had to find ways to make themselves invaluable to the authorities. Desvalls, was one of those men and knowing his vulnerabilities he was careful to maintain useful associations with those in a similar predicament, which afforded him freedoms or at least deflected unwanted scrutiny of his activities. Most people from all classes who would have given their lives for the Republic 20 years before, by now had lost heart. Remembering the murderous, bloody years, harboring vengeful thoughts for the misery and starvation, contemplating the outrages was too much to bear. They were tired of conflict and some, the ones who had forgotten most of what went before, had made the most of new opportunities.

Sebastian appeared to have the confidence of everyone he needed, and his polished diplomacy disguised any activities that might have caused concern. He also had the advantage, while not being wealthy, of owning a country estate hidden in the wooded hills of Montseny, where he was able to entertain; his neighbors either being those in whose society he was so comfortable they suspected nothing or locals who were indebted to him for regular employment. Xavi had visited the 16th-century farmhouse on several occasions as well as the family mansion deep in the Gothic quarter. Through Sebastian's social circle he was introduced to well-known artists and performers and perhaps more surprisingly there were lawyers, industrialists, politicians and some visiting foreigners at these stylish cocktail parties. Xavi was a popular attraction for the older men and had the ability to flirt efficiently enough to keep them at bay. He would play them off against each other, agreeing to meet them another time when no-one would know. The next time he saw them he'd roll his eyes and shrug his shoulders complaining of the possessiveness of another member of the group. As none of them would show their hand to the others, like a cat playing with his prey, he was one step ahead of their advances.

The gatherings would often begin with an opera at the Liceu or at a play and it was not until after the dinners with their families or friends had dispersed, sometimes at two or three in the morning, that they would drift off to enjoy their double life. But even when they were safely together in one apartment or other in the company of many like them, these powerful men kept their decorum deliberately tight and were always careful in their behavior. Although there were a few high-ranking policemen and military officials among them, if a scandal threatened they would not necessarily be able to intervene. If you made too public a display of yourself or were at risk of exposing the rest, you would not be invited back. There were clear protocols to follow.

At the Zurich, Xavi recognized some of the customers without greeting them. He wouldn't breach that familiarity unless someone happened to be a neighbor or a family friend. He hadn't explained any of this to Daniel, but felt quite safe with him. Despite their yearning to spend every moment together alone, they both instinctively resisted any behavior that would draw unwanted attention.

It was then he saw Desvalls approaching their table. Daniel recognized him. It was the suave, silver-haired man with his mouth twisted in that unreadable smile who he had met at the professor's office. It's Daniel, isn't it? How do you do, said Sebastian holding out his hand. I gather you are making remarkable progress with Professor Patxot's collections. We are most indebted for your work. It will help us a great deal. And I went to see the frescoes last week on a visit with the Museums Committee. Your cousin, the attaché, joined us. We are working with some American institutions.

Daniel was irked at the thought of Robert invading his place of work, his world. And it was too close to his new secret. Remarkable, quite remarkable, continued Devalls. 12th or 13th century they think. To Daniel's surprise Sebastian turned to nod acknowledgment to Xavi, narrowing his eyes slightly. So you know each other? Wonderful. How are your studies, Javier? Daniel noticed he was careful to use the Spanish pronunciation. Almost imperceptibly Desvalls started to move away from them but as he did so, he lowered his voice slightly. I hope you will both join us at a party I'm hosting after the concert at the Palau de Musica next week, and with a polite smile he continued to move effortlessly through the tables to greet two ladies in furs who fussed at his arrival.

Xavi pursed his lips, bright red in the cold air and smiled to himself. Without turning to Daniel, he sought his hand under the blanket, gently

held it and said there is so much I need to explain to you, Daniel. Things are different here, so far away from your home. I want to show you so much. Daniel kept his hand there, Xavi's slender fingers clasped over his. Everything was said in the warmth of that moment. Inside they ached for each other.

As they walked away, Daniel had explained how he had met Sebastian Desvalls and that he was involved with the work of the museums, advising the professor. Xavi asked him all about the process of examining and cataloguing and wanted to know what would happen to the collections once his task was complete. Daniel didn't know the exact details except that sometimes ownership could not be established or it wasn't possible to find the families to return them. He had been told that the more valuable items were stored separately and his descriptions of the less important papers and books were being translated into Spanish and prepared for the new center of national archives. Xavi was deep in thought about all of this for the rest of the day and kept asking questions about Desvalls' involvement. He wanted to tell Daniel so much he didn't yet understand but he trusted him and resolved to show him some of the parts of his life he hadn't yet shared.

Daniel was irritated by what Sebastian Desvalls had said about his cousin Robert at the café. He didn't want the invasion into this new life shaping around him. For the first time, he'd managed to make contact with someone completely on his own terms and within a couple of months he'd made this place his own. He was terrified of the possibility that someone from the world of before – anyone except Nate perhaps who would have cheered loudly and to whom he resolved to tell everything in due course – might be able to curse this paradise in which he found himself. Having met Xavi, new feelings had come to his body, sensations where they had never been. Naturally he had been subject to the same hormonal and bodily inflections as any other boy. But he'd missed out on the clumsy and shapeless pleasures of unformed desire which smooth out the rough edges of adolescence. He treated masturbation like a necessity rather than a joy and locked himself into a narcissistic state of self-exploration rather than developing bold sexual fantasies.

Sex came as a surprise to him. It was not at all what he expected, nor were his reactions. He wasn't sure why he had left this part of himself submerged for so long but he had imagined it to be far more formulaic. The reality was different and the results far less inevitable. That penetration was even possible was extraordinary to him and its heightened pleasures sent streaks of ecstasy through his body like an exquisite torture. He thought this was what it must be like to be struck by lightning.

Though he was a little younger, his body was more manly than Xavi's and after a summer swimming at the beach house in Long Island, brown and lean with a furze of light hair. He feasted on the porcelain white flesh of his lover, whose limbs were muscular and strong. Exploring the corners and rounds of his buttocks and legs, the bold archway of his navel and deep gulley of his groin, the strong peaks of his chest and soft plain of his back, sent shudders through Daniel as he satisfied this new-found hunger. The combination of love and previously undiscovered desire was becoming an irresistible addiction, conspiring in a constant and powerful demand for more. With every touch of his lips and skin on Xavi's body a burning intensity surfaced and deep inside his lover he found a secret place of solace, a place of orgasm so intense, he feared he would never experience anything like it again.

When he sat, Xavi behind holding him, chin tucked into his shoulder, ear to ear, legs, hands and arms around his, Daniel felt physical love for the first time and it often moved him to tears. The kind of love babies experience from birth, which had been denied to Daniel. The simple feeling of being a visceral extension of the other. Mae had been determined to endow him with survival skills, almost immediately immersing him in the world with no knowledge of physical connection. She held back from him what he needed to be frail, treating him with almost Spartan severity. When the instincts for this kind of love are dulled, a child cannot know how to come to terms with their own maturing body. There is simply a failure of imagination. Daniel wondered how he could have gone so long without ever embodying the spilling out of nature, the true uncontrolled joy of giving yourself to another person. Now he had finally escaped the prison he had unwittingly created for his emotions, the demands of his new-found freedom were strong. The power of their love was so intense that it carried them further than either of them were expecting.

Meanwhile life went on around them as normal and they saw each other as often as possible, separated only by necessary work and study. Daniel had paid his landlady four months in advance and she took little interest in his movements, quickly getting used to seeing Xavi come and go. They fucked relentlessly on the mattress on the floor in a tumbled mess of love and laughter and no-one in the world had a care for these two unknown men in their unknowable union. He'd always stay until Daniel was asleep, creeping out before daybreak to his own bed or to help the men bring in the morning deliveries. Xavi knew he should introduce Daniel to his sister and one afternoon, he was invited to lunch in her home behind the warehouse at Pintor Fortuny.

Elena had not inherited her mother's features or frame, having neither the aquiline features or spidery grace of movement with which her brother seemed to conquer the world. Her hair was pinned tightly to her head for convenience rather than style and she wore clothes like armor, making her look at least a decade older as well as in a permanent state of mourning. She seldom smiled and when she did it was usually in derision, which slanted her eyes and made her lips tighten around her mouth. Daniel noticed that she clearly resented her brother with his wide-open eyes and mouth full of laughter. Meeting him required no change in her demeanor; in fact, because she spoke no English, she was able to carry on most of the conversation over lunch through Xavi, hardly looking at him. Xavi knew that it would get back to her if Daniel was visiting upstairs, so wanted to allay suspicion by letting her think he was teaching the American to speak Spanish. Before they arrived, Xavi told Daniel not to show more than basic comprehension of their conversation, which forced them both to suppress their laughter when she thought he hadn't understood her bitter commentary about something or other.

Xavi's quarters were also accessible from an iron staircase outside the back of the building to the second-floor terrace, but no-one ever used it and he kept the doors of his small terrace locked except in the heat of summer. After thanking Elena, they came out of the front of the store where they found Don Gilberto, tugging at his waxed mustache and plucking up courage to visit the object of his continued affections. Xavi briefly introduced his student and pushed him through the gateway before he could answer the inquisition of questions from his sister's suitor. Another time, Don Gilberto, we have to study this afternoon. Ring the bell, Elena is in the parlor. They ran along the alley, up the stairs three at a time, fell through the door giggling, drank deep and long from each other and slept until late afternoon.

Daniel awoke on the scramble of bedclothes and opened one eye. Xavi wearing only his shirt, lay spread-eagled on the small sofa smoking, his long white legs tucked over the arm, tapping the burning end of a cigarette on the ashtray that sat on his taut, flat navel. He was deep in thought but smiled when he noticed Daniel looking at him and came to lie down next to him on the bed, resting his chin on his hands, kissing his face softly. How have you come to me, Daniel Sale? What are we going to do together, you and I? Daniel grinned and stretched out all his limbs, feeling hard against Xavi. The fog of self-denial he had used for so long to keep his balance in the world had cleared to reveal a new landscape of sexual urges he now didn't have any reason to deny. He could never have imagined thirsting so much for Xavi's experienced hands. For all his achievements and status, despite the sophistication his mother had applied at will in his upbringing, she had not prepared him for this state. Come, let's get dressed, I want to take you somewhere tonight. It's time you met some of my friends.

Chapter Eighteen

After a short tram ride, they jumped off and started walking down Carrer Marina. It was late now and as they made their way further down, the buildings on each side of the road started to clear and the street lighting disappeared. But in the light of the moon, Daniel could see factory chimneys and water towers ahead of them silhouetted against the dark night sky. To the left the giant frames of the gas reserves loomed towards them, as he realized they were walking towards the beach close to the area called Barceloneta where he had first set eyes on Xavi. Here a hotchpotch of low-slung factories were jammed up against each other so that it was impossible to tell where one ended or another began. These buildings were all closed up in the darkness but in between them were narrow lanes, sparsely lit with the occasional naked light bulb twinkling in front of them. He began to hear the sounds of habitation, laughter, dogs barking, mewling babies and radios bawling, all competing, thoughtless of each other. Careful, said Xavi as they made their way carefully along one of these ditches, it's muddy and they throw everything out here at this time of night.

Daniel resisted the urge to grasp his arm and followed his steps gingerly for a few minutes until they came to an area of open ground, surrounded by huts. In the middle people were gathered under a wooden-framed canopy with a large fire burning in the middle. A few dirty looking women next to it holding sticks which they used to balance large metal cooking pots on the embers. Someone shouted Xavi's nickname and suddenly people were greeting them both. Before he was able to introduce Daniel properly they had tin cups thrust in their hands and toasts were being made. It wasn't unpleasant, something between brandy and wine. With the bustle of people around them talking and the heat of the fire he quickly relaxed while people nodded and smiled at him. Once they had established that not only was he American but that he could speak some Spanish they were welcoming him to Somorrostro in their strong accents with unguarded smiles, revealing blackened teeth and bombarding him with questions, without ever waiting for the answers.

Some chairs were brought and a small circle of people formed, including them, while a meat stew was served in bowls by the women. Hey *Palillo*! Daniel looked behind him to see a familiar face emerge from the darkness, the raven hair pushed back with a bright scarf, white blouse and flowing red skirt. It was Lili, the girl he had met in the square. She looked at him and winking and put her hand on his cheek, so you are the friend of Palillo. She laughed and moved across the circle to greet Xavi in the usual way. He looked at her seriously. You missed class this week, Lili. You better be careful the children are speaking better than you now. I have a new boyfriend, Pal. He takes me out and buys me things, I learn from him. My mother says do what you need now, you only become a saint after you are dead, claro? Everyone laughed and the company continued in high spirits. Once they had eaten, the chairs and wooden boxes they had been sitting on were moved out and the circle was cleared. Someone in the darkness started playing a guitar. Lili began to dance.

Xavi came over to Daniel. He explained that they were in Somorrostro, the shanty town right on the waterfront beyond the big hospital. These people were Roma from Andalucia. They had been targeted in the war as the lowest of the low and were forced to keep moving on. But here they found work among others from the south and made something of a life, however poor and desperate, in these slum settlements across Barcelona. The Catalans were decent people and despite having nothing, would not turn strangers away. There wasn't much work but they could make shacks out of whatever they could find and some lived in tents. When there were storms, the surge of the sea sometimes swept their houses and even people away but as a community they survived. The authorities provided fresh water from a pump and local nuns ministered as they could, otherwise there was nothing but what they shared between them and the help they received from people like us.

It struck Daniel how much Mae would have loved to be here among these people, how she should have wanted to create order here in the chaos. More than he, she was hungry for experiences and wanted to know about life, she had a voyeuristic compulsion to observe the conditions of people's lives and to be part of them. He was pleased that he was here, knowing how the people who lived where he came from would fear this. That was why she had introduced him to those New York jazz dives, so he would witness life not as it had been constructed by his people with power and money but life as it should be, guided only by instinct, life lived only because it had to be, regardless of obstacle or trouble. What she punned as life up and down the bar lines.

By now the clack-clack of castanets had reached such a rate of repetition that Daniel's head was beginning to spin. Lili grabbed Xavi's hand while another girl took Daniel's and both were twisting and turning around them along with the whole crowd of people moving as one with exuberance and wild energy, until thankfully the song ended with a huge cry and everyone stopped to catch their breath. Daniel was drunk, there was no two ways about it, the hooch had gone to his head but happily so and he reached into his pocket for cigarettes, taking one before passing them round. He sat down with a thump on one of the boxes close to the fire while he smoked. At this point, a man with a scar running down the side of his face, looking like an old warrior joined the huddle of men talking to Xavi. It looked like a serious conversation but he couldn't tell what it was about and was too tired to care. A few minutes later Xavi came over, suggesting they walk Lili home if he didn't mind stopping off to pay his respects to her mother who had been unwell.

After cheerful farewells and embraces, the three of them set off through the maze of shacks and after a while found themselves outside a corrugated tin door. They went inside where two candles in jars on a table lit the room and an old lady sat asleep on a chair next to a mattress on which two young children slept. Lili gently shook her mother's shoulder and Xavi kneeled in front of her speaking softly. She looked at him, eyes half-open and nodded, raising her hand to his head as if blessing him. Without moving from her chair, she turned and looked towards Daniel, beckoning him over. He followed Xavi's example and crouched down while she muttered something to Xavi. He shook his head and standing up, kissed her forehead. On the way home he asked what she had said. That I should not let you suffer. I don't understand. She meant that there is no need for you to see these people living like this. But I wanted to share it with you. Seeing is knowing. One day maybe you can help me here.

The days and weeks passed as spring emerged from the dry chill of winter, the rustle of the leaves blowing along the sidewalks replaced with wet warmth of April showers and the green lawns of the Ciutadella park reappeared from the brown earth. At night after work Daniel and Xavi would often meet here and sit by the lake in the middle of the park, watching the swifts recently returned from Africa, swooping across the surface of the water to drink in the evening light, a constant carousel turning in the air. Did you know, Daniel told him, they only stop flying to nest and give birth. They mate and sleep on the wing. And they pair for life.

They were happy and their quickly born love soon became something strong. There were no dramas or jealousies, nothing to taint the pure strength of two young men, lustful and proud, none but the other to look up to. These were languid days, adrift on calm waters and apart from the secrecy in which they shrouded their friendship there had been no clashes to strike an ill note. They were hardly apart when time from their duties allowed. Even then there was nothing demanding or anxious. And Daniel became dependent on the force of these feelings. All was as it should be in the early term of love.

After leaving the park, they would go to eat in a tiny café on the corner of Plaça St. Pere opposite the convent before heading back to Daniel's place, where they drank beer and listened to Billie Holiday while they fucked in every possible way. Xavi could cook and had a small gas cooker, wooden table and kitchen sink in his room, so they would often eat there; and as the evenings became warmer they sat outside on the terrace, smoked, talked and read books. To avoid questions from Elena, Daniel would usually go home late from Pintor Fortuny. But sometimes on weekends, Xavi wanted him to stay, to feel his warmth next to him in the morning. On those nights, he pulled over the shutters, so they wouldn't be disturbed.

Some Sundays, Daniel went with Xavi to Somorrostro where he gave his English classes to a rag-tag group of women and children in a low brick building with a corrugated tin roof, chairs arranged in rows on the earth floor and a blackboard at the end. It was one of the few decent constructions here, built by their fathers and sons and paid for by the nuns who were midwives and nurses to the infants and the sick. The children turned up to their lessons, immaculately turned out and sat attentively watching their teacher. In daylight, he could see how precarious life was for Lili and her people. There were more than 10,000 living in this wreckage of stone, brick and rotting wood, protected from the sea behind an eroding escarpment of sand, like a besieged trench along the shore, cut through by filthy waterways washing their daily grime into the sea.

More than the ramshackle detritus of houses or the wild, unkempt poverty of it all, what Daniel noticed was the battle for cleanliness. Gangs of women at washing troughs or with galvanized steel buckets of water, pounding the dirt out of already threadbare garments, and right across the beach down to the tideline, tossed in the wind, in an act of defiant opposition against the misery of their lives they hung miles and miles of drying clothes and bedding. The clothes of these sunbaked children, brown as almonds, dressed in their clean best on their way to the weekly mass led by a Carmelite friar, were made more dazzling white by the victory of these efforts over their sordid surroundings. Against the hardship, there was true joy and laughter to be found here he thought, like you find in Harlem or the Lower East Side, where the only antidote to the toughness of life and poorness of opportunity is high spirits and sheer optimism. Daniel wrote to Nate. *I have been helping my friend Xavi in a shanty town by the sea. This afternoon I ran a conversation class for the girls while he worked with the children. They are all so polite, nothing like students at home. But they giggle and blush a bit when I talk which is odd given the way they make money. It's amusing that they all want to either own a store or find an American boyfriend. The respect they show Xavi in the whole area is touching. He feels so much for their condition and is very angry about the way the city authorities are building settlements out of the city with no infrastructure to rehouse many of the shanties. I'm sure it won't be long before this place is cleared. It doesn't look good to foreigners since Spain has joined the UN. I enjoy this experience, which I don't suppose I would have anywhere else.*

The two of them would walk home along the front, the children clamoring at their knees, laughing and screaming. They'd pick up the small ones up to ride on their shoulders, which made the rest noisier and from the mouths of the toothless old women they passed came smiles and mumbled blessings as if they were wandering apostles. They were greeted by all but the most surly and resentful, who knew nothing of Xavi's work and assumed they were rich boys, *pijos*, passing through for amusement. One day a drunk barged into them and started pushing them about, shouting abuse. Xavi pulled him off but within moments a small crowd came to their rescue, gathered round the man and berated him for his disrespect to their visitors. It surprised Daniel that this was one of the places he felt safe, albeit in the shadow of his friend. The sound of the gulls and the sea washing in the mist before the sun was high, reminded him of Long Island.

Chapter Nineteen

In the library, Daniel was gradually creating order amid the hush of ancient paper. Every day would reveal single treasures, fragments of lives and homes of which he knew nothing. For this reason he was impartial in the deference he paid to his charges. Important works, ancient correspondence or the mundane and banal ephemera of more recent activity, were all given respectful service. Sometimes he would find an existing catalog made by the original owners, not only making his life easier but setting the books or manuscripts in context to the personal passion with which they had been collected.

Naturally, the greatest delight he reserved was for his beloved maps; he encountered some real gems including a military campaign map in a metal tube casing from the Napoleonic Wars, a rolled 18th-century leather coaching map and a proposed expedition route of the Ivory Coast. There was even an urban planning document showing the first construction layouts of this city where he now lived. Best of all, he found two particularly fine Mallorquin portolans and an early Dutch sea atlas. They had been collected by a Jewish family from Girona who, the professor explained, had fled to Switzerland through France only to be captured on the way there and interned in a German concentration camp. These families were seldom far from the back of his mind and he mourned their lost ownership, ever conscious of the troubles they had faced. How strong your resistance to an invading force would have to be - especially of your own people - for them then to exile you.

Daniel imagined a lifetime of searching out objects of fascination, often by generations, only to have them snatched from you by a careless tyrant. Or to have to escape for your life with a suitcase, abandoning everything you have known as home, leaving all you have loved behind.

Some days Xavi would come up to meet him for lunch. But being there unnerved him and he would pace up and down, waiting for Daniel to break. They had discussed it many times. Xavi saw the value in what he was doing, for the preservation of the collections, particularly for the survival of Catalan culture which had suffered such harsh attempts of eradication. But at heart he was much agitated by the very injustice of the exercise. Daniel could see anger, carefully stowed away, start to surface. One afternoon he

was waiting in the university gardens for Xavi to finish class. He arrived in a sweat, furious and complaining loudly that he was going to leave the university, they could forget it, he was finished. Anyway, he'd been offered a job working with the new foundation for the Catalan culture and he didn't need their help.

It turned out that a recently formed student association, set up to support the workers and unions, had been proscribed by his professors, under pressure from the government. He had personally been called up to the office of his head of department, where he and the dean warned him not to cause any difficulties or the financial support for his studies would be stopped. He had argued with bitter resentment that this was an academic institution, supposedly free of allegiances. Weren't *Opus Dei* allowed to flourish, recruiting among conservative students? Daniel hadn't seen Xavi in such a state before and it took considerable coaxing before he returned to his affable nonchalance. Daniel suspected vaguely that there were things he wasn't talking about and the following week Xavi disappeared for a few days. Daniel found it hard; he didn't complain but he missed him desperately even if a day passed without knowing when he'd see his lover next.

The night of the choral concert in which Natalia's cousin was singing at the Palau de Musica, was the same night Sebastian Desvalls was also hosting his party, so the two of them turned out smartly. Natalia had never asked directly about Xavi, though she liked him and had become familiar with his presence around Daniel. The work they were doing on the frescoes at Montcada was attracting some international attention, she was enjoying a high regard among her peers and the museum had offered her the job of mounting the frescoes after the conservation was complete. She noticed that Daniel's Spanish had improved since he met Xavi and became fond of them both, so didn't mind keeping her suspicions to herself.

Secrecy was a habit of living here where it was always hard to know what people were ever really thinking. Sometimes this was more true with family than with friends, whom you choose after all for what you have in common, however indistinctly expressed. Families were not so honest with each other and rivalries between disgruntled relatives might be played out against political loyalties. Xavi told Daniel later that when they had all visited the exhibition of Romanesque church paintings, Natalia was giving him the subtle signs of being a passionate Catalan. He couldn't quite explain how but there was implicit meaning in expressions they used, which without giving anything away, told someone where you stand.

They met Natalia and her friend under the giant arches where they milled with the smart looking crowd, before making their way up the staircase to the hall. Daniel was astonished, for though he'd walked past it many times and marveled, he'd never found the opportunity to be inside the building. The extravagant confection of anarchic modernism and organic art flowing out of the walls of the building seemed the opposite of the people here. It was very Catalan in that. Ironic, he thought, that the vigor of the artistic imagination outwardly expressed in architecture all over the city, runs so counter to the deeply restrained nature of the people behind the facades.

The four of them sat at the side of the balcony where they looked over most of the crowd. Dressed in furs and black tie, the cultural elite and the people of power were all obvious from their indifference to any but their own. Like any municipal concert hall there were formalities of status in where people sat, which was seldom based on their love of music. These days, Xavi had explained, since the war, money was still an advantage but ostentatious wealth aroused suspicion that you were too close to the regime. As he surveyed this play of status taking place below them, Xavi directed Daniel's gaze to a couple in the stalls near the stage. He was balding and sitting bolt upright with his hands open flat on his knees as if he was about to deliver a sermon. Beside him a woman in a startling emerald satin dress and black stole with white gloves, her hair tightly combed back. Take a look. He's a judge. Judge Antonio Sabater. He's the scourge of the streets, the Caudillo's pimp, he imprisons anyone he doesn't like. The prostitutes call him *La Sabata D'Or*. You'd say Golden Shoe. But don't be fooled. If Golden Shoe gets you, it's all over. Daniel could feel Xavi shudder.

Daniel loved the voice of the contralto, with a mountainous bust bedecked in jewels, who threw herself and her voice with great drama around the stage. The auditorium had been designed for precisely this kind of performance and though Daniel wasn't familiar with the music, he'd seen opera and orchestral concerts with his mother. His ear had been adjusted to seek out the rhythm and tunes of jazz but it was impossible not to be impressed by any music in this setting. Though it was buttoned-up and lacked the laid-back atmosphere in which he loved listening to music, the sound was still joyful and shifted all around them. The interior of the hall came to life under its influence. The ravishing skylight poised to pour itself in liquid color over them, the sculptures teetering from the walls. It looked to Daniel as if these giants had been created to overwhelm, almost seduce the audience. Most of all he loved the public warmth of Xavi's thigh gently resting against his, while he half-composed a letter in his head to his mother, explaining the important work he was doing and that he planned to extend his stay.

After the concert, they joined Natalia's cousin and some of the choir at a restaurant before finding their way through a warren of streets behind the Plaça St. Jaume at two in the morning to the large wooden doors of the Desvalls mansion. Xavi nudged him and winked as they walked up the wide sweep of stone staircase to the apartments upstairs. Daniel hadn't expected this; the grand entrance was the same as the palace in Montcada.

He could hear the ripple of noise coming through the open windows looking down over the courtyard. In a far corner, a tall woman with white hair in a lace gown was standing at one of the windows, watching their approach. Gentleman, I'm so delighted you could join us. Holding out both arms, Sebastian Desvalls, sleek and debonair welcomed them and following Daniel's gaze. My mother. I'm afraid she has completely lost her mind. But it cheers her up to see the place full of people again, as it was in the old days. She loves these evenings. Come in, let me introduce you to some friends.

This was familiar territory for Daniel, he was skilled in the kind of social niceties that were designed to ensure people found out as much or little about you as you were prepared to give. He was fascinated by the mix of Barcelona life, young and old, men and women. The apartment, Sebastian explained, was the lower floor of what had been his family's home since the 18th century. But they could no longer afford to live in it following the collapse of the bank, so he and his mother had renovated this floor to occupy after his father's death. Elaborate tiles covered the floors, the walls were embellished with stucco decorations and the ceilings were painted with faded sylvan scenes of lovers and shepherds, which reminded Daniel of the Fragonard poster Nate had pinned to the wall of their room at college.

Each room full of people opened out into another through large double doors, one had wall chandeliers like exotic head-dresses where a group were singing wistful songs in Catalan round a piano. In the crush of another room there was a bar where cocktails were being poured in liberal quantities. Daniel talked to a poet who had written a play, complaining about the lack of opportunity for his art and a dancer with the ballet, who had studied under Balanchine in New York and grumbled bitterly how he resented coming back to Spain.

Two things happened in quick succession that set Daniel on edge. Xavi had gone over to Desvalls, leaving him talking to a glamorous woman who looked out of place in a gold lamé pant suit with a huge African necklace made from the teeth of some wild animal. She was married to an American film producer. From the corner of his eye he could see that it was a heated conversation. Both of them were trying to make it look harmless by smiling as they talked, shooting glances around the room to make sure no-one would get the wrong impression. But at some point, it became more animated and he could hear Xavi raising his voice. The next minute they parted and he walked out onto the terrace, where Daniel joined him. Is everything alright? Yes, yes, it's nothing, I will explain later, Xavi responded unconvincingly as he lit a cigarette and tried to smile. At the other end of the terrace were stone steps leading down to a garden overgrown with jasmine, the scent heavy in the warm night air. As they ambled along the terrace, he noticed two people sitting on a stone seat, an older man in a white dinner jacket, grasping at a smaller and much younger Latino, all white teeth and flashing eyes, who would remove the hand from his thigh laughing. The older man wiped the sweat from his forehead with a handkerchief and took something from his inside pocket. It all happened so quickly but before they noticed him, Daniel turned on his heel telling Xavi that he wanted to leave. Please don't ask why, let's just go. On the way home they stopped at the café where they'd first talked. Daniel explained that the man he'd seen in the garden with what he assumed was a rent boy, was his cousin Robert. Xavi raised his eyebrows. Didn't you know? He's always at those parties. Daniel took a few seconds to register.

Chapter Twenty

He didn't know what to feel, lying awake the next morning, with Xavi naked and beautiful beside him in the slow rise and fall of sleep. Apart from the shock at seeing his cousin pawing at the Latino in the dark, the idea that they were in any way the same hadn't occurred to him. But everyone else, well at least the people he knew there, seemed unsurprised, which was more complicated. He wondered who else had associated them at the party without him knowing. He had only recently met Robert but no-one here would comprehend that two cousins happened to be in the same city in Europe by chance. Did it look as though they were complicit? Despite his mother's indiscretions and the racy company she kept, she would never tolerate this in her own son. The thought that he might be exposed, made him panic.

Daniel knew himself well enough, that he could be neurotic and apt to selfishness but this was his first love and he considered his relationship to Xavi as something separate, different from the purely sexual impulse; above it in intention and action. This thought made him feel stronger, less offended, more able to fight off the demons of doubt and fear. What they had could never be tawdry like the desperate mauling of his wretched cousin.

While Daniel didn't exactly look down on people, he hardly wavered in his opinion that what he did, the life he steered, the decisions he made, were better informed and more carefully enacted than most other people. He'd inherited that from his mother. So far he had singled out only three or four people in his life whom he truly admired and respected, people he trusted. What worried him more was the idea that he and Robert were now unavoidably connected by more than the tenuous threads of distant relation but by a common aberration, something that could harm them equally, that he would be no better and that back home everything Mae had etched into his upbringing, would be lost. An anger seethed inside him that he could lose so much from that chance evening.

What he didn't know is whether Robert had seen him. He thought not, but he would ask Xavi to speak to their host on his behalf the next day. It was essential that his presence at the party, this love affair, the reason he wanted to stay in Barcelona, remained a secret. Xavi was also anxious when he awoke and agreed to see Sebastian, saying that anyway he should apologize for storming off. Daniel was a cautious optimist for all his misgivings but he could tell there was something going on with him. Xavi was distracted and talkative one minute and deep in thought the next. He knew it had to do with the conversation with Desvalls but Xavi assured him they hadn't fallen out. It crossed his mind that perhaps they'd been lovers once. There was something unspoken between them and when they'd appeared to argue, as if they were both worried about something secret between them.

The next time he saw Xavi, his misgivings were put to rest. He reassured Daniel that no-one had alerted Robert to his presence and that his cousin was far too drunk to have noticed anyone in the darkness of the terrace. The younger man was an expensive rent boy and they had both arrived drunk. This was a complete breach of the unspoken rules of these parties but to avoid a scene amongst his friends, Sebastian had discreetly pushed them into the garden, from which there was a gate under the building back into the courtyard through which he could usher them out after a respectable interval. It seems there had been a scene because Robert was refusing to pay and the boy was refusing his advances. Sebastian had to intervene and paid the boy on condition that he would agree to see Robert home immediately. A driver was put at their disposal. Xavi laughed as he recounted this but Daniel was horrified. From deep down in the pit of his stomach surfaced an illogical fear that this distant cousin might be the undoing of all that had made him happy. What if Robert had been exposed, disgraced by scandal and recalled? By association he would be implicated, the family name would be drawn in. The reality of the transaction for sex had made his cheeks blush with shame. How could he be so careless and brazen? But it was clear from what Sebastian had told Xavi that all of these possibilities had been averted and clearly no-one else had made any connection between him and Robert.

Sebastian had invited them to stay the following weekend in his house at Montseny, where they could walk in the woods and swim. They would take the train to the small station at Sant Celoni on the Thursday evening and he would collect them by car. It was nearing the end of June and the full heat of summer was approaching. By afternoon, the breeze from the sea threw off the smog that cloaked the old city, revealing skies of violent blue. On these days, Daniel would open the balcony doors of the library all along the side of the building. It would bring a change to the parched air inside, papers rustled under the gentle persuasion of an imperceptible wind, like a zephyr breathing these ancient sheaves into life. He would sit on his stool sorting and documenting, the ritual of a faithful votive.

On the morning of their trip, he'd packed a small canvas backpack to take with him and would make his way straight to the station after finishing at the library. On his way to work he stopped at his usual café where a man was recounting something excitedly. Suddenly, he recounted with an air of being an important messenger, there was a very loud explosion that made my windows shudder. He had jumped up and run to the balcony. There was nothing in the road below but his neighbors started to run out of the houses looking where the noise had come from. A small crowd had gathered and next thing there were police cars and firemen everywhere. Guardia Urbana arrived in vans and someone came running down the streets saying there'd been a bomb somewhere else in the city. As he spoke, the people in the café who were listening intently, looked more sad than worried. A woman in the corner started crying while her friend was comforting her; an old man muttered about the war starting again.

Daniel spent an anxious day at work but when Xavi didn't turn up to meet him, a dizzy panic came over him and he decided to head back to his room, slowly making his way through the streets. Halfway, he changed direction towards Pintor Fortuny. He walked into the warehouse and asked the men if they'd seen him. They pointed him in the direction of Elena's parlor behind the office and with more courage than usual, he walked up to the door and knocked. She had seen him coming and was untying her apron and checking her hair in the mirror. Daniel stammered the news of the explosion and the crowd and that they were supposed to be meeting and he wanted to know they were all safe. Elena who was never friendly, always the cold side of courteous, thanked her brother's friend for letting them know. She hadn't seen Javier for some days in person, but could hear he was upstairs the night before and he'd helped with the deliveries that morning when she was out at mass. She'd happily pass on his concerns but couldn't see any reason why he'd have been in that area.

Daniel crossed over town to his own place and as he came down the square, he was relieved to see Xavi sitting at the café under the tree. He pulled up a chair next to him and asked if he'd heard what had happened. Xavi looked a bit distant, slightly dazed, as he pulled on a cigarette. Then he smiled, yes I heard it was a bit of a mess up there, the local party office and two other bombs, nobody hurt it seems. I'm sorry I didn't make it over to the library. I had to meet someone. But I think we shouldn't go tonight. I told Sebastian already. He downed the rest of his beer, stood up and tossed some coins on the table. They went upstairs. Love making for them had become focused and intense, they sought one another out, knowing exactly how to touch and push, the sweet release of completely giving up one's body to another. Later in a restaurant eating tiny fried fish and ripe tomatoes, they noticed the city in a state of high alert, police everywhere looking around for suspects. It's a little dangerous right now, they will look for anything or anyone suspicious. It would be better to keep a low profile. The two of us. We do stand out a bit. Let's go back to my place.

You are both in the sea. But you can't swim. He holds on, keeping you afloat, treading water until suddenly he just goes dead in your arms. You try desperately to hold him up. But he starts to sink in your grasp. Daniel woke up in a cold sweat with Xavi's arms tight around him, their legs crooked together, breathing heavily behind him. It was almost dawn as the light crept under the slats of the blind. Daniel turned and gradually opened his eyes to look at Xavi. The love he felt was palpable, not just the physical lust that tore at him but a sense of wholeness, that everything up until now had been for this. And now it could not be undone, he was inescapably drawn into love for this man, his hero, at once all the men he had never known, father, brother, friend. When they kissed, he sank into a pool of golden liquid. When he came under Xavi's touch, it was like exploding into a million pieces. And afterwards, waking up amid the smell of sweat and semen, latched to each other limp and soft, was as if all the bits of him that had been destroyed had come back together and the yearning and desire was reborn.

Desvalls had decided to postpone his trip to the country, so they did not go out of town that weekend. But two weeks later one Saturday morning, they left early for the station, a sweet odor of rain in the streets. Daniel wasn't sure if he was being too sensitive but people seemed subdued and lost. At the station the police were out in force. Xavi was unperturbed and whispered to him it's the ones not in uniform, the ones that look like us, we have to fear. They were stopped at the platform and their papers were checked before they sauntered onto the train, arriving around midday at Sant Celoni, a low-slung town beneath a green sward of mountains. Sebastian was there to meet them at the station, greeting them warmly.

It was immediately a relief to Daniel, to be out of Barcelona. The previous days, the week since the party had presented things to unquiet his mind. But here he was comfortable. It felt like Connecticut, the small town, the trees, the mountains. Here he could breathe air fully. We need provisions on the way home, Sebastian said as they jumped in the car, Xavi in the front seat and after picking up supplies of food and wine, they were soon snaking their way up and out of town into the mountains. As they drove through the trees, it was as if he could smell things for the first time, the pines, the ferns, the heavy moss, the gasoline fumes as they accelerated round the corners, up and up. It transported Daniel back to trips with his mother, he threw back his head, full of a sense of adventure, happy to be here, with him.

They talked excitedly in the front at the top of their voices over the roar of the car with the wind in their ears about nothing in particular. Sebastian pointed at something they passed and Xavi shouted that his family had been in the area since the 16th century. He slowed down to show the famous chestnut trees to Daniel, and explaining that his family's oaks had supplied cork to the monastery near here. The monks had made the only wine grown on the mountain and every year gave a cask to the Desvalls family in return. The story goes that during an invasion his forebear had avoided capture by hiding in one of the barrels and rolling down the mountainside to safety. Daniel sat back, half-listening as the town disappeared beneath them, giving way to a landscape of undulating greens and reds.

A moment later, the car reared off up a track curving round a steep escarpment, with walls on either side, which opened out to a meadow surrounded by tall crooked trees, beside each trunk a neatly piled stack of bark. The source of wine corks had never occurred to Daniel. At the end of the meadow, there was a low stone building with an archway in the middle. The car screeched to a stop at the side of the building under the trees. The three men walked down some steps leading to a courtyard, around which the main house was built. Welcome to the Desvalls' *masia*, El Mas del Roure, the Oak House, he told Daniel. It used to be a working estate with more than ten families living here but last century, when my family opened the bank, we turned it into a hunting lodge and somewhere to escape the heat of the city in summer.

Windows set into the rough cast walls looked onto the three-sided garden courtyard and a loggia ran across with flower beds on either side, ending in terraces leading down to the woods. This is my little piece of England, he laughed. We'll have lunch under here and they dropped their bags on the stone step by a large set of doors, making their way to a table under the loggia next to a well, already set for lunch. They drank white wine from the Penedes and ate bread, *fuet* and cheese. Sebastian told Xavi to show Daniel the room they were sleeping in. The house was huge and it was at the far end next to the terrace in the eaves of the timbered roof looking across to the sea in the far distance. Daniel's gaze took him to thoughts of Long Island. Xavi came up behind him and kissed the nape of his neck. Shall we go swimming? There is an incredible pool under the waterfall. Not such a long walk from here.

You could see the sky reflected in the clear water and the heat of the sun beating down made plunging into the icy water all the sweeter against his tingling skin. The two of them spent the afternoon alone lazing on the rocks and swimming, feeling each other hard and urgent. It was a little piece of paradise for two people in love. They had no care for what was around them and slept off the afternoon in the shade of the large boulder jutting out over the pool. Late in the day, as the sun fell from the sky, they came home to find Sebastian in the kitchen.

Up here, high in the mountains, there's a chill at night still and the old stone walls never lose the centuries of dampness, so we'll have a fire later in the study. While Xavi fetched logs from the storerooms, Daniel sat in the kitchen watching him prepare dinner. He was impressed how deftly he worked, I learned all this from my mother, he said when he noticed he was being observed. It's a rabbit stew cooked with garlic and rosemary from the mountain with smoked paprika, dried peppers and hazelnuts. I pound that with the heart and liver of the rabbit to make a *picada* sauce, it's not too spicy for us Catalans but has a little heat, he said, as he took two rabbits from a covered bowl and cut them into pieces with a blackened steel knife.

Daniel talked about the museum and the collections and explained that he was hoping to stay longer to complete the work, that Exhampton might allow him to start the January semester. Sebastian smiled in response and let Daniel chatter away about his fascination with Mallorquin portolan maps and the history of the ships that sailed on these seas, pleased that he seemed relaxed enough. He liked the young man and wondered how he would react when he was fully aware of the circumstances of this weekend.

They ate at the vast oak kitchen table, rough with the grain of centuries grooved into it and scrubbed clean of the mud and blood of a thousand feasts. Afterwards they licked their fingers clean and removed to a wood-paneled room where the embers were glowing in the vast stone fireplace. Sebastian poured them each a glass of cognac and they fell into the threadbare sofas squatting in front of the fire. The room was full of books, family objects, paintings, antlers and a pair of flintlock pistols mounted on the mildewed walls. It smelled of damp, dust and time. Daniel felt quite at peace.

Chapter Twenty-One

Sebastian settled into the sofa opposite them, I've enjoyed meeting you Daniel and because Xavi is a friend of mine, I want you to know something about me. He explained that his parents had sent him away to boarding school and then university in England because his father had planned for him to open a branch of the bank in London. It was the 1920s and he passed his childhood with the children of the upper classes. His father, once an influential player in the Republic recognized that to survive he had to play both sides. Although he secretly bankrolled the Catalan uprising, he was always careful not to let anyone know his business, keeping friends where he needed them. He was saved from execution because a large portion of his business in Madrid was with the southern landowners, so when the capital was taken, he was put under house arrest. By this time Sebastian had come back from England and unbeknown to his father was running supplies to the Aragon front at Zaragoza, where he was also captured. The Falange needed someone on the inside to feed them news of Russian support for the communists, so he was recruited as an agent, an offer he'd accepted because by now his father was very sick. This gave him leverage with the Companys government by feeding disinformation to the Nationalists and somehow he'd managed to make it through the war without giving much away. Because he had equally arm's-length trust from both sides the new regime had never searched El Mas del Roure, where he had given refuge to the maquis as they were driven north to France.

An angry peace came and the Barcelonians quickly drew a fragile veil over the punishing years of resistance. The deceit and betrayal were covered over and somehow Sebastian managed to avoid discovery. Neither side saw me as friend or traitor, and I was able to keep both dependent on my loyalty without knowing it. I attribute this skill to my English education, playing the long game I learned on the cricket field and the ability to defend any side of the argument in the debating hall, without allegiance for the cause. While I despise the Fascists, there was too much self-interest from our own internal political factions. In the end, the truth we had to face is that they were guilty of destroying our chance of winning. Meanwhile my father had died of pneumonia before the long siege ended and the bank had collapsed. But somehow because of my background, I was given an unofficial diplomatic post negotiating for the new government with the British and to cover my activities I became a dealer in fine art. And once again, my activities here were indulged by the rich Catalan families who needed to raise funds.

Meanwhile I have been quietly supporting the work of the Anglo-Catalan Association. Cultural renewal and recognition are the long road towards regaining what we've lost. No-one really believed that this could have gone on for so long, that we'd still be under a dictatorship so many years later. I managed to persuade the interior ministry that by allowing just enough Catalan to flourish among academic scholars, it would look good to the United Nations and distract from political activism. That's how I met our mutual friend here. When the university was finally allowed to embark on teaching some courses on Catalan linguistics, I went to an opening reception and met Xavi. It was only later that we discovered our fathers had known one another.

Xavi who had been silent to this point, his head leaning back on Daniel's shoulder while he sipped at the cognac, sat up. Desvalls continued. For some of us, the war has never ended. But we were betrayed by the arrogance of our own people. As Catalans we have been invaded countless times, not only foreign powers but our own people have tried to suppress our customs and language, to blockade our ports and deny us our independence. You have to understand that more than anything what the Spanish hate us for is our defiance, we dare to deny that church or state can have power over us, beyond our own rule. We don't submit. We see the constant struggle of an aggrieved nation as our national cause.

My social position makes it easy for me to move between different groups. They think I am amoral which is helpful to me. I trade in unattributed antiquities with no allegiances except to myself. It has taken me years to establish this position. No-one exactly trusts me, or considers me capable of doing anything except to serve my own interests. They tolerate me, they come to my parties, feigning friendship, particularly some of the old families who saw their opportunity after the war and have done well from it. They fool themselves into thinking they can look down on me when the truth is that they are the ones taking advantage of their own people. But we are human, Daniel, above all. And of all people, the Catalan often figures himself to be more human than anyone else. For him there are no burdens of suffering or injustice so great as those he has endured. We are paralyzed by this and continue to accept meekly the slow erosion of our identity, like the moldering mansions up and down our city, once extravagant in their desire to impress, now crumbling to slums.

I wanted to do something about this, to wake my people up, to continue the opposition to complacency. I have used my reputation for divided loyalties to support this struggle. But I do so with incredible care, never to implicate myself or my friends. However careful you are, everything is noted by someone. When you saw us arguing, it is because Xavi wants to protect you. After the bomb, when Xavi's friend was arrested, we had to stay in the city and carry on as normal so we wouldn't be suspected.

Later as they lay in bed, Daniel thought about his portolans, how most had been born from this Catalan inventiveness and survived the centuries to prove it. At a point in history, the power and skills of Barcelona in trade and seafaring had made it the greatest power in the Mediterranean. He had seen with his own eyes copies of the ancient Catalan sea laws, universally adopted, many still in use, known as the Consulate of the Sea, the *costums de mar*.

The next day Desvalls let his guests sleep late into the day and after breakfast, all three of them walked high up into the mountains. Daniel thrived on instinct and remained reserved until he had judged he could trust someone. He felt that uncertainty surrounded Desvalls but he was pleased that Xavi had this friend, it gave him some assurances for his safety and was pleased to be in their confidence. The new-found discoveries gave them so much to talk about. They swam and ate, and the next morning drove back to the city.

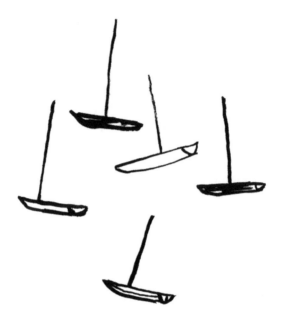

Chapter Twenty-Two

By August a dense heat fell on the city like a heavy blanket and the nights were stifling. Those who could leave went to visit families in the countryside and those who stayed hid in the shade behind closed blinds. The young took to the beach where they courted one another or looked from afar at the objects of their desires. Daniel had planned to take some time off and they decided to take the train north with their bicycles to Girona and then to Sadernes, where Xavi's cousins lived.

First, he wanted to finish some work on a particular collection, so that he could hand over a complete catalog to Patxot before the vacation. Therefore they planned to leave at the end of that week. Daniel had been spending almost every night over the summer at Xavi's place. Because they had their own entrance onto the street, their movements went more or less unnoticed by Elena, though Don Gilberto was her faithful spy and kept any news from the street as enticing information to insinuate himself into her company. But Xavi was wise to him and knew how hot his interest was for Elena, so pandered to him, suggesting all the right things to say to her with great seriousness and a vague threat of what might happen if the strict confidence of their conversations was betrayed.

A few weeks before Daniel had heard back from the faculty head at Exhampton, who had agreed he could start the second semester of the year, so he had written to Mae at Gideon's Farm explaining that he would extend his stay here. He was dreading her response and decided to call her to make sure she wouldn't contact Robert. She put up a slight struggle, but he timed his call well just as she was off to Newport for the Jazz Festival and couldn't linger so supposed he knew best, resigned now to her son being his own man. He was already anxious about what would happen after Christmas when he'd have to return. There was the gnawing realization that he had to face their separation at some point. He'd wondered about asking Xavi to come to New York. They could rent an apartment, he could teach, they'd be happy. But knew deep down that taking Xavi away from here would be impossible. Xavi had strong ties to his home and family. So much of his identity was in his love for this city. They were both locked in what seemed like an inescapable sense of duty to others and he could not yet see how he could extricate himself from his mother. By now Daniel trusted Desvalls

and sensed he had Xavi's best interests at heart. He might ask for his advice.

In the early hours of the morning they had planned to travel north, Daniel awoke with a start, for a moment unsure of what Xavi was doing. He tried to talk but he felt a sweaty hand over his mouth. A flashlight was pointing directly in his eyes and thinking it was Xavi he started to wriggle and tell him to stop when he realized that Xavi was also beside him struggling, his head in the bolster trying to speak. Then he felt a grip on his forearm and somebody spoke in Spanish into his ear. Get up quickly, be quiet. He looked around and could see two other flashlights. There were three men in the room, two in shirtsleeves one of whom was standing at the doorway, the other forcing Xavi down on the bed and the one next to him in a leather jacket and cap. You whore faggots make me sick, he said pulling Daniel off the bed onto the floor before he could protest. Get dressed, quick. Xavi meanwhile was twisting and struggling to get up while the man holding him from behind on the bed with his arm around his neck and hand over his mouth, spoke calmly in his ear. Listen Ferran, you have two choices, neither is good for you. You're coming with us you little fucker, but you do it quietly unless of course you want us to wake up the whole street, your sister maybe, the neighbors? If you want a scandal, I can drag you downstairs for the whole place to see. Xavi nodded, his eyes scared and wild, looking over to Daniel.

Meanwhile Daniel was in a daze, pulling on his pants, no idea what was going on. The man demanded his passport, so he fumbled through his clothes to find the identity papers he'd received from the consulate. After scrutinizing it by flashlight, he put it in his pocket. Well, Mr. Sale, the fun is over, his top lip curling up under the black mustache. You two have some explaining to do. Daniel was taking nothing in, with the adrenalin pumping through his heart, he could hardly concentrate on the impossible task of getting his shoes on. On the other side of the bed, Xavi pulled on his pants, shirt and jacket before being handcuffed. You are both coming with us. In separate cars. Say goodbye, girls! The other men laughed and marched out of the room with Xavi between them, down the stairs into a waiting car. You will come with me, Mr. Sale.

The lightbulb in the room flickered. A moth kept fluttering into it until the final singe sent it tumbling towards the table where its tiny body struggled with a last twitch of life. Not for the first time since being in Barcelona, Daniel had no idea what to do or think. As usual nothing in his experience had happened to prepare Daniel for these circumstances. All the careful reflexes Mae Farwell had groomed in him, had not included this. While Daniel was fully aware that homosexuality was illegal, it had never occurred to him that to protect their love, he needed to be anything other than discreet. Which they were. So how had they been discovered? Had someone informed on them?

At any other time of crisis, he would have immediately called his mother. She always had a solution and certainly would never have put up with seeing her son treated this way. But he didn't know what he was doing, he hadn't talked to anyone or been told what would happen. Why had they separated him and Xavi, was he safe, what had just happened? The sinister man with the sweaty palms and mustache left him here and locked the door leaving him in the room with only a table and two chairs. It smelled like it had been scrubbed with bleach and he shuddered.

By now the legs of the moth had stopped moving and Daniel must have fallen asleep because the next thing he woke up with his head resting on the table. The policeman was standing in the doorway, a cigarette hanging out of the corner of his mouth. As he closed the door behind him, Daniel focused on the flaking blue paint on the walls of the empty corridor outside. He sat down opposite. So, my young American friend, as you can speak Spanish let me say this. You think you can come here and behave as you like. You think we are just like you, don't you. Your motherfucking sailors ruining this city, keeping our wives and children awake at night, fighting in the bars, paying our women for sex. This was a rotten city before we cleaned it up and taught them some manners but then you Americans come thinking you can take over the world. But we are not like you, we do not like you, we don't want to be like you. Do you understand. There are strict laws against deviants. You and Ferran, fucking perverts. You're no better than delinquents, like the Gypsies and drunks. You see we cannot have you faggots infecting the minds of our children.

But you are the lucky one, my friend, spitting his cigarette on the floor and grinding it under a shoe. My superiors tell me that you are with the consulate, which gives you some kind of diplomatic status. So I can't throw you in the cells or cut your balls off, which is what I would like to do because I will lose my job. I have to let you go. Before I do, let's be clear about something. I don't give a fuck for you or your government or anyone else. I was brought here to this dump of a city, to keep the streets clean of your filth, so whatever you are doing here, it's over. You are no longer

welcome and if you stay I will personally make it my business to expose your behavior publicly. You have a week to get out of Barcelona for good. Do you understand? He threw Daniel's passport on the table.

Daniel, who could hardly keep up with the implications of what he was saying, stammered a yes and looked blankly at him, wide-eyed and scared. He could hear his teeth chattering but could do nothing to prevent it. What about Javier Ferran? You can forget about your little boyfriend. He doesn't have your privilege. He is involved in something far more serious than fucking his American bitch. Whatever happens to him, you can blame yourself. You think we can't see you but we know exactly who you are. All of you. Now get up. He stood up, scraping the chair along the floor and Daniel followed him out of the door, past other closed rooms along the corridor, down three flights of stairs, where a policeman in uniform stood at an entrance which he unlocked. Daniel walked out into side street, blinking, his eyes raw and stinging in the sunlight. He had no idea where he was, anxious if anyone would see him looking so disheveled and desperate. But in the anonymous city, the most significant events of your life are nothing to the passing glance of a stranger. He walked down to the end of the street, realizing he was on Via Laeitana. The drivers of the cars on their weekend jaunts, the newspaper boy, the toothless hunched old woman, the young lovers out walking, the priest followed by a dog, all going about the business of the day in their city, with no place for Daniel in their hearts. While he had been arrested, taken to prison, separated from Xavi and released, their lives had simply progressed a little further without noticing anything at all. The existence he had created for himself here had been destroyed in a single act. He had no clue what to do first. The two people he needed most to give him aid in this disastrous moment were unable to do so. For the first time, he was truly alone and had to make his own decisions about what to do next. Without thinking he allowed his feet to take him to Plaça de Llana.

Chapter Twenty-Three

Three days later, Daniel sat upright on the side of the narrow bed, tears streaming down his tanned, gaunt face. On either side, his hands were anxiously grasping the iron frame. Try as he might, he couldn't bring the conflicting sensations of his mind and body into order. The gathering noises in the tiny square outside his room seemed to deafen him. Children making their way noisily back from school; street sellers emerging from the cool corners of the damp alleyways; local drunks arguing with the street dogs, store owners greeting each other loudly across the square as they unlocked their doors for evening trade. And above them caged birds on the balconies, uncovered from the afternoon heat, began to sing as neighbors gossiped between them.

He looked desperate as he stared terrified at the wall before him. Suppressing the cries inside him, he turned his face up to the ceiling, stretching out his features so that he looked like a wild animal impaled. He tried to breathe more calmly but his heart still thumped as he looked around the room. This had been his haven but now he was to be expelled from it, back into a world he no longer knew. One in which he couldn't be sure he could survive. The painfully short-lived love and laughter in this room was gone. Replaced by panic and fear.

He gazed at the wooden cross above his bed; a portent of the monasticism that was to dominate his days beyond this time.

On a square wooden table, positioned between the open balcony doors sat a neat leather pack and beneath it his suitcase. Again and again he considered his predicament, arriving always at the same conclusion. There was nothing for him to do. He had to leave. The threats to his safety here. The fear of reprisal, a scandal.

That morning as he was collecting his few possessions into the case, he realized he'd left the leather pocket book in which he had kept his journal in the room above the warehouse. It was too late to go back there, he'd been warned off ever returning. His only record of the time they had spent together, now banished to ashes in the fire grate of Elena's kitchen. Almost without noticing, this city which had drawn him to her heart, had done with him.

He went over the arrest in his mind, desperately trying to find a clue of how this had happened. And so quickly, without warning. They'd met after work as usual and sat in the dying light of the day on the edge of the pond in the park, watching the carousel of swifts swing in low to drink on the surface of the water and rise again. Then they'd walked back to the warehouse, stopping only for beer and some provisions, which they cooked and ate on the terrace. They smoked and talked until they had fallen naked into each other's arms on the bed. They hadn't met or talked to anyone. They were both relaxed and full of chatter. Nothing he could remember about the evening brought him any clue of what happened next.

A dull pain hung close in around him. Every few moments he stopped breathing, as if holding on to a last thread of hope that something, anything, might happen, even now, to reverse time and halt this nightmare.

But all avenues of aid had been exhausted. If he stayed, he'd be murdered or imprisoned on some trumped-up charge. Nobody here would help him, fearing the unwanted attention it would bring. The evening before he had walked down to the *barraques* to look for Lili. He found the Gypsy with the long scar on his face but she hadn't been seen for days. It wasn't safe here for him. The place was crawling with police. There had been a gas explosion nearby and they were using it as an excuse to clear their homes.

Now everywhere was dangerous and the people who had most cared for him were gone. Elena had refused to see him. He knew she blamed him because he'd managed to corner Don Gilberto in the street. He was sweating even more profusely than normal and kept wringing his hands and rolling his eyes and grimacing at the whole affair.

There simply was nothing else to do. The city which had barely begun to open her heart to him, was withdrawing her favors. When you cannot survive on your wits, she cannot protect you and she will cast you out.

His heart beat fast and his head was spinning as he stood up. He would have to take the train, as planned. But even in these last minutes he resisted, pacing the room, his fists clenched, hammering at his head with tears streaming down his face. What lay ahead for him would be as painful and bitter as those last few days.

As the bells of the cathedral rang a quarter hour, he slowly turned to have one more look around the room. He walked to the table, picked up his bags and made his way silently down the steep stairs into the square. The landlady's children were playing on the doorstep and gazed up at him as he passed. He could not return their smiles and shook off the hands grasping at his. He crossed the street, turned around and looked up at the window of the room where they had spent so many nights talking, smoking, drinking. It had been a time, he had thought, that could hold him forever. Now he wasn't sure what could keep him alive.

The moment he turned his eyes back to the street before him, a savage creature crept from its lair, reared on its hind legs and in its vast paws caught his heart and tore it clean in two, then crawled deep inside him.

The time before, as he came to think of it in the years that followed, faded in and out of focus and eventually dissipated, lost in the dark, eventually almost entirely submerged. But there were moments when thin shards of time would catch the light, sending pangs of steel sharp pain into him. He'd close his eyes and force the feeling, the splinter of recollection deep down again, out of sight. And what grew around him was a reluctant, heavy silence. One for which he could never be thankful.

Chapter Twenty-Four

Tears soaked Chester's beard. It was past two. He was leaning back on his chair with his feet on the heavy oak desk in his office, reading the entries from Daniel's notebook and the letters he had written to Xavi as he was forced into this hurried, heart-rending retreat from Barcelona. He'd written more letters from Gideon's Farm on his return, which had been sent back bearing the blunt news, written on the outside of an envelope, *deceased*.

What can this have been like? How must he have felt? The sheer torment of exile from his lover was bad enough. How he had faced the terror of these circumstances forced upon him, Chester found hard to imagine.

The letters were not descriptive, indeed they hardly referred to the places where they were written, except for a French city or the name of a London hotel. They attempted at best a cheerful tone, like letters sent home from the front line, talking of times in the future when they'd be reunited and normality would be resumed. Trying not to let Xavi think he's lost hope, Daniel exhorted him to write back, asking vainly if he was being treated well and fed properly. The letters began with banalities, to prevent him from incriminating his lover any further with intimacy, though the agony was palpable enough to Chester. They soon built to a crescendo of grief, missing him desperately, unsure how he could go on without him. Tones that were demanding, pleading, begging, desperate for details of where he was, for just a glimmer of hope, were scratched helplessly in ink, like threads woven into the brittle paper. Daniel had told Chester that he'd never truly experienced his own emotions until he had met Xavi. It was clear from the letters and that they were rapidly dwindling, receding into incomprehension, like losing a language.

He contemplated his own split with Christina. It couldn't have been more different. Sure, there had been anger between them at first but their parting was public; documented and discussed by lawyers and therapists, among their friends and with their children. He couldn't imagine if everything he knew was taken from him without warning and he was left with the shell of his life but no vestige, no record of what had gone before. Now it was over, he and Christina were open and had a tolerable friendship; they would always have the weld of parenthood, their girls provided a common ground on which they were able to parlay.

He thought about the many one-night stands he had, the would-be relationships that came to nothing in his life, all forgotten now. For Daniel, this brilliant, funny, handsome man, there had only ever been one. His intensely brief and passionate love affair open and shut in a heartbeat, never spoken of to anyone, drowned forever. What an extraordinary man, to have taken all that inside and locked it away. Then to find room in his heart for Lydia, for a different kind of love. She must have known, she must have sensed that more than anything else this man needed her nurture. He was sad that he'd never met Daniel's late wife. Doubtless they presented a formidable partnership, a lifeline that helped his friend survive the gnawing canker of loss. Chester's heart was swelling, growing towards Daniel.

Picking up the whiskey glass on his desk, he held it above his head, emptying the very last sweet drop into his mouth. He decided another would help him to sleep, leaned over and flicked off the lamp. As he shut the door of his office behind him, there was a noise in the kitchen and he found Tabitha getting herself a glass of milk from the fridge. Once he'd poured the whiskey, she curled up next to him on the sofa in the dark, only the streetlight casting its yellow shadows across the room and the sound of dumpsters somewhere in the distance setting off to rid the city of its trash. He loved his firstborn daughter's knowing patience, she was one of those beings who from the moment she'd come into the world, looked like she'd been through all this before and knew, regardless of anything, that it would all be fine. She'd smile and hug him when he was mad with something Christina had said or after a difficult call with a client. That feeling, his daughter, nestling her head in his belly saying I love you Daddy, don't worry, don't let it get to you. That feeling was all the reassurance in life he ever needed. She had a confidence and serenity he'd never had, not the same at all as her mother's intolerant temperament but as if she could actually see into the future and was certain about everything, for all of them. He would often walk into a room or find her sitting in the park while Chloe was running around, sitting quite still, looking out into the distance with an almost saintly look on her face, not lost or daydreaming but beatific, as if she could see a vision. She was guiding them all steadily towards a place of safety and they all relied on her for that. He'd applied that skill he'd learned from her in his friendship with Daniel. As he sat there in the dark, Chester thought he knew exactly what that expression meant when someone said what a comfort their children were to them. He got that totally. His girls truly brought him joy, the kind that lifts your heart every time.

Tabitha's breath was steady, her small frame rising gently as she slept, head on his lap. He picked her up and carried her through to the bedroom, laying her gently in bed and pulling up the bedclothes around her. He kissed them both, went to his own room and undressed. As he lay in bed, his heart was sad for Daniel, alone, bereft in cities that cared nothing for his suffering, places he'd have to pretend, as he had continued to do for the rest of his life, that everything was normal. When he'd arrived in London, he booked himself on a flight back to New York and left this part of his story behind him.

Outside the bedroom window he could see a soft down of snow beginning to fall. Tomorrow he'd call Daniel.

Daniel laughed to himself, sitting in the back of the cab, relieved and annoyed with himself. Labyrinthitis. The meeting with the specialist had shown no indications of unusual memory loss and the expensive MRI scan had produced the image of a brain in good shape. It turned out that the discombobulation, the motion sickness, his surroundings going into a spin, the tightness in his chest and shortness of breath, the ringing in his ear and dizziness were caused by an infection in his ear. The blank moments, the loss of balance were made worse, the doctor suggested by extreme anxiety. The circumstances of mourning. He was being subconsciously paralyzed by grief, his physician told him. And the infection was causing him to have the equivalent of panic attacks.

He ran his hand along the rumpled vinyl of the car's upholstery, feeling his fingertips sticking in the grooves, where black tape was holding their threadbare surfaces in one piece. He'd allowed fear to absorb him for far too long and he had a chance to do something different. To ascend from the labyrinth into the daylight, come what may. How strange, he thought, to have assumed I was losing my mind, how easy that would have been, for so many reasons. Almost as if I'd willed it to happen. But how much I have left to do at 77, how many things I still need to achieve.

Since Lydia had died, he'd been going through the motions, living his life at one step removed. He'd fallen back into the daze he'd been in before he met her with nothing obvious, no significant purpose to engage him, except what was literally within his arm's reach. He could hear Lydia telling him to make contact with life and people. For though they'd avoided meaningless company for its own sake, she was never without a project or some research activity taking her far into the future. A future she couldn't make now, so

he had to do it for her.

It was astonishing to him but he had to acknowledge the maps were no longer enough. He had to find a way to make peace with the world outside, beyond his territory. He wasn't sick and knew that he had to take his part again. Having lived an interior life, it was time to emerge, to meet whatever was waiting for him and accept the consequences. He part wished she was here but was also grateful, in a way, that he could resolve it himself, just as he had started. He had Chester too, a good friend. She would have adored him straight away, taken him to her heart. He could see her diminutive frame from the porch, both hands grasped to his arm, showing him round the garden where she'd continued Mae's work, pointing, talking and asking questions about everything she could think of. She had an enthusiasm for new people in whom she found originality. He was a one-off and she'd have admired his style, the twinkling eyes and the astonishing smile that emerged behind his close clipped beard. She'd have relished his expertise and loved a clever man, reveling in a feverish necessity for detail. Most of all, though half his size, she would have insisted on being hugged by him and doing so in return, before issuing forth her deep, conspiratorial laugh. Daniel knew that she would have taken what was happening now entirely in her stride, like the most natural course of events. He felt her guiding presence now so much, among these affairs; her calm trust, that unique intuition to know what was needed. She was always able to strongly resist or quietly accept with equal measure.

In the afternoon, he brewed tea from smoked Chinese leaf and pored over his history of Fairfield County, a 19th-century tome of biographical sketches and illustrations of the men, the dignified and pious pioneers with their whiskers and frock coats, who had built Greenwich and its surrounding towns. The Sales were a prominent family, established from the time of his first mentioned forebear Thomas in the late 17th century, when the Dutch gave up their claim to Connecticut. But Daniel had never been able to make the obvious connection with seafaring which would have led to his understanding of the provenance of the Sale portolan, another anomaly in their heritage. No-one knew where Thomas Henry Sale had come from, except that he was reputed to have travelled from Pennsylvania and settled in Greenwich. As the story went, the boards of the chart were discovered wedged into the lid of the Sale box. But why was it put there? The curious historian had tried unsuccessfully to unravel the story and hoped now that he would learn more with Chester's help.

An opera was playing on the radio, a recording from the Met, *Norma* he thought but had never been able to distinguish one grand opera from another. It was a dramatic backdrop to his contemplation at the table, leaning on his elbows, the burnished vapors of fermented black tea rising from the cup in his hands. He found himself for a moment back in the library at the College of Architects 50 more years before, wondering what became of Patxot and Desvalls. Had Lili survived whatever had happened there? In the years after he returned home, he'd simply taught himself never to think of that time and somehow managed to cut off Spain and even Europe entirely from his consciousness, as if by excising it from his *mappa mundi* he could not be touched by its poisonous past. His research had refocused on cartography in the Americas and in Asia so he wouldn't have to see the name of that city in the comings and goings of his study. Then by the time his mother had died, it couldn't resurface. Those he loved had never pushed him and he'd managed quite successfully to keep the memories at bay. Robert Denton Sale, his cousin, had avoided him, marrying soon after returning from Barcelona. Mae had insisted that they attend. It was quite unbearable for Daniel, who was unable to look Robert in the eye and they escaped early. After that, except for Mae's funeral years later when Robert proudly introduced a pair of flaccid teenagers, wide-faced and edgy like their father, they never met again. He had no idea if he was still alive.

The day after he was released from the police station, Daniel in his desperation had been to see Robert at home. His cousin was not to be prevailed upon and had made no sign of sympathy or recognition of his predicament. If you have become embroiled in scandal, Daniel, this is the last place you should have come. It is most inconsiderate of my support that you would consider risking my position. My job demands the most sensitive of relations with the authorities and however your behavior has compromised you, or offended them, I simply cannot help you. I suggest you take their advice and leave as soon as possible. When Daniel mentioned Sebastian Desvalls who knew his friend Xavi, Robert's brow furrowed and for a moment he looked away in disbelief before bringing the conversation to an abrupt end, without acknowledging any recognition of what Daniel was referring to.

The Sales, thinking of what his mother had always said to him, were a disloyal, self-serving family of despots. Your father wanted to escape them which is why he loved flying. Do better than them, Daniel.

How disappointed she would have been, knowing he'd fled his duty, how horrified she'd have been by the circumstances. She considered herself a fearless New Jersey dame but like all drunks the more she secretly threw back the more she relied on a show of propriety to cover her tracks. Sodomy among her *avant garde* friends was one thing but she wouldn't hear of it for her son.

Chapter Twenty-Five

As a child, winters on Round Hill arrived with aplomb and without warning. Just as quickly as it came, all the domestic accoutrements of the festive season were uncovered. Bright lights in windows, log piles, the smell of wood burning, cold weather clothing and holly wreaths produced an atmosphere of uncharacteristic neighborliness. The houses with their meandering gardens, formerly sequestered by leafy no-man's lands of forest between plots, became part of a new landscape of etched patterns, connected by freshly trodden paths in the snow. The leafless trees were now waymarks, guiding the inhabitants to and from each other's doors, where cars couldn't go until the snow-plows made it up the hill to clear the roads. The frost hung heavy on the branches and hedgerows, roofs were laden with ice, and smoke crept up into the wintry skies from the fires of countless furnaces and fireplaces, from the grand to the homely. Brightly dressed children played and built snowmen in the low winter light. It could be a scene from any century in history, from Bruegel to Van Gogh.

Something about winter brought people together here, created a community of endeavor, stomping feet and clapping gloved hands against the cold. Winter was the great leveler, both common enemy and shared pleasure. People couldn't move far from their homes and so were forced together in anticipation of Christmas, when folks set aside their petty territorial and social grievances and greeted each other, neighbor to neighbor and without necessarily looking one another in the eye, uttered heartfelt seasonal wishes.

It was no different at Gideon's Farm. For Daniel, it became a lighter place in winter, the sun shining through the beeches and poplars and its reflection on the snow covering the lawns and garden brought a savage brightness into the house which for the rest of the year was softened by more diffuse sunlight. When he woke that morning, his spirits were lifted by the sun glinting off the white covering of snowfall from the previous night. He clambered out of bed, put on a plaid dressing gown, stumbled bleary-eyed to the kitchen, made a pot of Orange Pekoe Ceylon and went to sit in the morning room overlooking the porch, savoring the strength of the tea and considering the prospect of the days ahead.

It had been a huge relief to be reassured that he wasn't losing his brain to disease, that his mind was medically sound. But this was accompanied by the burden, the sense of responsibility that now he couldn't hide from what lay before him, excused by dementia or worse. Sitting there as he had for more than 70 years and as he might for another 10 or even 20, he questioned, as he had many times before, if he'd just been wishing his life away. After that brief dazzling fire of love, all these winters had crept up on him, covering over his life, in a blanket of snow, season by season. What had he given to this world of note, he thought? Perhaps in his small area of scholarship, in the orphaned maps he had restored, in the historiography of early seafaring, perhaps in these he had left a slight imprint, a vague contribution to learning. But what was it worth? It wasn't progress, he hadn't served to spin the globe any faster on its axis, none of it had any real meaning to anyone outside his narrow expert universe. The only thing that had ever mattered, his one chance at really living life was with Xavi and that had been taken away from him. What he had always blamed himself for, was that almost without a struggle, until now, he had yielded to that tragedy which life had thrown him.

He could be grateful for the human contact he and Lydia shared for 30 years but couldn't help wondering if all along she really wanted more, that in the end he'd disappointed her too. The vines she had grown around him, were they after all, grasping unquenched at a possibility that he was too blind, too selfish to see? Had he really brought her happiness? She knew he felt these things and had always sought to reassure his fragile self-confidence. Our life, he remembered, is perfect equilibrium. Daniel went upstairs to dress warmly for a walk. Since he couldn't make it to swim he was determined to test his limbs somehow.

The lunch with Rosa had been arranged early the following week and he had no idea what to expect. He contemplated the act of making his final confession to a member of the Ferran family. Would he be forced to admit that it had been his love for her uncle, their inseparable summer which had ultimately caused his death? Rosa had not been at all accusatory in the manner of her letter and her tone in subsequent emails, perhaps more worryingly, was vague and distant, apologetic almost. As if she hadn't wanted to disturb the peace of an old man. What she couldn't have expected was that it had created the opposite effect. The ghosts were indeed rising from his past but disturbing them had made him feel alive to his surroundings in a new way. As he marched through the snow, his frozen breath perched just at the end of his nose, his earlobes tingling in the icy air. Like Rip van Winkle, he thought, awoken after years to a new world, transformed from his old self to a newer, younger man. Daniel had let so much of life happen to him and now perhaps, there was enough time to change that, whatever lay ahead.

He'd turned down the path at the back of the house, where the slope led to the Cabin jutting out into the woods beyond, and decided to take in the full boundary, skirting the neighbor's wall, crossing the bridge over the little stream, heading back up on the south side where the balsam poplars ran along the side of the lane and back through the garden. The wood thrush sang from the top of the dogwood tree and Daniel could hear a woodpecker prizing at the birch bark above his head. He was shattered at the specter of Xavi, so long faded. In a way, he hadn't fully let up his resistance to thinking about him, properly, about it. That would have to come later. After next week, the lunch, then he would allow himself to reflect on all that that happened. Knowing that he had Chester around had helped so much, he'd already learned to lean on him a little and was grateful for the way he and the girls had shown their concern for him. Next week. Next week everything would be different.

Lunch was booked for 2.30 in the basement dining room at the Exhampton Club. There was a table he liked, slightly out of sight between two pillars, where he could avoid Rudy Brubaker who often dined there. When he spotted Daniel, he insisted on engaging him loudly in pointless conversation or introducing him to his lunch companion ostentatiously as the man he'd learned everything from. Daniel had stayed overnight at the club to give himself time to have breakfast, visit the gallery and walk back through the park to make sure he was composed. In the morning, he sat looking at one of his favorite paintings, *Before Dinner* by Bonnard, with the two women lost in thought, only a tiny dachshund expectantly gazing at the table.

Daniel had made the reservation for the mid-afternoon in a cheerful nod to what he remembered of Spanish customs, and as he hardly ate in the middle of the day it didn't matter to him. Chester was going to join him in the bar beforehand. If Rosa arrived with her husband, he would stay for lunch; if she was on her own, he'd make his excuses. Daniel didn't think he'd want to be alone with a stranger but felt it would be less intimidating for Rosa.

He was nervous, sitting in the bar clasping his hands which felt clammy, habitually rolling his thumbs around each other, while Chester chattered

to distract him. He'd suggested to Daniel that they could take up Nate's invitation to fly down to Palm Springs for Christmas, as this year the girls would be with Christina's parents in Napa. They could fly back through San Francisco and pick them up on the way home. The girls would love to see him again and it would give them a reason to escape.

As he was talking, over his shoulder approaching their table, a tall fair-skinned woman with slightly graying tousled black hair was following a waiter. Suddenly Daniel was swept back in time, as the boy loped across the square towards him that first night they'd met in Barcelona. He stood up and Chester turned around, moving to one side to allow them to greet each other. Rosa, he said holding out his hand and then instinctively without thinking, Daniel smiled, tears already in his eyes, and opened both arms to embrace her, you are most welcome here. They were beaming at each other entranced, like long lost friends, so after he was briefly introduced and some small talk, Chester could see they'd be fine. He made his excuses and left them to it.

Daniel was smiling broadly, he kept taking her hand in his and looking straight into her eyes, I'm so pleased to meet you. He had no idea what she was going to say but couldn't stop himself looking at her intently as if trying to find him behind that face and those eyes, that were so like Xavi's. Any anxiety that he was going to be blamed or accused of anything dissolved after a few minutes. Gently she returned his gaze, calling him Professor and then Daniel in the most affectionate tones. When the waiter had brought a glass of champagne for each of them, Rosa looked a little serious. I promised to myself that before anything, I must say this from everyone in our family. Daniel, it has been a terrible thing. What happened to you and to my uncle. It was my mother's doing. She was a complicated and sometimes spiteful woman but even she confessed her sin and asked for your forgiveness at the end. This is why I have come here. To ask this from you.

Daniel could feel hot stinging at his eyes and looked down. People often kill the love in themselves, Rosa. Let's try not look back with anger or sadness anymore. Whatever you tell me, I have waited such a long time. He laughed. I didn't even know I was waiting for you.

Taking her arm, they went down to the dining room, which was almost empty. This used to be the swimming pool, he told her, until they moved that to the roof. It gives me the feeling of descending to the underworld, so you can be my goddess this afternoon, patting her hand. He was entranced by meeting this lovely woman, a living record of his past. They ordered and Rosa recounted the story of her mother's marriage to Don Gilberto, converting the warehouse to a grocery supplies emporium, these days a great favorite with tourists. Daniel appeared calm as Rosa described all these memories, some images he could remember. Inside he was desperate to know anything, just some sad facts about Xavi that would help him be at peace. He daren't ask Rosa about her uncle directly. Upsetting her, given the circumstances, was the last thing he wanted. But she looked him straight in the eye, now taking his hands in hers and gave him such a look of Xavi it sent a shiver all around his body.

Daniel... I know you must want me to tell you what happened. You are going to find some of this difficult to hear. It is certainly painful to describe it. He could see that there were tears in her eyes and he leaned over, Rosa, I feel today like I have known you all your life, you remind me so much of him, as if suddenly he has been given back to me. Perhaps that is some form of justice. I have lived a long time and faced many shocks in my life, just tell me what you can and don't worry about my feelings, I think we are friends. Nothing can hurt me anymore. I would like to know the truth.

Rosa looked at him with concern and such care. First of all, you need to know that it was not your fault, the arrest, it was hers. In those days you know, two men together, it was a scandal. My mother had been concerned that Xavi was getting involved in politics. So one evening, she thought he was alone and came up the stairs at the back of the terrace. She stood at the door of his room and through the blinds could see you both together. She said that she did not know what to do. She was so jealous of my uncle. It had been her job, she felt to give him all the opportunities in life but take none for herself. She thought he was in danger of throwing all that away. She couldn't understand what she had witnessed, she knew nothing of your devotion lying together on that bed. She only knew it as mortal sin. And because she was always desperate to win favors in heaven, she went to confide in a man she knew who was a Jesuit priest, whom she turned to for advice when she needed to feel more devout. She confessed what she had seen to him, asking for his help to save her brother. She did not know that she was playing right into the hands of the authorities. What she had told him was not in the sanctity of the confessional, so he informed the police. Apparently, he had some connections with a committee of men who were dedicated to cleaning up the city, a group that was working for a man called Sabater, a judge who was known to be the scourge of the city.

It all flooded back into Daniel's mind. The smell of stale cigarettes on the hand over his mouth, the last flare of Xavi's frightened eyes in the flashlight, the interrogation room, his exile. Apart from his most cruel dreams, until now he'd swept away these memories, he'd kept the images of the past submerged, drowned at the bottom of his life. The unbearable sadness and his impotence to change anything had prevented him from truly living, and the failure to do anything brave had been a lifetime's burden. Suddenly now they surfaced, it was like looking at an ancient photograph album of lost lives, including his own. His smile had faded but Rosa kept going.

By now they had finished eating and had both ordered double espressos. I don't know how much you were aware of Xavi's political activism? He was part of a resistance group funded by rich, influential Catalans. The face of Desvalls joined those other specters hovering in the middle distance of Daniel's memory. It made complete sense. They were looking for a reason to imprison him, to get him out of the way. They knew the sons of many of the maquis would always give them trouble and they accused him of conspiring in a bombing in Barcelona, to get him out of the way. You see Daniel, none of this was your fault and what my mother did, not forwarding your letters. Or his to you. Her blaming you, knowing all along that it was she who was responsible. But even though she had unwittingly made it easier for the men who wanted Xavi dead, hers were the worst of the crimes because they could have been avoided. I will always find it hard to forgive her for this.

It took a few moments for Daniel who had been listening intently, leaning forward and then back, folding and unfolding his arms, unsure at all how to sit, to register what she'd said. That there was a piece of Xavi, however slight, here, so close to him, kept his heart beating fast. As calmly as he could he asked, there were letters to me? There was one, she said. Rosa picked up her bag from the floor and reaching in, retrieved a manila envelope. Inside is a letter Xavi wrote to you from prison. He had it smuggled out to my mother. But she refused to forward it. All these years she kept the letter hidden with her secret.

Chapter Twenty-Six

Daniel was adept at diverting pity; something he'd inherited from a woman who'd seen her husband's burned corpse. A lifetime spent avoiding the intrusion of others into his inner world made him a past master. He learned from childhood a technique that enabled him to both deflect his mother's smothering insecurities and cover for them at the same time. He needed for her not to feel inadequate as a mother, the thought of which would set her off into a narcissistic spin with him the central victim of her lamented failures. Daniel sheltered other people from his pain and never talked of his past experiences, not even with Nate or Lydia who both guessed at likely tragedy but respected his right to privacy.

As Rosa sat looking at Daniel holding the envelope, he became aware of how concerned she was for him, how after all this time, she was feeling guilty for him, showing him pity. He looked at her calmly, betraying none of the shock and turmoil raging inside him. Dear Rosa, thank you from my heart for coming here and sharing this burden, it has been incredibly brave of you to tell this story. You can imagine that it has come as a great surprise to discover this, that things were not as I had thought. He couldn't yet speak his name for fear of what might come from the utterance and he could hear how formal and unemotional he was sounding. But please, just give me a little time to take it in. This is the beginning of something new, wonderful even but I am an old man and it takes me much longer to think about everything. I hope we can get to know each other very well and that you will tell me everything about your uncle. The emotions were playing close to the surface and he had no idea how long he'd be able to keep this up. I would like to read this letter first, and you'll understand that I had probably better do that alone. Can we arrange to meet again? Can I call you later or tomorrow? Now you must enjoy your vacation with your husband and daughter. He agreed to call Rosa the following morning to decide when to meet.

Daniel stood at the top of the steps of the club entrance to see her off and as she disappeared through the revolving door the hand of something almost human began to grip at his throat. He fled upstairs to his room, where he sat down on the bed. A single sheet written in that familiar hand, small and neat, in Xavi's newspaper English, as he used to call it. He could see him now quite clearly standing before him, the unruly long black hair just revealing the nape of his neck, diamond eyes astride the long, slender bridge of his nose that arched over his mouth, the full lips, the hollow beneath his throat, his chest and arms disappearing into the billowing white shirt. Daniel somehow knew that as soon as he read this letter this image in his mind might disappear forever. This letter was written from prison, from the place Xavi had died. It had sat there in a drawer during half a century of guilt and denial and fear and recrimination.

He rocked back and forth on the edge of the bed, arms locked around himself, his ears ringing, not daring to read it, trying to slow his breathing down, to stop the room from turning. He'd always been philosophical about life, finding the means to rationalize most things that happened to him. This was different. Everything had been scaffolded around this brief encounter, this one and only love affair. A life he hadn't been brave enough to fight for, so he covered it up, buried it deep away from the light. He'd always planned to go back for Xavi; he could hardly contemplate the ease with which Elena had dispensed with him. Anger and grief were locked in combat, their claws scratching at his skin. How could he have been so blind; the boy who never allows himself to be the victim. It turns out that was a fiction he'd created, he'd been the greatest victim all along. Every day had been shoring up the fragments of broken possibility.

Daniel, my love. I am so sorry that you have had to face this alone. I was not expecting anything of this kind to happen to us and I am still trying to find out how. All I can tell you is that our friend was also arrested, though I think he has now been released. I have not had any contact. I want to tell you that these months we have spent together, for me they transformed all of my hopes and dreams. I want nothing but to be with you, even to find a way to come to America, so that we can start again together. I am being accused of crimes that have nothing to do with me. I was involved in some student action before I met you but I had decided to give all that up. When you saw me arguing at the party, it was because I told our friend that I would not risk putting you in danger. After our trip to the countryside, we agreed that I would not be involved. What I have with you is more important to me than the memories of the past. What happened then cannot change but we can make a new world together. The police are difficult with me though and they have wanted to arrest me for a long time. They want revenge for my father. They are saying I was involved in the explosion in the city last month. There is no evidence that I am involved. I do not know who told them about us but they knew when and where to find us. I am writing this, hoping to get it to Elena, so she will pass it to you. I know you will have visited her and that she can be harsh, but please be patient with her for she has suffered from life and means no harm. I don't know if your connections have helped you but if you have left already, please don't forget me. They can't keep me here forever and I will wait for you. At the close of every day, I will wait at the place we meet, where the swifts come down to drink in the early evening light. Please write to me at my sister's address, she will find a way to get letters to me. I must go now, I can't let anyone see me write this. We don't know who is betraying us. I miss you Daniel, my friend, my brother, my love.

After leaving Daniel, Chester had taken the subway home, where he picked up the car and drove to the conservation lab. We can't date it exactly and it has none of the carving or ornamentation you'd expect on a Jacobean family strongbox, the restorer told him, but it's English oak and we can tell that the hinges and the padlock clasps were hand-forged. They were added later with the handles on the side, almost certainly fitted for ropes, probably to be carried on a packhorse. We can't tell you any more about its origin except one of our researchers has run a search of the settler passengers' lists. We can't find a Sale but she found a Thomas Salesbury arriving at Upland, Pennsylvania on a ship called *The Amity* sailing from London in 1687. We'll let you know if we find out anything else.

Chester thanked him for the favor and carried the box to the car wrapped in the blanket taken from Daniel's home, still reeking of mothballs. He wondered how his friend was getting on. She seemed like a nice woman, possibly more nervous than Daniel. They had struck up a rapport like long-lost relatives. He'd agreed to return downtown to collect Daniel, so drove into the city to avoid the rush.

Elements of Daniel's revelations were echoing his own experience. Like lots of guys, he'd been interested in other men way back but had never acted on it, assuming the feelings would pass as unintended as they had arrived. And to some extent they had. College and university passed with little angst for Chester. Apart from the usual drunken blunders, awkward dates and occasional girlfriends, student life had continued for him, mostly free of intense sexual encounters. He was studying hard to escape forever the joyless mundanity of his parents' existence, so hadn't allowed the drama of sex to interfere with his ambition. In fact, it was the absence of melodrama in his childhood from which he inherited a solidity and calm, envied among his friends and colleagues. Soon he was in a law practice,

had met Christina and the world moved too fast around him to allow time for any serious doubt about things like sex. It was only the guilty sense of exhilaration he experienced after they split that caused him to reflect on the possibility that his interests might lie elsewhere.

Up to this point, he had never noticed any undercurrent with the gay people he knew, no sense of shared energy. They treated him as a source of strong masculine bear hugs, usually to assuage their broken hearts but never, he thought, an object of desire. He was definitely handsome, with a broad, bright complexion and alert, laughing eyes. The Edwardian beard he'd recently cultivated gave him the look of an avuncular king and beneath his stylish hipster look he was naturally muscular; an unashamedly big man next to the svelte and smooth gays he knew with their perfect apartments and carry-on dogs.

It certainly never occurred to Chester that any of them would be attracted to him sexually, so he was taken aback one night when he allowed himself to be picked up at a party. He was happy to roll with it and see what happened. The man was older and Chester took to the sex, allowing himself to explore freely. It was suddenly clear how much he'd been missing in his sex life. He hadn't known it was possible to experience selfish pleasure while fully satisfying someone else's desires. With Christina, he'd dutifully considered it was his role as a man to give her pleasure but had no idea he could demand much beyond that. She'd more or less fallen into the other role, being satisfied without any thought for what might pleasure her husband more than the occasional blow job.

He was aroused by the grain and weft of the older man's body, the pliant furrows of his soft skin like well-worn wood, the sound of their bodies together, like waves over sand. It was a powerful and sturdy lust, in which Chester happily enrolled, excited by the shifting play of control and submission.

After two months of regular fucking, the sculptor, who was used to getting his own way among his coterie of feverish followers, became increasingly demanding and appeared to have at least one other boyfriend. When a threesome was proposed, Chester, who was a pragmatist, reckoned he'd had sufficient self-discovery and could spot an unhappy ending looming. As an assiduous parent with the well-being of his girls at the forefront of his mind, he'd never brought his lover to the apartment and hadn't even considered that he would tell them about this. He disappeared from the crowd of wannabes, quislings and hangers-on without a head turning in his direction; pleased to have explored a new sexual adventure, though not quite sure what to do with it. He was happy to have time to contemplate and enjoy the feeling, untroubled by any complicated emotional demands.

His cell rang. It was Daniel. It had been quite an afternoon, the lunch with Rosa had been a delight but he'd learned some remarkable things. He was tired and thought he'd like to get back to Greenwich. Perhaps they could meet somewhere first. Chester explained that he'd been to collect the box and could be outside in half an hour to collect him.

Daniel stood outside on the sidewalk under the canopy in his heavy coat, scarf and cap, the lights and embellishments of festivity all around him adorning every available prominence. Despite the snow, indeed because of it, people were in high spirits. Christmas in New York harked back to lost innocence, lights flickering in windows, carols piping onto the streets, everyone wrapped up against the cold. Snowfall in the city signified a time when people looked hopeful because they'd overcome the odds of the year and it was important to celebrate. Chester pulling up in his restored Rambler completed the picture of 1950s clean-cut cheerfulness. The doorman opened the passenger door for Daniel and put his bag on the back seat with best wishes for the season. For a moment, they sat looking at each other in silence until Daniel turned away and Chester knew just to drive. Then, like an exhausted child, without any shame, Daniel started to shake, his chest heaving as he sobbed there in the car next to Chester. He put his arm over Daniel's shoulder as they crawled through the Manhattan traffic.

Forced from the confines of its sullen lair, the incubus that had long petrified Daniel in guilt and despair emerged from the shadows, reached out of his body and fled into the night beyond.

Chapter Twenty-Seven

He lay in the bath, up to his chin without his toes touching the end, the steam rising from the water wafting clouds of pine around him. After sitting in the car for more than an hour hardly moving, with Daniel tired and exhausted, Chester suggested they drive down to Brooklyn and decide what to do from there. When they got up to the apartment, Daniel slumped on the sofa without taking off his coat and within a few minutes fell asleep. Chester placed a cushion behind his head and laid a rug over him. He hated seeing Daniel's poise diminished like this. He wanted to shake him back into life, to see his vitality and quiet optimism return. He'd go out for provisions, certain they'd not be driving upstate tonight.

Thirty minutes later he reappeared, Daniel woke up to the sound of the elevator and keys in the door. He looked momentarily confused, wondering where he was. Chester put his bags down on the table and sat down next to him. How are you feeling? Washed out. That's only to be expected. This isn't an experience anything could have prepared you for. Listen, I hope you don't mind but I don't want you to go to Gideon's Farm tonight, not just the traffic but I think you should be here with me, where I can take care of you. We need to talk about this and work out what to do. He put his hand on Daniel's shoulder. But mostly you need to rest. Daniel did not resist. He felt the comfort surround him, surprised at how readily he accepted the invitation. Trust was something he had so rarely allowed himself, it was time to let that go with Chester. Here, I bought some tea, why don't you make us some while I fix you a bath and cook some dinner. Then we'll decide on a plan of action.

Daniel stood in the kitchen, waiting for the kettle to reach its rackety boil, staring out of the window at the brownstone opposite, not focusing but feeling curiously free. It was an empty feeling, bereft of something that had lived with him for so long, longer than anything. As if he'd had no peripheral vision up to that point, now as he looked about him the landscape opened up and he could see everything clearly as it was. As he poured the tea, familiar music floated up the corridor from the bedroom. He and Chester sat at the table listening to *Winterreise*. I downloaded this recording after the recital, it's so beautiful, something between ghostly and angelic. He wanted to say that it reminded him of Daniel but changed his mind. They sat in silence, listening to the lament of the lost lover on his icy journey, uncertain where it will lead him or how he will find his way back on a path to peaceful rest. It was too much like Daniel, thought Chester taking his case and coat down the corridor into the bedroom where he had laid out towels, pajamas and dressing gown.

Daniel had to start to take on what he'd learned but still needed to know the full story. Though the torture of their parting, the raw wound of separation had never left him, the living Xavi had long been buried. That late summer when he'd returned from Europe, he shut himself up and performed life just well enough to manage his mother's expectations, aware that she had no appetite for upheaval. She knew not to push for answers, frustrated that she was unable to exert more influence, desperate to see the parts of herself she had supplanted, shaping and reflecting him back in her image. But this was an unwelcome victory. She recognized that a part of him was lost to her forever, because despite having strong suspicions about the cause of his withdrawal, she had taught him to trust no-one. Especially now as it turned out, his own mother. She'd raised Daniel to be his own man; he would never be hers.

Daniel had every intention of flying back to Barcelona and continued to write his regular airmail letters, reduced to returning home every evening for a signal of hope in the mailbox. He threw himself into his research until early the following spring, the letters were returned to him, inscribed with that fatal message. The tragedy affected him in a surprising way. It was as if he had already lamented the end of the love and the time they had spent together. He'd crushed those happy memories into dust and the news of Xavi's death came like a dagger which he used to commit a form of living suicide, driving the truth of his love deep inside and burying it in that dust. By sacrificing part of himself, sealing off his life from the perils of human contact, he would never have to face this agony again. Restricting the ways he encountered the world, narrowing his vision, he could half-live, stay safely in the shelter.

The long, cast-iron bath was a dramatic statement on a platform in the middle of the bedroom at the end of the huge bed with its elaborate carved headboard. The heavy drapes were drawn, and Chester had lit candles which cast a flickering warmth all over the room. It occurred to Daniel, how much Chester reminded him of Lydia. Unwittingly he'd found a friend, someone like her who knew how to care for him. He'd had a talent for that, for finding people. Nate too, but he'd continued the friendship as it had been, without interference. As he finished his tea, listening to the songs of the feckless wanderer, he dried himself, pulled on Chester's pajamas and in that childish state emerged to the rich smell of tomatoes and garlic, a bottle of red wine and Chester in his apron, mixing salad dressing. You must be hungry. Daniel smiled shyly, thank you. For a moment, he was sitting at Marta's kitchen table. This is a strange time, here I am, an old man with a past I thought long consigned to ashes. It has come to find me and I am so grateful we met. I really don't think I could have taken it this far without your support. Things have a habit of working out, Daniel, they really do. Daniel felt renewed under Chester's gaze, like first sunlight on the skin. Over dinner they decided to call Rosa first thing in the morning and invite her over for coffee.

Daniel went to sleep in Chester's bed, as his friend cleared the table. He drifted off, with the comforting smell of his friend on the pillows. The warmth of companionship was slowly returning to him, reawakening a memory. He imagined how it was at the weekends with Chester and his girls, filling that bed with laughter and plans. He had loved Mae, and she wanted the best for her son, believing the best gift she could bestow was to teach him to fend for himself. When he was a child they'd hardly ever stray into each other's rooms. So that time, when he really needed her to prevent him from falling off the edge of the flat earth, neither knew how to reach out. Her mothering had been intense and ruthless. The cost of that single-mindedness had forced them both into a mutually narcissistic existence.

Daniel slept soundly but his dreams were troubled, sewn-together fragments of the day. Stumbling through a field, deep in snow, dark woods gathering around him, large black birds cawing overhead, a full moon, white and threatening. He was trying to run towards the lights of a drab, dank cottage, sinking into the snow, calling towards a figure silhouetted against an open door. He was trying to force out a warning, but his mouth wouldn't open, he couldn't be heard, the little house was sinking faster, there was nothing he could do to prevent it being swallowed into the ground. He reached out towards it then woke up in the darkness. Uncertain but determined to come out of hiding to face it.

Later that morning Rosa, with her husband Carles and daughter Alba, had arrived at the apartment. They all sat round the table drinking coffee while Rosa spoke uninterrupted, grateful to be unburdening herself.

She continued to explain that when Xavi was arrested, the police were determined to make an example of him. They couldn't find any evidence or witnesses to his involvement in acts of violence, only a few posters for an anti-fascist student march which never took place. He'd endured torture and solitary confinement until the perpetrators were finally rounded up and charged without his name ever being brought up. By all accounts when the authorities realized their mistake, it was clear they didn't want to be exposed for the torture to which he had been subjected. They shifted the charges to petty crimes of degenerate behavior and delinquency, racketeering and organized prostitution. They could easily arrange informers against him for these crimes and his arrest with the American, with you, was the perfect cover.

Rosa looked at Daniel and took his hand, as if she was helping him over an obstacle. He was still confused, unclear how she knew all of these details. And he knew instinctively that what she was about to tell him would be hard. You know about Sabater, yes? The name rang familiar. He was a Spanish judge with a terrifying reputation. From nowhere, under his breath, Daniel said Golden Shoe, as he remembered Xavi pointing out the sinister man at the concert. This was a time when the regime was still exacting revenge on the city. We Catalans always refuse to comply with bullying. We can be very conventional but we will never submit to the tyranny of Spanish morals. The judge was cleaning up the city streets, sending teenage prostitutes to sterilization centers, imprisoning drunks and Gypsies. Worse, he was encouraging the doctors to experiment with methods to force homosexuals to change, electric shocks to the brain. Her voice was breaking, her husband and daughter were looking into their coffee cups, as if they wanted to swim away in the sadness of it all, but Daniel looked straight ahead, modulating his breathing.

It was only at this point four or five months after his arrest that my mother heard any news from him, a short note from Badajoz jail. This must have been the time she returned your letters. Then she lost him again until after petitioning the court, she was told that uncle Xavi had been sent to a prison somewhere in the Canary Islands. A year later he was transferred to a secure psychiatric hospital near Malaga. She was able to visit him once there. What she found shocked her. His speech was slow and he'd lost sight in one eye.

He'd been incarcerated almost 15 years before Franco died. Even then the new government would not grant him and many other prisoners in his position an amnesty or pardon. Rosa suspected that her uncle had not wanted to return home to Barcelona and four years later, only when the hospital was closed, did he return to the city, a broken man. With my uncle, who refused to change, they had gone one step further and performed an operation on his brain – a lobotomy. Whatever they thought it would achieve, it destroyed him.

We tried to help him fight. By now there are many organizations battling the government for compensation but he wouldn't get involved. He moved back to a small apartment in our building and took a job as a gardener in the Parc de Ciutadella where he worked for 20 years, a gentle, withdrawn man who spoke only to me and the birds he fed every day in the park.

Rosa, there is something I don't understand. What are you telling us? He was looking into the eye of the storm of Xavi's life, tortured, lobotomized, imprisoned and worst of all he hadn't been there. Xavi, he is still alive? She let go of his hand, got up from the table, walked to the window, staring outside for a moment in the silence surrounding the table. She turned around. Yes, he is alive. I'm so sorry; I just didn't know when would be the right time to tell you. Yesterday, you were so happy when I met you, I didn't know how to say it. She looked at him. Until my mother died, I had never heard of you. He never mentioned you. I'm sorry, Daniel. There is more.

This was all too much for Daniel, he sat speechless, his head spinning in his hands. They'd been apart all this time, separated by that faithless, forgetful sea between them, parted by the ocean of their lives, unable to find a way back to each other. All that had remained of their love was slow and continual destruction. Everything was as normal, Rosa smiled sweetly with Xavi's bright hopefulness, frightened that she'd made a mistake. He stood up and walked round the table next to her and took her hand. Rosa, I have sacrificed my life to the certain knowledge that I was responsible for his death. Meeting you, hearing this story, has changed everything, changed me. And I am strong enough to bear it, please don't spare me. Tell me the rest.

Rosa continued to explain that Xavi had retired 12 years ago but continued to spend almost every day sitting in the park by the small lake and walking by the sea. A couple of years ago he began to slow down and sometimes got lost in the city. It wasn't a problem, as many people knew who he was and would guide him home. It was hard for us to tell if he was sick, as he hardly speaks anyway, until one evening he was knocked down by a cyclist and had to go to hospital. After running some tests, the results were more serious than we had imagined. Something to do with the scar

tissue from the operation caused a tumor in his brain.

Daniel steadied himself against the wall and looked bleakly at Chester then back to Rosa. There was no way of disguising what he was feeling. He couldn't focus now on what she was saying. He needed to think. He needed to hold it together now, sensing a vertigo creeping around him.

Please, I'm sorry, looking at Rosa, who suddenly seemed sullen. Something about the way her eyes narrowed at him reminded him of Elena. Was this part of her revenge from the grave? He had to get out of this room, into the air, to steady his breathing. Do you mind if I take a moment, I need to clear my head. I'm fine, seeing their alarm.

Chester followed him into the hall. You can take the elevator upstairs to the roof, wear your coat, it's cold but we have some chairs there. Take your time, I'll keep them occupied. After 30 minutes he returned, cheeks flushed with the cold, tears in his eyes. Are you ok? Daniel nodded, his facial muscles were tensed, tight with grief. He felt as if he didn't know what was happening again, desperately reaching out for something familiar. This was torment and he was just a vulnerable old man. He had to get back to the farm. He'd be able to think about it there.

Chapter Twenty-Eight

Chester drove him back to Greenwich and when they arrived at Gideon's Farm, Ade was busy in the house with his cousin, a shiny girl with fiercely bleached hair. She'd started helping Daniel around the house in recent weeks. He trusted Ade who had a good instinct for making himself invaluable. Working for Daniel was a pleasure. The two men gave each other time and talked freely, as they walked round the house, Ade reassured Daniel where he could make the house more secure and issuing orders to his cousin when he spotted something needed fixing. The meeting left him in a surprisingly positive state of mind, knowing the unwieldy property would be cared for while he was away.

When they'd gone, he and Chester sat in Lydia's study and booked their flights to Spain. Are you sure you want me to come, Daniel? Wouldn't you prefer to be on your own for this? Daniel laughed. You are the first person I have allowed to see me weep, Chester. I wouldn't blame you for wanting to escape but I'm not sure if I can allow it. I've run from the world for so long and you're so much part of this story now, I hope you don't mind that. It would mean the world to me if you came. We both know it won't be easy. I can do this with you around me.

That evening he called his friend and apologized for a lifetime of omissions. Nate had pulled a muscle playing tennis and was recuperating on his terrace with painkillers, the usual glass of Saint Veran and cigarettes. They talked for two hours. Nate was taken aback at his oldest friend's unaccustomed frankness but responded calmly. Dan, we've been through so many years together and have shared so many experiences without ever really sharing each other. I figured you just wanted it that way. I should have asked. Perhaps there is much we should have said, my dear friend. Now we don't need to. This overweight, heart-diseased Creole may be old but whatever you need, just ask. You are in safe hands with Chester, I know he also has your best interests at heart. Yes, well thank you for that too, Nate. He showed up; you seemed to know just the right moment. You've always known Nate, haven't you? Always one step ahead. You and Lydia. Who did I think I was fooling? No-one Dan, no-one. We were complicit too. We wanted what you wanted. Today folks need to announce everything to the world, to reveal their innermost secrets with the utmost indiscretion. They weren't hidden, it wasn't things we kept from each other, we just took care to protect what has been inviolable between us. I for one, am grateful for that. I love you, I always have and am one among many others who have. Only none of us really knew how to say it. But not one of us has loved the less for that. Now, go and find the ending to this story, Dan. I can come at a moment's notice.

It was a relief. His oldest and newest friends had not flinched and he knew that if Lydia had been alive, she would have encouraged him to do this. She was curious and followed a trail like a bloodhound. It was at the heart of what she did, her research. She would pick up on what appeared to be a passing comment in a letter or an insignificant note in a margin and trace it to source or destination, often leading her to discoveries about her subjects that others missed. She said that it was in the commonplace facts of a life that scholars can find the remarkable.

His past was being thrown in the air, after years of deliberate silence he didn't know what to say. What had Nate thought all these years? He'd let that time, those decades just slip passed, without really noticing. It must have been obvious that something had changed when he returned to New York. The channel he'd cut between them, full of the things they'd tacitly agreed not to discuss with each other, had never been crossed. One thing was clear. He needed his oldest friend now. It was not too late. He could change things. Even if he couldn't alter the past, there was an opportunity to seek resolution, a rare gift to take charge of a life bound up in disaster.

Xavi was still alive and that was heart-breaking. The thought of the wasted years, that they could have been together, it was hard to bear. But talking about it for the first time, he felt those threads working loose. He could be free of the trammels he'd wound himself up in. Though he'd been laid bare and open, he felt strong and purposeful. Recounting this scarred history had left his body taut and alert. Whatever faced him now, there was only one direction he could take, to sail into the storm and accept what was to come, fighting for those he loved, as they had done for him. For the first time, the journey was uncharted but he no longer felt his life was dwindling into the dissolving distance. It was not too late, after all, to dare beyond the edge of the map. He had to go to Xavi, to find him again.

They would fly out on Christmas Day, two days after Rosa returned. He admired her desire to correct her mother's injustice. She had flown to New York to confront the past but with absolute faith that it was the past. She insisted nothing could change and that Daniel must only expect the worst.

That took courage. For all that, she felt a grace could fall on them. She liked him. Maybe something of her uncle had stayed with them both, the time they'd spent together felt like decades elided to a point of time. He could remember lying on the beach, their two glistening bodies in the sun, Xavi saying that if this was their last moment it would be locked in time like the sound of the sea in shell. Now Daniel had to hope what he'd stowed away would be full of the sound of that same sea.

Barcelona. The streets, sidewalks and alleyways unfolding and merging back into one another, these are the constructions of time, the waymarks of worn pathways, shortcuts and rat-runs, laid down by countless footsteps through generations of existence in one place. Those unknown lives busy with the essential details of their days; some rush inexorably from departure to destination, others shuffle unnoticed along the cobbled lines. Children balance on the cracks between sidewalk stones or step carefully on only the horizontal slabs, chalk-marking their games in the grit. Old men waiting for action on street benches, kick the edges of their heels in the dust, grinding cigarette ends beneath once war-weary feet, now buoyant in trainers. They know that these streets studded with countless spat-out gums, will never need their resistance again. And the buildings, once pockmarked with gunshots now earmarked for luxury, slumped together above the undercurrent of drains gushing with the effluent of a million homes. Their doorways and steel shutters, still witnesses to the intricate wheeling and dealing of the furtive and the bold are now the canvas for final protest, these last rebels daubing a relentless language of unintelligible graffiti across the exits and entrances of everyday lives, meaningless scars across the eyeline, signifying nothing. All this crowded in on Daniel on that first walk across the city. In the early morning the city was noisy, as he remembered it but now with new sounds and faces demanding their right to flourish. It was at once the same and completely different.

They'd landed mid-evening, taking a taxi to their hotel, something international and unremarkable on the Ramblas, close to Pintor Fortuny. Time contracted and expanded, circled at high speed around them. From the window of the car the brightness, the lights, the color rushed past him. He was leaning from the balcony again, everywhere a tangled mess of wires bringing light, sound, cold and heat. He could hear the competing sounds of news, jazz, dogs, babies, birds and the street vendors. Here more than anywhere people extracted more sound from the silence, more light from

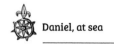

the darkness.

It was impossible to know what to expect, Barcelona banished from his mind for half a century, had only come back to Daniel in these last few weeks. Franco's death and freedom had come such a long time ago, his painful memories were unrecorded in the new life here and as they drove past the Plaça Catalunya he could tell the city was well in her swing again.

Though he was excited to be here, Daniel was anxious to make it easy for Chester and wasn't at all sure how to deal with this sudden exposure himself. It was past midnight, so they decided to eat in the hotel and get some sleep to readjust. Chester could explore tomorrow while he visited Xavi, that way they'd have something to compare, new discoveries together, a common version of the city where they could meet, not a map of the tragedy so long past.

But Daniel knew he would not resist retracing old steps. He slept fitfully for a few hours, images of the past flitting frantically into sight and disappearing as quickly. It was light when he woke, so he got up, dressed quietly and ventured out, turning in the direction of the dawn light and the sea.

The way gave up to him unconsciously, one of those well-trodden paths, as if he could trace what the city had forgotten. With little effort, he found himself standing in front of the cathedral. A desultory group of late-night revelers called over to him but he carefully crossed over Via Laeitana to the market square, close to where the old police station was slumbering in her vantage point, unmoved by the presence of his return. Santa Caterina was busy with lorries and porters, the mingling smells of meat, fish, tomatoes and pungent freshness uncovered vaults of memory. He remembered how that smell would turn rancid and cloying in the stifling heat of the day. The roof of the market had been replaced and he took coffee in a bar where the porters drank beer and cognac underneath the new spectacular wave. He was surprised at the ease with which he knew what to do. The dank streets were the same, the buildings teetered around him, balconies adorned in laundry. Then there he was, minutes later, standing again in Plaça de Llana looking up to his point of departure. Fifty-one years ago, the last place he took note of, the final snapshot. His eyes filled with tears, the place where his heart had closed up to life. From here, his feet alone had carried him to the station that would exile him forever.

The café had gone and the laundry replaced by ersatz storefronts. But the pharmacy was still here and the baker, and it struck him that the children he left on the doorstep might live here; they still needed bread and medicines. Life continued for these people oblivious, not just to him but to anything outside their own means of survival. He followed the instinct that was pushing him on, burrowing through the maze of alleys that emerge at Santa Maria del Mar. Then around the corner there was Montcada, now fully famous as the museum. How little time had passed in the days of this palace, he thought, placing his flat palms on one of its great blocks of stone, heft from Montjuic. These buildings have cared nothing for the allegiances or rebellions of the city's inhabitants, despite their chiseling and hammers. He'd been one of the last of those invaders, cutting away at the walls to save the thinnest skin of art for posterity. The stone was warm under his hand but with no longing for him or any other who'd come before. He'd bring Chester here to see the room where they found the frescoes: no, he'd find wherever they are exhibited, that would be better. Let's not drag him round a mausoleum of my past.

Daniel made his way back along the old port, now a handsome boulevard and turned up the Ramblas to the hotel, satisfied that the city was still within his stride and that the ghosts he'd expected were only those he carried with him. On his return Chester was up, had slept well and was looking fresh and beaming, happy to see Daniel in a new setting. They went downstairs not with a burden of responsibility, more a sense of mission, knowing they'd done the right thing to come here. Over breakfast Rosa called from a hospital to say that Xavi had been admitted overnight. Pressure from the tumor had caused a stroke. There would be some more tests this morning, so she would call later to let him know when he should come.

Chapter Twenty-Nine

Chester lay in bed that first morning, aware that Daniel was out of the bed and moving around in the room. He heard the door close quietly. He was amazed how Daniel was taking all this. Only a few days ago, he'd seemed helpless. Now his decisiveness in making this trip had changed all that, given him a purpose like a medieval knight, a quest that wholly depended on him. As if he'd been waiting for just this to wake him from sleepwalking. Of course, he was pleased to see the transformation and couldn't help observing his every move. Here was a strong-willed man, striking out, undeterred by what lay ahead. He'd thought it was unfamiliar territory perhaps, after so long. But Daniel looked at him in the taxi, this place is etched on my heart, it feels the same as it did then, I can smell the air.

Chester thought of his father, a meek undemonstrative figure who disappeared into the shadows of their home, serving his purpose, no more than that, never reaching out, never holding an opinion or daring to be noticed. When he'd died a few years before, his mother had simply swept up behind him as if she'd been anticipating his departure.

Here was Daniel, almost youthful – the same age but bold, emotional, handsome and healthy. Chester couldn't imagine what he must feel like, facing up to this part of his life. Perhaps he'd also been waiting for this moment? Years of shouldering responsibility for the death of the only man he'd loved, then discovering that person is still alive but on the brink of life and with an unflinching instinct to forgive those who'd caused this wrong. He hadn't heard Daniel utter a single recriminatory remark, he bore everything with poise. No wonder his expansive heart was growing towards Daniel's. He felt the need to help him, he was pleased to share in the revival of this spirit. Though he feared these days would not be happy ones, he saw his friend was prepared for the worst; sometimes he'd whispered how blessed he felt to have been given his chance to speak his love again, to find voice for these years of silence.

After breakfast, they left the hotel in a more somber mood with Rosa's news, conscious now of occupying time until Daniel could visit the hospital. They turned left towards the Pintor Fortuny warehouse but walked right past it before Daniel realized the mistake. At street level the whole facade had changed where the entrance had been and the building had clearly enjoyed a flashy restoration of the smart apartments above. They walked through the automatic doors in the middle of three large glass arches entering a grocery store announcing its luxury products as authentic delicacies. Slim-hipped boys and girls in aprons bustled about rearranging garlands of dried chilis and dusting off mountains of canned fish. Daniel seemed not quite to get his bearings, pointing at the corner of the double-height ceiling where hams were hanging next to shelves stuffed with inaccessible delicacies. A young assistant following Daniel's upward gaze, asked how he could help in immaculate English, but Daniel thanked him with a lingering smile. I guess I was his age, he told Chester as they left, puzzling how his past fitted into this postmodern emporium with its faux vintage decor. It certainly wasn't like this.

Outside, Chester took him gently by the arm. Are you ok with this? Sure, he paused, looking up at the building again. I'm glad in a way. They have removed the place it happened, it's now suspended in the air. I guess I was thinking how it would look, the place where that vengeful murder happened. It was murder. It murdered us, everything we had. And now it hangs there in the air with the hams, and those kids selling those culinary souvenirs have no idea, thank God, not even a flash of insight about it. Their lives are better for it. And ours. We no longer need to pay homage to that. Better it is a shrine to tourism. Perhaps that's some kind of justice.

This really was all quite surreal, revisiting someone else's past in such a raw, unfiltered way. There was nothing between Daniel and his worst fears now. Chester was pleased just to be there for him of course, but had no idea at all how they would manage it. He'd started to rely on the smell of Daniel's shaving cream and his old-fashioned cologne. The strength of what he felt was scaring him, how quickly it was happening. But it would be selfish to steal this moment, he had to let Daniel live through it and see where they ended up. He intended to be a steady rock for him but now that role was changing. Daniel was emerging from the carapace of time, powerful and elegant, a new being ready for new life.

They had coffee at the Zurich where the city passes back and forth and talked about how they met. Daniel teased him about just how Nate had orchestrated their meeting and asked him if he'd endured one of those interminable dinners at *Le Veau d'Or*. There were moments of silence when he seemed jolted into remembering what he faced or looking around him, specters of the past walked by. The medication he'd been taking had steadied his reactions. His balance and breath had returned, his anxiety was less raw and brutal.

They'd shared so much in these past months, it wasn't always necessary to ask questions. Chester carefully navigated around Daniel without the fuss of talk, letting silence speak when it was required as they wandered into the city.

They found the building where Patxot's library had been, now a cultural foundation, the exteriors cleaned and restored to impressive 19th-century facades. Daniel walked around open-mouthed, happily orienting himself until drawing his breath, he gave a chuckle of delight on finding the library, his room intact, almost as he left it. More than that, the shelves were full of books, his books, those unhappy orphans he'd cared for. The lady curator with strange hair, listened rather drily while Daniel burbled on about working here and his story of the collections. She started to warm to him but as they were talking a message came through on Chester's phone. It was time for them to go.

They had to take a car from the hotel to Bellvitge, outside the city, where Rosa and Alba met them outside the oncology institute, a white, sleek building. Both women looked haggard but happy to see Chester and Daniel again, embracing them like family, grateful for their presence. The sun was disappearing behind the Ordal mountains and a cold wind pushed them indoors. Everything gleamed, throwing off the smell of surface wipes and floor cleaner. In the corridor, they were introduced to a specialist and Rosa explained these were relatives of her uncle who had traveled very far. Daniel could remember the look of optimistic defiance that cancer doctors get from daily defeat. But he was gracious and preoccupied and went off in search of some other battle. Chester took Daniel aside quietly to tell him that he'd wait for him, however long, not to worry, if he wanted him to go and return later to fetch him, whatever. Daniel felt rendered childlike by hospitals but now he just wanted to see Xavi, to set his eyes again on this man who had haunted his life with their lost love.

They left him at the door. He walked in gently shutting the door behind him. A bed was on his left looking out to the blood-flecked evening sky over the Llobregat plain to the sea in the distance. He looked around the room. There were flowers, a plastic bottle of water and a silent radio on a bedside table. Various medical machines were pulsing with tiny lights on the other side of the bed, connected by a tangle of life-sustaining tubes and wires, like jetsam washed up at high tide. Daniel walked round to the end of the bed silently. There was an old man with his eyes shut, breathing

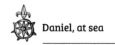

heavily, propped up on two pillows, neatly tucked in like an Egyptian king, his sinewy arms brown against the sheets resting alongside his body. Half of his head was shaved and bandages ran around the skull, completing the image of a war wounded hero.

Daniel gripped the metal frame of the bed, swallowing hard, impotent, realizing with anguish that he did not recognize the person lying in front of him.

He'd almost expected to see him as they'd parted and here was a battered, diseased old man, nothing like he'd known. Daniel was overcome with shame, desperately needing to feel something, to have a moment of recognition. There couldn't be no meaning to this moment, not now, not after they'd been through so much. Time slowed around him. He leaned heavily on the bars of the bed frame, wanting to scream at this man to wake up, to recognize him, to remember what they'd been. How could he sleep now? Xavi? Almost a whisper and then in a single moment it was all there. Slowly the old man's heavy lids rose, his eyes opened wider as if gazing at a vision. They were Xavi's eyes, the bold young man who lay on the pillow next to him for what seemed a lifetime. He looked intently at Daniel who was speechless reaching out inside to him, rooted to the spot. His lips shuddered slowly into a smile like the wings of a timeworn butterfly, as his mouth carefully shaped each sound D-a-n-i-e-l. His eyes closed again, for a moment lifting the fingers of one hand, as if beckoning Daniel to the bedside. He moved round the bed and sat down, picking up Xavi's hand, kissing it, placing it on his face, holding it gently under his. Xavi turned very slightly with great effort towards him, Daniel leaned forward and kissed him with the same tenderness, still holding his hand. Xavi smiled faintly and whispered, one word at a time. *Daniel, sabia que tornaries*. I knew you'd come back Daniel. He put his head down on the bed still holding Xavi's hand, trying to suppress the sobbing in his heart, the tears now flowing, sadness and joy. Yes, finally we are together again. What a life it has been. He was tired, closing his eyes, feeling the slow pulse of life flowing between them.

He was a young boy again, standing at the seashore, a long white beach stretched out before him, the sea lapping at his bare feet. Running now, the water splashing at his legs. There was no sun but all around a brilliant white haze. On the horizon he could see a small boat sailing on a flat sea towards him, he could see someone on board, a tall woman, she was waving at him, moving gracefully and laughing. A seagull circled above the boat, or it was a flag shimmering in the wind, he kept running towards the boat but couldn't get near it. Then from the opposite end of the beach, there was another boy, faceless, running along the sand, getting nearer the boat, crashing his legs through the waves, he reached for the side and the woman held out her hand to help him aboard. They were laughing and clapping and dancing around on the deck, hugging each other. He cried out to them to stop, to wait for him, he was running, out of breath, then leaped into the sea. It was deep and the waves were getting higher. The boy on the boat started to ring a bell attached to the mast. Ding. Ding. Ding. The woman was turning the sails around and they began to speed through the waves. He was sinking now, his arms pulling at the sea, glimpsing the boat further off, barely visible through the waves, but he could hear the bell. Ding. Ding. Ding.

The alarms of the machines were ringing and brought the nurses rushing into the room. Daniel opened his eyes and for a moment didn't recognize his surroundings. Gently one of the nurses took his hand from Xavi's and helped him to stand up. Rosa realizing what had happened, immediately put her arms around Daniel, held him tight for a moment, then carefully steered him out of the room.

Chapter Thirty

The early morning August sun warmed his face, creeping through the beech trees, dappling across the lawn. Daniel stood at his bedroom window, hands deep in the pockets of his dressing gown, pleased with what he could see. Today was his 79th birthday and they'd decided to make something of it. He felt like celebrating. It was important to show how much this meant to him. Everyone else was excited by the prospect too, making an effort to join him for the occasion. It had to be joyful and carefree, a party to remember. So many of his birthdays had passed here, not unhappily but not with that kind of atmosphere. He was fed up with being contained and the last year had shown him just how much of life there was left to live. He was full of shared purpose and projects. He'd had companionship on the road but after Lydia he assumed he'd outstayed his welcome. How wrong he'd been and she would have seen that right away. Today he almost felt coltish and couldn't wait for everyone to come, to feel the warmth of contact, to celebrate something together he'd never dreamed possible in his life. Nate and Chester had made him promise not to do anything, he should just concentrate on enjoying his day and writing his speech. They had Ade to help them, his sister had ensured the house was gleaming and the caterers were booked to arrive at lunchtime. He'd drive downtown later to collect flowers at the market.

If there was one thing that he'd learned from Xavi's death, it was that he still had time to look forward, to relish the last of every day and to share that pleasure with the people he loved. So much of his life had been a closed, locked-down thing, a burrow from which he'd occasionally emerged blinking before retreating again at the slightest sign of danger. It wasn't that he was a timid man but so much possibility had remained unexplored. In a matter of months, the once blank and empty seas of future days had become full of new people and activities. They wanted him to be part of their personal dramas, they needed to inveigle Daniel into their hopes and dreams and he was happy to do that for them. Most of all his own story had quite changed in direction. Rather than fading to a distant, indistinct pulse inside him, his heartbeat had become stronger, beating faster and louder than before, as if Xavi had given him his life to live too. Today of all days, he would be celebrating with the friends who would become his new family.

When he told Nate he just raised his eyebrows, turning down the corners of his mouth in that wicked smile and insisted that this was a ceremony of late flowering. He needed to concentrate on his speech. There was so much he wanted to say, happy with the prospect of being unguarded and talking out loud about everything that was happening. Every one of the people coming to the party had to be thanked individually for helping him get to this.

He pulled on a pair of jeans and a plaid shirt, made strong coffee and went downstairs to the Cabin to talk to Lydia, the one who was missing from this important day. He threw open the door of her study to welcome in the summer day. Already on the terrace, the air was full of the hum of bees on the lavender bushes and a flock of monarch butterflies fluttered above the mass of purple asters, drinking in the dewy morning. She would never have let him throw away this opportunity to be happy, to finally find a way to encounter his life as it was always meant to be. She would have said that Robinson Crusoe had been rescued, brought back to humanity. She had been his woman Friday, got him here, helped him survive. Now, today he could let her go, she could fly to her own place of peace.

Walking down the steep red brick steps leading from the terrace to the wild garden below, he felt quite at peace. Over the spring and summer, he and Ade had undertaken a project together cutting a wide path through the meadow grasses and laying paving stones where the feathery yellow senna and white peonies vied with foxgloves and blazing star. Down there, with the Cabin above them, he'd built a trellised walkway, wrapped with climbing roses under which they set a white painted, cast-iron bench, decorated with vines and birds bought in a Philadelphia house sale. A few yards off, they'd built up a stone bird bath. Lydia had found solace away from her poets in Mae's garden and took on its guardianship with great seriousness, keeping a journal of the year's tasks, planting with care, patiently tending newcomers and established time-servers without favoritism. She allowed room for whatever wanted to share the garden at Gideon's Farm, reporting the visits of hares, pine squirrels and possums with equal delight. Daniel thought this would be the right place to remember those he loved and where one day he wanted his ashes buried. He'd taught Tabitha and Chloe to sit quietly here, waiting to see what visitors might come. It thrilled him to see them so at home here, exploring to their heart's delight with squeals of pleasure and breathless accounts of new territories they'd conquered. He loved sharing these places he knew so intimately, that were part of his being. Created as a haven, in fact it had only ever been a castle fortified for two misfits. Now it was coming alive with the sound of people. Daniel was determined it would be the home it should always have been. As he sat on the bench, the wood thrush with her speckled breast dropped down from the trees above and perched on the side of the stone bath. She dipped down to drink and fixing Daniel with her beady eye, splashed her rusty green wing feathers in the water.

The four of them had sat outside the hospital room in the naked artificial light, waiting for the doctors to complete the official process of death. Chester was yearning to reach across the divide of the corridor to Daniel. The Ferrans looked blankly sad and Daniel leaned back against the wall, with his eyes shut. He was holding onto the brink, trying to shut out the invasive sweet odor of cancer. Silent orderlies appeared with brisk cleanliness to move the equipment out of the room and then ushered them back in to sit with the body. Xavi's eyes were closed. He looked peaceful but it pained Daniel that he could not find the person he had known there in that room. The flash of recognition, their brief reunion, the passing of Xavi's spirit into his, was a final blessing on their unlived lives. This is why he had come. Nothing had ever alleviated the numb ache of their separation, both men had been locked away, only able to observe a world in which they could not participate. But what had remained was free. Remarkably the intensity of what they'd had for those few short months had been held to them by the tiniest thread, just enough to stretch across time. Xavi's last sacrifice was to hand something of life back to Daniel.

At that moment, the door of the room opened to reveal a thin, old woman, immaculately dressed in black and fur, raven hair pulled back from her face, wearing huge dark glasses over a deeply lined, tanned face. Rosa hurried to the door and spoke to her quickly in Catalan. The woman looked over silently at Xavi. Then as she removed her glasses, revealing myopic eyes and a face streaked with mascara, she walked over to Daniel. For a few moments he was confused. Then a smile broke from her face and he knew immediately. Lili? It can't be you. Silently tears flowed as they embraced, the distant survivors of a disaster. She was the only witness, the one person both men had been able to confide in. They both turned to face Xavi, Lili squeezed Daniel's hand tight in hers, holding it up to her lips and then leaned over and kissed Xavi's forehead, speaking quietly to him while she did so, incanting an unintelligible benediction.

They left the room together, followed by Chester. He politely stood a little way off. Lili reached out her jeweled hand to him. This is my friend Chester. *Mi encanta.* The way she pronounced every syllable reminded him of Xavi. How entranced he'd always been by the way they spoke. She rolled Chester's name in her mouth and smiled at him. I can't believe it, Daniel, she said in perfect gravelly English. Here we are again, old friends, so sad, such a tragedy for us all. My God, so much has changed. I only found Palillo by accident, you know. I escaped to Cannes and married a rich Englishman, she held out her rings and laughed. I lived in London for many years. After he died, I began returning here every winter. I have an apartment looking over the sea, close to Somorrostro. There is so much to tell you. She sighed, so much heartbreak. But we must look forward, he of all people would expect that from us. She turned to Chester, took both of his hands in hers and looked up at his eyes. She kissed him on both cheeks and then Daniel. I can see he is looking after you. We need this love at our age. We must talk about it all very soon. By now Rosa and Alba had come out of the room. Lili talked to them for a few minutes, put her sunglasses back on and left them, marching with determined momentum into the bone-white, hygienic distance. Now there is a story, Daniel turned to Rosa. Did you know? She smiled. Yes, but she asked me not to tell you, she didn't know how it would be. I think she was anxious about seeing you.

By now it was after midnight. Xavi's body would be taken straight to the crematorium. so Rosa drove them all back into the city. She invited them up to the apartment where Carles was waiting with food, coffee and cognac. The whole floor of the building had been renovated into a loft, opening up the rooms, uncovering the original tiled floors and exposing the terracotta curved furrow ceilings. While they sat round the kitchen table, Rosa put a record down in front of Daniel. I found this. He immediately recognized it as the cover of Brubeck's *Time Further Out* with the Miro painting on the front. Another piece of the past washed up here, he laughed. This makes the years disappear quickly. It took him straight back to the warm nights lying out on the terrace here, drinking beer, listening to jazz. Come and look now. Rosa took his hand and led him to the back of the apartment, down some steps and out through the heavy sliding glass doors. We extended it across the building, you'll know this view. You don't mind me showing you I hope, the record? I want you to have your memories. I found this, it fell from the record sleeve. I waited until we were alone. It's you and Xavi. A square two-tone photograph. Two young men with backpacks, slightly out of focus standing beside their bicycles, one with his arm around the other's shoulder. In the background, what looks like sheets hanging on lines. And the sea. It was Somorrostro, at the seafront. Where they had first met Lili, where she lived. He stopped and looked at Rosa. You know I loved Xavi, your uncle, all my life. But my heart was broken then and I have wept so many tears, worn the wounds so heavily inside. Now I seem to have a choice. Either I can become an old man and disappear into this final tragedy or I have to see it as a gift that Xavi has given us. He has given us to each other, he has given us all this opportunity to do something different. Who knows how long I have left? Seeing this photograph, the record, being here back on the terrace, nothing stops, everything and everyone is here with us still. This is where I was alive, Rosa, and I need to live again. I must forgive and let go of the past. Even your mother, even Elena for she could never have known what she was doing and it must have tormented her when she realised what she had done. I know what that has felt like. It's time for us to put all that away and move forward. Rosa was smoking, Daniel reached out and took the cigarette from her hand, swallowing the cognac and drawing in tobacco. Let's celebrate now we have found each other. That's what I want to give him. And if there is somewhere after this, he won't have so long to wait for me. He put his arm around her and looked up to the night sky. The eerie piano riff of Brubeck's *Bluette* was floating on the air around them, Daniel was at ease, strangely here he knew just what to do, who he was, how to be.

The two men walked the few blocks to their hotel around 3.30 in the morning, still preoccupied with the day's events. The city hardly took a breath in its unrelenting refusal to sleep as if making up for the years lost to desperation and hardship. The streets teemed with light and life. As they left, Rosa remarked that they looked unsteady and tired on their feet like children and to be careful. Get some sleep and come over tomorrow, we can talk through the plans. In the elevator it crossed Daniel's mind how completely content he was with Chester's company. This friend had become a mainstay, steering him safely through these waters with intuitive steadiness. Daniel had always needed to be looked after, he attracted guardians. Every time he'd faced trouble in the last few months, reaching out, he'd readily found Chester.

Tomorrow he had to fly back to the States to collect the girls. Daniel would have to fend for himself for a while. They went into the suite and turned to wish each other goodnight. Daniel hesitated. Today a life had diminished, a soul had flown. But in its wake an imperceptible mantle remained, a gossamer thin film of love hung in the air. As Daniel felt it fall around them, something fearful melted away. The look in Chester's eyes called out to him and just as he had done, so many years before, that Christmas with Xavi, he relinquished himself. He closed his eyes in the warm embrace and felt the soft, malty breath of the man he loved upon his lips.

The shutters on the balcony windows in that little room, up the winding stairs at Plaça de Llana, long rusted shut, crumbled to dust and the light flooded in.

Daniel went upstairs to check the rooms were prepared. The changes pleased him and the house was breathing for the first time since Lydia's death. They'd occupied it neatly enough between them but it had never fully opened up to them. They were focused on the distractions of the esoteric and domestic contentment was simply a condition of that existence. They had not been able to live in it as Daniel's mother had, sweeping about gracefully with no purpose except to fill her days with indolence, a place she could safely keep Daniel, a home for them both where he could grow.

In truth it had become musty, a sarcophagus of time past. That is, until Ade's men had torn out its entrails of pipes, replacing the veins of the house, reviving the original decor, renewing its lifeblood. Now it was a place to be lived in again, no longer a shrine or museum. He stood at the balcony looking down into the drawing room below where he'd watched Mae's parties as a child, he too felt restored. Today it was to be a place of celebration again.

He'd placed what was now known as the Sale Box, prominently on the side table by the windows of the inner hall. He wanted people to see it and enjoyed telling its story to anyone who asked. It would be going to the new library at Exhampton to be reunited with the portolan with which it had shared history, the secrets of this family's past, more than three hundred years earlier. Daniel had just finished the article he'd been invited to submit for the *New York Review of Books*, sure their readers would enjoy the historical surprises it revealed about the early settlers, equally certain it would upset anyone who still traded on their Sale connections. It amused him to think of his mother's delight at the thought of a family scandal, so far back, literally on the quayside. Lydia too, she'd be rubbing her hands in manic glee, issuing forth the ribald chuckle she normally reserved for reading bad reviews of colleagues who'd slighted her.

Nobody could begrudge the unanimous decision of the university trustees to repay his generous bequest by naming the building in his honor. The Sale Library would be his academic legacy. The rest of the family financial portfolio, which still ran to many millions, would be put into an international foundation in Xavi's name to support political freedom. He'd asked Rosa and Chester to be the founding trustees. He never cared about the money. But now he wanted it to be useful.

The story of the Sale history he'd told to *Greenwich Time* had already sent ripples across the pool of Fairfield society. Sitting on the porch in the sun with the reporter, who'd been dispatched to write up his donation to Exhampton, he'd felt liberated and told her his own news. Her interview had unsettled sanctimonious New England church folk and upset local right-wingers as had the news of his marriage to Chester. But since the interview, old and new neighbors recognized him from the paper. When he went to the store they wanted to pass the time of day with him, possibly hoping for an invitation. But apart from a few old family friends, acquaintances from the swimming pool, hiking companions and colleagues from the faculty, they would hope in vain.

After waiting decades, he was breaking the chains that had held him down. Whatever Mae had taught him, it was to think freely, to resist the clutches of convention. He liked to think she'd be pleased that now, late in the day, he was about to fulfil the dream that had been taken away from him, rejected that past. Today laughter and music and a new family would take up occupation here and he was excited by the prospect of what he had achieved in that, stitching back up the fragments of the years. What he'd lost with Xavi he'd found in these new generations, people who looked to him to be the scion of their lives, who wanted him wholly and only as he was. A purpose was clear, being alive he could help them to live better lives, open lives, free of chains.

Daniel and Chester had moved to the larger master bedroom at the front overlooking the woods cascading down Round Hill, the fragment of sea in the far distance. It had been his mother's and then Lydia's. The adjoining dressing room had been refitted and in the bathroom the griffin-claw bathtub had been raised on a platform from which you could see across the garden to the walnut copse. After showering and getting dressed in a blue linen shirt and white pants, he went to check the other rooms where

his guests would stay for the weekend. The Ferrans would sleep in his old bedroom, Alba was coming down later on the train from Grand Central and would camp in the Cabin with the girls. Chester was collecting Lilli from La Guardia and Nate was arriving with a chauffeur.

As he went through the rooms, he threw open the windows to welcome in the breeze and decided he'd call the florist to deliver the flowers. The whole house would be filled with agapanthus, white dahlias and sky-blue delphiniums.

Once he was happy that the house was ready, Daniel sat down on the porch rehearsing the day's events in his mind. Above him a pair of swifts wheeled in the azure sky.

Afterword

When I was 16, at school, I had a lover. For a year or two we had a sexual relationship. Two years after we left school, he hanged himself.

To realise, sometimes at a very young age, that you are different, that what you feel is different from everyone else, is a profoundly separating experience. And most people who realise they are gay, at some stage in their sexual awakening find themselves floating alone on a sea of emotional and psychological separation. For some, knowing they are different, accepting that they will never fit into a straight world, this is too terrifying a prospect.

The lucky ones, like me, somehow find the strength to seek dry land and to meet others like themselves. Others, luckier still are embraced by their family, friends and society and the difference they felt while accepting themselves, disappears. But even today in societies where homosexuality appears to be tolerated there are many, many people who never reach dry land, who float unfulfilled, lonely and desperate, unable to accept their sexuality. They often live double lives, outwardly denouncing their true feelings, while seeking fleeting physical satisfaction. Sometimes they live their whole lives, many decades, without ever accepting or acting upon their true feelings. This is true, even today.

It is certainly within living memory that life was like this for all gay people. Lives spent hiding, searching out glances in crowds, scared of being entrapped, blackmailed, raped, beaten and abused without ever being able to speak the truth or seek justice.

This book emerged from two stories I encountered. The first was someone I knew. An elegant, erudite, wealthy seventy year old man who, though clearly gay and interested in the company of gays, lived his whole life in monastic chastity. He was terrified of sex. One evening, in an uncharacteristically unguarded moment, he told me that he hadn't made love to anyone since the suicide of his first and only lover, fifty years before. A time when he could have been sent to prison. He could never speak his grief. Instead he became an eminent lawyer.

The second is the story of Barcelona, where the tough and spirited Catalans, survived under the brutal reign of Franco. The dictator had a personal and vengeful hatred for these people, who had been at the centre of resistance against fascism during the Civil War. And for almost four

decades following his victory, he exacted a prolonged humiliation upon the city and its inhabitants. But the Catalans never lost their culture or defiance. Somehow despite repression, they remained strong.

In 1952, as part of an economic agreement, Franco gave the US Navy's 6th Fleet Barcelona port as a base on the Mediterranean. As a result, the city found itself awash in sailors on shore leave and for all of the obvious reasons, the black market flourished and the city was brought alive with music, goods and habits from across the world. Needless to say the sexual desires of the sailors were at the forefront of this metamorphosis. Women sold their favours and started to learn English, while their pimps traded silk stockings, chocolate and American tobacco. The city was being reborn into the place we know today. And as the decade grew on, Barcelona's gay community grew in confidence, men seeking each other out in parks and at stations, theatres and cafés. Stolen moments of sexual abandon among the ruins of the Raval and the shadows of Montjuic, passions played out at high risk in all levels of society from the Liceu Association to the barraques along the shoreline.

But this did not suit the Francoist authorities at all. And as result they targeted marginalised groups who undermined their conservativism. They wanted to purge the city of petty criminals – the drunks, the homeless, gypsies and pickpockets. And while they were at it, those who epitomised human frailty and moral weakness; the mentally ill, the disabled and the sexually effeminate.

One man in particular casts his grim spectre over this period. His name was Antonio Sabater Tomàs. He was a judge and had been responsible for extending the city's vagrancy and delinquency laws. He became the self-appointed guardian of Franco's moral code and had a particularly vicious focus on homosexuals, sanctioning the arrest, torture, extended imprisonment and medical 'curing' of thousands of gay men.

Many of these innocent men, after being taken to Barcelona's notorious police station on via Laeitana (still there today), were sent to prisons around Spain, places like Bajadoz and Huelva and even the Canaries, where they languished for years. And even after Franco's death, the amnesty which immediately freed all political prisoners, did not extend to homosexuals. It was not until the repeal of the social dangers law 3 years later in 1979 that they were released.

Armand de Fluvià i Escorsa, Antoni Ruiz and the late José María Rialp, all lived through those times and willingly and freely told their stories to me. I salute their courage and am indebted to them for allowing me to plunder what I learned about their lives as young gay men in Barcelona during the 1960s.

I owe a debt of thanks to them and a number of other people in researching, writing and publishing this book.

To my friends and tireless readers Simon, Joyce, Sim, Richard and my sister Emma who painstakingly read manuscript versions, each in turn falling in love with Daniel Sale. To Gretchen Hefferman who has been so enthusiastic in publishing me under her Backlash Press imprint, Rachael Adams for designing the book and my dear and talented friend Robert Littleford for his illustrations. Also my soul sister Carlos van Oosterzee, who gave me insight to the Catalan character, translated for me and encouraged me to learn some of the language.

The following people guided my hand in ensuring that I had the right cultural and historical information. Gema Pilar Pérez-Sánchez at the University of Miami, filmmaker Javi Larrauri, Josep Bracons Clapés from the Museu d'Història de Barcelona and Luca Gaetano Pira, queer photographer who has documented the lives of those affected by Sabater's 'Social Dangers' laws under Franco.

Finally, thanks to my husband Glynn for being the love of my life.

Philip Dundas, 2020

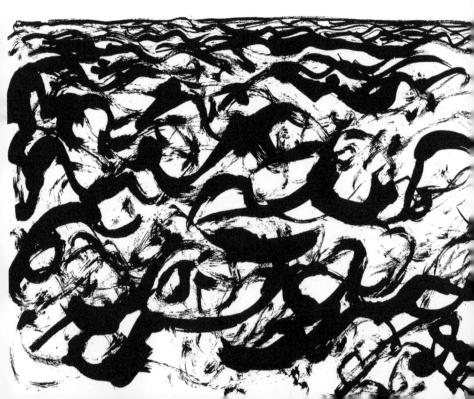

Photograph © Sim Canetty-Clarke

Brought up on a farm in Scotland, Philip realised he was different before he knew he was gay. After leaving school, he jumped on a train to Kings Cross, leapt out of the closet and danced through the 1980s with all the boys in town. His first book *Cooking without Recipes* was inspired by teaching his elderly widowed father to cook. *Daniel, at sea* is his first novel.

Philip lives in London with his husband and dog.